HER FOOTBALL STAR EX

RICH AND FAMOUS SERIES

CHERRY
BLOSSOM
ROMANCE

HER FOOTBALL STAR EX

JUDY CORRY

Cover Illustration by Wastoki

Cover Design by Judy Corry

Edited by Precy Larkins

For my daughter Janelle

Also By Judy Corry

Rich and Famous Series:

Assisting My Brother's Best Friend (Kate and Drew)

Hollywood and Ivy (Ivy and Justin)

Her Football Star Ex (Emerson and Vincent)

Friend Zone to End Zone (Arianna and Cole)

Stolen Kisses from a Rock Star (Maya and Landon)

Eden Falls Academy Series:

The Charade (Ava and Carter)

The Facade (Cambrielle and Mack)

The Ruse (Elyse and Asher)

The Confidant (Scarlett and Hunter)

The Confession (Nash and Kiara)

Ridgewater High Series:

When We Began (Cassie and Liam)

Meet Me There (Ashlyn and Luke)

Don't Forget Me (Eliana and Jess)

It Was Always You (Lexi and Noah)

My Second Chance (Juliette and Easton)

My Mistletoe Mix-Up (Raven and Logan)

Forever Yours (Alyssa and Jace)

Standalones:

Protect My Heart (Emma and Arie)

Kissing The Boy Next Door (Lauren and Wes)

<u>Coming Soon:</u>

Hideaway With You (Addie and Evan)

PLAYLIST

"Notice"—Thomas Rhett
"Small Talk"—Katy Perry
"Die From A Broken Heart"—Maddie & Tae
"Unkiss Me"—Maroon 5
"Drunk Me"—Mitchell Tenpenny
"Not Over You"—Gavin Degraw
"One Good Reason"—Hunter Hayes
"Just A Dream"—Nelly
"It's Quiet Uptown"—Kelly Clarkson
"Marry Me"—Jason Derulo
"Some People Do"—Old Dominion
"This Love"—Taylor Swift
"Return To Love"—Andrea Bocelli [feat. Ellie
Goulding]
"Unconditionally"—Katy Perry

1

EMERSON

"CONGRATS ON WINNING THE CASE," my paralegal, Kira Zigler, said after the judge had sentenced the defendant to six months in prison. "I knew you were worried about having enough evidence to convict him, but you pulled through once again."

I smoothed my hands along my pencil skirt and stood. "I couldn't have done it without you finding that last-minute witness, so thank you."

Kira really was a lifesaver. Without her help, I probably would have lost my first case of the new year.

And I couldn't have that. I needed this year to be better than last.

"Do you have any plans to celebrate your win tonight?" Kira put her bag over her shoulder, pulling her long and braided brown hair out of the way of the strap.

I shrugged and put my tablet into my bag. "I'll probably end up taking a bubble bath or something," I said. "Vincent won't be dropping Jaxon back home until after dinner, so I should have just enough time to get one in before I have to get Jaxon to bed."

I was missing my son who had been with my ex-husband for the past couple of days, so having him back with me again would be a reward in and of itself.

"A bath sounds nice," Kira said, and I was thankful for her kind comment, instead of looking at me like my life was so dull and boring these days.

My life hadn't always been this way, though. Before the divorce, when I first started practicing law and was winning my first cases, Vincent always made such a big deal out of it. Every ruling in my clients' favor was worthy of celebration, and he would insist on taking Jaxon and me out to the fanciest restaurants in Denver where we'd wine and dine until we were so full we could barely walk out of the restaurant.

But that was *before* our marriage had fallen apart.

Life was a lot different now.

"Are you and Derek doing anything to celebrate the Dragons winning the wild card game?" I put my bag on my shoulder and led the way out of the courtroom. "He's got to be excited about that."

Derek was one of the defensive ends for the Denver Dragons, the NFL team my ex-husband, Vincent Lake, was the star quarterback for. And in the six years that I'd followed the team closely—ever since I first met Vincent and fell in love with the sport at the same time I was falling in love with him—the team hadn't made it into the playoffs.

"He's on top of the world right now." Kira smiled, her brown eyes sparkling with pride for her fiancé. "The whole team is."

"I bet. It's pretty exciting."

"Did you watch the game with Jaxon then?" She glanced sideways at me as she pushed open the door that led to the big hall of the courthouse.

I tucked some of my blonde hair behind my ear. "He went with Vincent's mom and sister to the game since it was Vincent's weekend to have him. So, no, I didn't watch the game."

"Knowing you, you were probably working all weekend anyway." She gave me a knowing look.

I shrugged. "You don't win cases without preparation."

"Well, you missed a good game."

"That's what I've heard."

We passed by the lawyer we'd just gone up against, standing in the hall with his legal team. We'd already shaken hands in the courtroom earlier, so I simply smiled at them as we continued toward the exit doors.

"So you never said what you were doing to celebrate

Derek's win," I said to Kira as we walked down the steps. I pulled my wool coat close as the January air sent a chill through my body.

"My mom is cooking a special dinner for Derek and me tonight. So we'll be heading over there once he's back from his workout."

"Does that mean you'll also be doing more wedding planning?" I raised an eyebrow.

"Of course." She smiled. "You know my mom will make any excuse to get us to her house to do wedding stuff. I think we're finalizing the seating arrangements tonight."

"I bet Derek's excited for that." I laughed, trying to imagine the big, tough guy who tackled other big guys for a living caring about those particular details.

"He's a pretty good sport. He says he's just happy the planning is almost over and we'll be getting married next month."

They had purposely planned their wedding for two weeks after the Super Bowl was scheduled. That way, if the Dragons actually made it that far this year, the wedding wouldn't interfere with it.

And if the season ended sooner than they wanted, he'd still have something to look forward to in February and they could spend the off-season honeymooning.

We made it to the parking structure where I'd parked my dark blue Mercedes. Kira and I had driven to the courthouse together since her car was in the shop. I opened the back door and set my bag on the seat next to Jaxon's dinosaur booster seat before climbing in behind the wheel and starting the engine.

"Speaking of table arrangements," Kira said as she turned to me after we'd buckled our seatbelts. "My mom was hoping to have the final count tonight and you're the only one who hasn't sent the save-the-date card back."

I was the only one?

Man, their friends and family were on the ball. I could have sworn it wasn't due back to them for another week at least.

I put my car in reverse. "Are you talking about the card where I'm supposed to declare whether I'm coming alone or with a date?" My lack of enthusiasm at announcing my single status to all of her friends and family showed in my voice.

"That would be it," she said timidly.

Could I pretend I wasn't familiar with the proper etiquette for save-the-dates? Vincent and I had eloped to Vegas after all, so we'd never had the chance to do any of the wedding-planning stuff.

But since I knew better, I decided to just go with the truth. "I'm still trying to decide whether to beg a random guy to pretend to be my date or not."

"I hope you're not serious," Kira said, her voice rising with shock.

I gave a non-committal shrug.

"I really doubt you'd have to beg anyone to be your date," Kira said. "In fact, I'm pretty sure Cade has a major crush on you and would do anything you ask him to."

I laughed, remembering how I'd gotten the twenty-two-year-old law student at the front desk to pretend to be my best friend's date last month when she was trying to make her now-boyfriend see what a hot commodity she was. "If I wasn't four years older than him, I might actually consider it."

Cade *was* pretty cute—almost as tall as Vincent, even. Though he definitely had the physique of a guy who worked at a desk instead of the muscular giant I'd been married to.

But the four-year gap wasn't that bad—especially since Vincent had been five years older than me when we started dating my sophomore year of college.

But that was just the thing. I wasn't a cougar.

If I was going to bring a date to a wedding where my ex-husband was set to be the best man, I needed to at least bribe someone believable.

Which reminded me...

"Do you know if Vincent is bringing a date?" I

studied the traffic ahead, hoping not to seem too interested in her answer.

"I, um, I can't really remember off the top of my head." There was an awkwardness in Kira's tone that told me she didn't really want to try to remember that particular fact, either.

I glanced sideways at her. "If he's dating someone, you can just tell me."

It wasn't like I could really expect to find my next soulmate before my star quarterback ex-husband found his.

He may have decided to stay in our small town of Sutton Creek to be closer to Jaxon instead of moving twenty minutes away into Denver, but that didn't mean I expected him to stay home alone on the nights he didn't have our son.

Kira cleared her throat. "I don't think he's dating anyone seriously, but yes, Derek might have said something about Vincent bringing a date."

My fingers tightened around the steering wheel.

I made myself take a calming breath before I asked my next question. "Do you know who he's bringing? The new physical therapist they hired after Victoria quit, perhaps?"

Kira shook her head, a hint of compassion in her eyes at my mention of Victoria. "The newest physical therapist is a fifty-year-old male, so I don't think you'll need to worry about that."

"Well, I guess that's good. Having such a distraction had probably kept the players from recovering as quickly as they should have in the past."

Having a female help with Vincent's rehabilitation after his Achilles tendon injury had proven too much of a temptation for him to resist.

Which was why I was in this predicament of needing to find a date in the first place.

If he'd just come home after practice like he was supposed to that October night over a year ago, instead of going to the bar and getting drunk before running into Victoria who was drunk and on the rebound herself, we'd probably still be married. And I'd have a date to weddings lined up for the rest of my life.

"Maybe he's bringing one of the cheerleaders?" I asked, still trying to figure out who he might be seeing now. "Or maybe one of the super fans who always seems to find out which hotel the guys are staying at before their in-town games?"

"Would you believe me if I told you I honestly don't know who he's asked?" Kira looked like she regretted bringing up the topic of plus-ones in the first place.

And I felt guilty for making this about me when the wedding was a celebration for her and Derek. It must be hard being close friends with a couple who got divorced.

Vincent and I had been the ones to set her and Derek up in the first place. It had been the perfect match since both guys played for the same team while Kira and I worked together. We'd always had the same weekends off to go on trips together. They adored Jaxon, and once Kira and Derek were married, we had planned to ask them to be his godparents.

Things had been great.

Until they weren't.

And now, since I was one of her bridesmaids and Vincent was the best man, I would be forced to look at Vincent across the aisle as Kira and Derek said "I do."

It made me sick just thinking about being at the wedding with him, but not "with" him.

And, of course, all the other Dragons teammates and their wives would be there to watch it and judge me.

Since we'd never gone public with the reasons behind our divorce, all sorts of rumors had spread through the gossip mill that was the Dragon Ladies. I could only guess what they had said about me when they heard that I'd filed for divorce from the living legend that was *Vincent Lake*. The tabloids had certainly raked my name through the coals with all sorts of crazy conspiracy theories.

"What are you thinking about?" Kira seemed to study my face when I pulled up to a stoplight a block from our office building.

"I'm just imagining seeing the other Dragon Ladies again."

"I bet everyone will be happy to see you," Kira said in her delusional, happy tone.

I snorted. "Yeah right." They were never happy to see me, even before I stopped trying to be their friend.

I had always been a bit of an outcast from the circle of Dragons' wives—being one of the few who chose to have a career of her own instead of staying home and raising babies.

Could I bear sitting at the singles table with everyone watching and whispering about me? Because there was no doubt in my mind that the ringleader of the group, Chelsea Stockton, would have all sorts of things to say about me and the downgrading of my social status since the divorce.

"How upset would you be if I suddenly got the flu on your wedding day?" I looked at Kira with innocent eyes.

"Don't even think about it." She shook her head. "You're a bridesmaid. You will be at my wedding."

"Then I guess I better find a boyfriend quick because there's no way I'm showing up alone with all those people just waiting for me to fail."

I needed someone tall with broad shoulders.

I started making a list of my preferences in my head.

Brown hair would be ideal, since I had a major

weakness for guys with darker features. A strong jaw was also a must. Eye color didn't really matter, as long as his eyes were vibrant with life...

I continued piecing together the physical attributes of my ideal man in my head as we drove down Main Street, scanning up his imaginary torso in my mind's eye. A torso held a guy's heart and securing that for the long haul had turned out to be one of the trickiest parts for me.

He definitely needed to have big, strong arms to hold me tight as we danced at Kira's wedding. And a little scruff on his jawline wouldn't hurt, either. I was a sucker for guys like that.

My mind's eye pieced together my dream man's face. But when the eyes came into focus, I gasped, because my mind had betrayed me.

I thought I'd been piecing together a dream guy whom I'd never met, but when the eyes formed, I realized I hadn't been conjuring up someone new at all. Instead, I'd just re-imagined my ex-husband.

Ugh.

And the exercise had been going so well.

"Maybe I need to give online dating a shot," I mumbled as I switched on my blinker to turn into the parking lot of our office building.

Our tiny town had a grand total of three single guys close to my age. And since one of them was my ex-husband, and the other two were even less charming than him, my best bet was to find someone online.

"Did you say something?" Kira looked up from her phone, like she hadn't quite caught what I'd said.

I pulled into the parking lot and turned to Kira, trepidation filling my chest. "Do you think I'd look completely desperate if I tried online dating?"

"Not at all." Kira gave me an understanding smile. "Everyone is online these days. And it's way better than the alternative of spending hours in a bar or coffee shop just hoping a guy will hit on you."

"Plus, it's probably better guys know up front that they're getting two for the price of one," I said, hoping to sound more confident about it than I really was. I could put that I'm a single mom right on my profile instead of trying to figure out a way to naturally bring it up in conversation.

Because, while I saw Jaxon as a major blessing and I was so thankful that I at least had him in my life, I knew a lot of single guys in their twenties would see it as a drawback. It would be good to just narrow things down right away.

I was quiet for a moment, just watching the snow softly fall on the windshield as I thought about actually putting myself out there again.

Sure, I could stand in front of a court all day every

day and barely break a sweat. But put myself out there for guys to weigh the pros and cons of dating me?

The thought gave me hives.

Kira must have sensed my growing anxiety because she touched my arm. "You've only been divorced for a year. You don't need to rush into anything if you're not ready."

I sighed. "But your wedding is coming up whether I'm ready or not."

I needed a date. I couldn't show up alone.

"I could always set you up with my cousin Marty," she suggested. "He's still single. He's even asked about you a few times."

Marty-pickle-breath Johnson had been asking about me?

I scrunched up my nose as the image of her cousin came into my mind. He wasn't exactly ugly, but his resemblance to Mr. Collins in the latest movie adaption of Pride and Prejudice was uncanny.

And the fact that his personality was also nearly identical to Mr. Collins would be almost comical, if he wasn't so awkward to be around.

Kira must have seen my expression because she hurried to say, "I know he's not exactly your tall, dark, and handsome type. But he just got his Ph.D. in Physics, so what he lacks in looks he can make up for with intelligent conversation."

Not wanting to seem completely shallow, I shrugged nonchalantly and said, "If I'm still dateless a month from now, I might take you up on that."

Keyword: might.

Which meant I would most definitely be taking some photos and setting up an online dating profile as soon as I got home from work tonight instead of taking that bubble bath. Because there was no way I would have Marty be the guy I spent the evening trying to make my ex jealous of.

2

VINCENT

"DON'T FORGET TO GRAB PETRIE," I told Jaxon after parking my dark gray truck in front of Emerson's house on Monday evening. "You don't want to miss him when you're going to bed tonight."

"I got him," he called from behind me. And when I climbed out of my truck and opened the backseat door, my blond-haired, brown-eyed, four-year-old son was indeed holding the mangled-looking, black-and-white stuffed cat in his hands.

We really needed to replace his favorite stuffed animal. Petrie had definitely seen some better days.

I waited for Jaxon to unbuckle his seatbelt and when he was ready, I helped him out of the truck and onto the wet asphalt drive.

Before shutting the door, I grabbed the backpack

with his special blanket and raccoon stuffed animal tucked inside—the things he needed to sleep with no matter whose house he was staying at. "Ready to go see your mommy?"

"Uh-huh." He put his little hand in mine and looked at me with a big smile on his face. "I bet she's going to be so excited to see me."

"I bet she is." I chuckled lightly, loving the enthusiasm Jaxon always had about him. "I bet she's been missing you the whole time you were with me."

I knew I missed him whenever he was with Emerson.

Missed both of them if I was being honest.

But I would just keep that information to myself.

We walked up the path to the two-story Craftsman-style home Emerson and I had custom built a few years ago, and I couldn't help but feel the twinge of remorse that came every time I dropped Jaxon off.

This beautiful home had once been a place of peace and love for our family—the place I could come to after a long practice or game. But now it was just a reminder of all the dreams and plans Emerson and I used to have for a future that would never happen now.

Jaxon and I stepped onto the front porch, and I was just about to knock on the door when Jaxon pulled on the handle and opened it.

"Mom!" Jaxon called in a loud voice as he stepped into the entryway. "I'm back."

"Hold on, bud," I said when he was about to stomp right into the main part of the house with his wet snow boots. "You need to take off your boots before you go walking on your mom's nice, clean floors."

I didn't need Emerson complaining about me not respecting the rules she'd set up for *her* house since I'd moved out.

Even though she argued all day in court, that girl was never too tired for a fight if I gave her the right ammunition.

Jaxon seemed to remember how serious his mom's no-shoes-in-the-house rule was because he stopped in his tracks and went to sit on the bench next to the entryway closet and took off his boots, letting them drop onto the rug.

When it looked like he was just going to leave them there, I crossed my arms. "Is that where your shoes are supposed to go?"

Jaxon's shoulders dropped. Then after rolling his eyes and sighing like I imagined a teenager would, he said, "I was going to put them away."

"I was just making sure." I raised an eyebrow. "It looked like you were leaving the room."

Jaxon could be the sweetest and most polite four-year-old in the world, but either he was hitting puberty about nine years too early or his preschool teacher's teenage daughter had been helping out after school again, because he was definitely picking up this new attitude from somewhere.

He jumped off the bench and opened the closet where he and Emerson kept their shoes and dropped his boots into a basket.

"Good job, buddy," I said, when he closed the door.

He smiled up at me, the sass from a second ago already gone from his face. "Now you can come see my dinosaurs."

I looked around the entryway and down the hall, wondering where Emerson was. She usually came right to the door when Jaxon got home.

"Maybe I should go make sure your mom is home first and see if she's okay with it," I said. Even though I usually came into the entryway, and sometimes even into the living room when I dropped off Jaxon, I hadn't gone upstairs in this house since the day Emerson packed my bags for me and kicked me out.

Which had happened just over a year ago.

If I was to just make myself at home again and head upstairs without Emerson's permission, I'd most likely get an earful about how it wasn't my home anymore and I shouldn't act like it was.

But Jaxon must not have heard me because he called, "I'll race you to my room," before disappearing down the hall and up the staircase. So I quickly slipped off my shoes and started after him.

The music from Emerson's favorite singer, Incognito, grew louder the closer I got to the center of the house. And when I reached the end of the hall and peeked my head around the corner, I found my ex-wife sitting on the tufted cream couch in the living room with her arm extended above her like she was taking a selfie with her phone.

"Um, hi," I said, clearing my throat to get her attention.

She must have really been in the zone with her pose, because at the sound of my voice, she startled and dropped her phone onto the couch cushion.

"Vincent!" Her hand went to her chest as she turned in my direction. "H-how long have you been standing there?"

"I just walked in." I slipped my hands into the pockets of my joggers. "We weren't sure if you were home."

"Yeah, sorry I was..." She glanced back to where her phone was sitting on the couch and flipped it over, screen down. Then she got to her feet and faced me. "I was just listening to some music to unwind."

But the guilty look in her green eyes had me wondering if there was something more.

Why did she look guilty? Did it have something to do with the selfies she was taking?

Had she been sending photos of herself to someone?

Her hair and makeup looked fresh, almost like she'd touched it up since getting home from work. Emerson always took good care of herself. But after being married to the woman for almost four years, I had learned to pick up on the signs of when she was dressed up for something special.

And that navy-blue dress she wore was fitted to her slender frame in a way that I knew it wasn't what she wore to court today.

A surge of unwanted jealousy pulsed through my veins.

Who was she all dressed up for?

I darted my gaze around to make sure I wasn't about to meet a new boyfriend of hers. I didn't find anyone, so I forced myself to take a deep breath through my nose and released it slowly.

Forcing a calm expression onto my face, I said, "Jaxon wanted to show me his new dinosaurs in his room. Is it okay if I head upstairs to check them out?"

"Oh, sure." She smoothed her hands down the sides of her dress, drawing my eyes to her feminine curves. "I'm guessing he already ran upstairs?"

"He seemed really excited."

"Go ahead and go on up then." She waved her hand

toward the stairs. "I just have to wash my dinner dishes and I'll be up to put him to bed."

I looked at the dishes on the coffee table that I hadn't noticed before.

Did it make me a bad person for feeling relieved that she'd eaten alone instead of having just gotten back from a dinner date?

"Is something wrong?" she asked, when she noticed me staring at her empty wineglass and plate.

"No..." I shrugged, hoping to come off disinterested. "I was just looking at your dishes."

Her eyebrows knitted together. "You were looking at my dishes?"

"Yeah..." And to avoid going into just what exactly interested me about them, I cleared my throat and said, "Is that a new dress? I don't think I've seen it before."

"It's the bridesmaid dress I'll be wearing to Kira and Derek's wedding." She looked down at her outfit briefly. "I was just trying it on again to make sure it still fits after the holidays."

"A bridesmaid dress?" I asked, confused. "I thought it was traditional for brides to pick out ugly bridesmaid dresses for their friends?"

Because if that was the case, Kira had failed in that department. Emerson just might outshine the bride on her wedding day if she showed up looking like she did.

Not that I would dare tell her.

"So it looks okay?" She did a little turn to the side, the low backline revealing a good portion of her tanned skin.

"Yeah." I swallowed.

Looking okay would be an understatement.

She's not your wife anymore, I reminded myself.

I made myself look at the oversized clock on the wall behind her instead of raking her in even more.

Emerson had always been a beautiful woman. She had the looks of a supermodel but the heart of a small-town girl. It was something that had attracted me to her in the first place.

But even though she was easily the prettiest girl in every room she stepped into, she never seemed to know it.

She must have noticed the admiration in my eyes, though, because she let out her cute, contented giggle and said, "Good. Hopefully that means my date will like it."

My attention shot back to her face. "You have a date?"

"Mmm-hmm." She bent down to pick up her dishes, avoiding my gaze.

"Anyone I know?" I asked, even though I knew I shouldn't look like I cared.

"It's a secret." She shrugged and started walking toward the kitchen.

"A secret?" I raised an eyebrow and followed her.

"Yes."

Why was she being so mysterious all of a sudden? Was she trying to make me jealous?

Because it was working.

"Would those selfies you were taking when I walked in happen to be for this guy?" I asked, unable to help myself.

She stopped walking momentarily, as if the question startled her, but after a short pause she looked over her shoulder with sultry eyes and said, "It's really none of your business, but yes, maybe they were."

And the jealous pit that instantly hit my stomach with her affirmation that she was dressed up for some other dude was not pleasant in the least.

"Kira said you were bringing a date, too." She stepped up to the sink and started rinsing off her dishes. "Sounds like you've been busy off the fields as well as on."

I frowned. "Kira said I had a date?"

Emerson nodded. "She told me today after court."

Why would she say that? I had told Derek that I might show up with one of our teammates' sister-in-law if his wife arranged it.

But nothing was set in stone.

And if I was to be honest with myself, I knew that there was a part of me that had hoped Emerson would show up alone so I could continue with my New Year's resolution, which was to convince her to forgive me and maybe remind her that even though I had screwed everything up, we did have something worth fighting for.

"Anyway." She set her plate on the bottom rack of the dishwasher. "I hope we can both enjoy the wedding without feeling too awkward about seeing each other and our dates."

"Oh yeah, sure," I mumbled, feeling my heart sink from my chest to my stomach. "I'll be on my best behavior."

She put the rest of her dishes in the dishwasher and then turned back around to face me. "Are you bringing anyone I know?"

"Um..." I said, wondering if I should just admit that Kira was misinformed about my plus-one status. But deciding I'd rather play the game she was playing, I said, "My date is a secret, too."

She raised her eyebrows, "Really?"

I nodded. "Yes."

Especially since it was a mystery to me at the moment as well.

Looks like I should probably tell Chelsea Stockton to go ahead and set me up with her sister after all.

Emerson seemed like she was about to say something more when Jaxon's little footsteps sounded on the tile floor.

"I've been waiting *for-ever!*" he said in his impatient voice, his hands balled up into fists and resting on his waist. "Aren't you going to come see my dinosaurs?"

"Yes, of course." I stood up straighter. "I was just talking to your mom for a minute." I held my hand out for him to take and lead me up the stairs. "But let's go see your dinosaurs before it's time for you to go to bed."

———

"*TA-DAH!*" Jaxon said with a huge smile on his face as he gestured at the row of colorful dinosaurs he had lined up on the bookshelf next to his bed.

"Wow, those are so awesome!" I said, taking in the various dinosaurs that looked like they belonged in the movie *Jurassic Park*. "Is that a Utahraptor?" I pointed to the brown ferocious-looking creature covered in feathers.

He nodded, his face growing more excited that I would know the name. "That's my favorite one."

"I thought so." I smiled and went to sit on his bed so I could get a closer look. "It looks awesome."

He grabbed another brown dinosaur, which had its mouth open and a spiky tongue sticking out. "And this is the Velociraptor. It's my other favorite." He put it in my hands and said, "Let's fight."

Jaxon picked up the Utahraptor, which was clearly

the bigger dinosaur of the two, and we started a little dinosaur battle, adding in the others from the lineup as the game went on.

I was just about to have a green Tyrannosaurus Rex join in on the action when I noticed, out of the corner of my eye, that Emerson was watching us from the doorway.

"Is it time for Jaxon to go to bed?" I asked, setting T-Rex back on the bookshelf.

Emerson nodded. "It's already eight o'clock."

"Five more minutes?" Jaxon turned to Emerson with a hopeful look in his brown eyes. And I found myself hoping for more time with him as well. I hated that the amount of time I could spend with my son was now dictated by a custody agreement.

But she shook her head and said, "We have to wake up early in the morning, so you'll have to play dinosaurs with your daddy another time."

Jaxon sighed loudly, and I worried he would throw a fit. But he surprised me by saying, "Fine," and started setting his dinosaurs back on the bookshelf.

And as he put his dinosaurs back the way he had them earlier, I glanced around his room for the first time. A wave of nostalgia hit me. Even though it had been a year since I'd been in his room, nothing had really changed. Emerson had changed a lot of the decor in the entryway and living room—switching out the old family photos for newer photos of just her and Jaxon. But on the wall across from me were the newborn photos Emerson had framed and the last family photo we'd taken all together in front of an old barn.

I studied the photo for a moment, remembering back to the day it was taken. Jaxon was almost three and Emerson's hair had been shoulder-length at the time with a few streaks of dark pink underneath. My arm was around her waist, holding her tight against my side, and she was holding Jaxon in front of her.

I specifically remembered her telling me she wanted to hold Jaxon for the photos because she was self-conscious of the slight bulge she had in the stomach area after suffering a miscarriage the month before.

I'd told her she looked great and that it was hardly noticeable, but she had insisted on holding him anyway, because she didn't want to look at those photos and remember the sad times.

I tore my gaze away from the photo and found that Emerson was watching me.

Could she see the regret that had washed over me as I studied what was once *our* happy family?

"That's his favorite photo," she said, an uncomfortable look on her face. "I tried to put it away one day, but he threw a fit and wouldn't let me."

And with those few words from Emerson, my heart broke a little for my son.

I watched my little boy who thrived on organiza-
tion line his dinosaurs up in just the right way. On his
bed, he had put his stuffed cat Petrie next to his
raccoon, Bandit. He was already a little perfectionist
like his mother, and though he may act like a normal
four-year-old boy most of the time, the fact that he was
so attached to a photo of his family back before I'd
broken it reminded me of just how much damage I had
caused.

One stupid night, when I'd let my guard slip too far,
had ruined everything we'd built together in one fell
swoop.

My stomach knotted, and I scrubbed a hand over my
face. What I wouldn't give to go back and redo
everything.

Go back and tell myself not to drink so much before
bumping into Victoria that night.

To stop feeling sorry for myself and my injury and
the worries I had about my career.

To stop letting the pain from the miscarriage and
infertility and Emerson's desire to go back to work again
put a stupid wedge between us.

To stop feeling threatened by the fact that I'd
married a strong and independent woman who didn't
need me like my patriarchal upbringing had told me a
good wife should.

To stop letting the hard things in life put distance

between us when we should have been holding onto each other tighter.

One night had ruined everything.

And I'd regret my decisions for the rest of my life.

"Thank you for putting your dinosaurs away," Emerson said to our son, breaking into my train of thought. "Now it's time for you to put on your pajamas and brush your teeth."

"Okay," Jaxon said and went to his dresser to pull out the dinosaur footie pajamas Emerson's housekeeper had folded in the second drawer.

Deciding that was probably my cue to leave them, I stood and started toward the door.

I was just about to walk past Emerson when she spoke, "I forgot to tell you earlier, but congrats on winning the wild card game this weekend. That's got to feel so good after all these years."

"Yeah." I looked at her, trying to push away the thoughts of the past so I could be normal right now. "It's pretty exciting. I was worried we might not pull it off when we were so far behind at the beginning of the fourth quarter, but the guys really came through for me."

"That's what I heard," she said. "Kira told me how close it was."

Kira told her?

My heart sunk as I realized what that meant.

Emerson hadn't watched the game.

All these years of talking about the day when the Dragons would finally advance in the postseason, all the times she'd told me she couldn't wait to cheer me on as we did it, and she hadn't even watched the game?

She must have seen the disappointment in my face because she glanced down at the plush carpet and said, "I had a big case to prepare for, so I wasn't able to watch it."

A big case?

I cleared my throat and forced a smile. "And how did it go?"

Her face brightened. "It was a lot like you said your game went. I didn't think we'd be able to pull it off, but we actually won."

The look on her face when our eyes met made my heart stop for a second. I loved seeing her like this. So happy and full of life.

"That's so awesome," I said, and the smile on my face was genuine. I really was happy that she was doing well in her career. Even after everything, I wanted her to make her dreams come true.

In the past I would have pulled her into my arms and hugged her after hearing such great news, but even though the urge was still there to celebrate like that, I forced my arms to remain at my sides.

Because we didn't do that anymore.

We hadn't touched in over a year.

She hadn't let me touch her since I confessed everything to her that night.

Our eyes locked, and I worried she could read everything I was thinking in that moment. So before she could, I cleared my throat and said, "Anyway, I have practice early in the morning, so I better get back to my apartment."

"Oh, yeah." She stepped back, almost like she too had gotten caught up in the moment we'd been sharing. "I-I have an early morning as well."

I turned back to Jaxon, needing the distraction. "I'm going to go now, buddy. Come give me a big hug before I leave."

He had finished changing into his pajamas and was just working on the snap at the top.

"Here let me help you with that." I crouched down on my haunches, knowing that was the one part of footie pajamas that he still had a hard time doing on his own.

He ran to me and lifted his chin so I could snap the part of his pajamas together. Afterwards, I pulled him into my arms and kissed him on the cheek. "Have a good night, buddy," I said in a soft voice. "I'll see you in a couple of days."

"I'll miss you." His little arms squeezed my sides tighter. "Sleep well, Dad."

I gave him one last kiss on the cheek and stood, and

when I glanced back at Emerson, I saw a hint of tears in her eyes. But she quickly wiped them away so I couldn't be sure if they'd really been there.

"Have a good night, Emerson," I said, my voice coming out thicker than I wanted.

"Good night, Vincent." She gave me a curt nod. "I'll bring Jaxon to your apartment on Thursday night."

I nodded. "I'll see you then."

And then I forced myself to walk down the hall, past the closed door that would lead into the bedroom I once shared with Emerson, down the stairs and then out of the house. I climbed into my truck and drove back toward the apartment where I would sleep alone for the next two days.

These nights when Jaxon was with Emerson were the longest.

At least I had a game to prepare for this weekend because it would make the time go by faster until I got to be with my son again.

Some days it was easier to live with myself and the mistakes I'd made. But tonight wasn't one of those.

3

EMERSON

WELL, *that was an interesting drop-off,* I thought as I walked back downstairs after reading three Paw Patrol books to Jaxon.

The drop-offs were usually brief. A quick hi and an update on what Jaxon had going on during the time we were separated, and then a quick goodbye.

We didn't usually talk about anything else.

And we most definitely had never broached the subject of either one of us dating again. I had been avoiding the sweet moments between Jaxon and Vincent for the past several months because I knew exactly how they made me feel.

They made me miss *us.*

Our family. And all the good moments we'd had when we were all together.

While watching them play dinosaurs together and witnessing the sweet way Vincent hugged Jaxon and helped him with his pajamas, I had to remind myself that just because Vincent was a good dad didn't mean that we should still be a family.

Because he hadn't been a very good husband.

At least, he hadn't been a good one when it had really counted—when he'd been presented with the option to choose me when someone else was right in front of him.

He'd betrayed me and all the promises he'd made to me when we'd gotten married.

And I couldn't trust him anymore.

So instead of reliving the past again for the millionth time, I made myself a cup of my favorite chamomile tea and sat at my kitchen table with my laptop to do something I'd been putting off for way too long.

I'd about died of embarrassment when Vincent caught me taking photos for my online dating profile, but he seemed to assume I was sending photos to a guy I was dating, so I wasn't going to correct him. But letting him believe I had a guy already lined up to be my date for the wedding only made it even more essential that I actually find a date.

So even though I was tired and had to get up in less than seven hours, I started typing my personal information into the dating website I'd researched during dinner earlier. It was one that I had to pay for, so hopefully this meant the caliber of guys would be a bit higher than the free hookup sites I'd seen.

I wasn't necessarily looking for forever, but I needed a date to Kira's wedding who would look impressive to Vincent and the Dragon Ladies.

I can't believe I'm actually doing this. I shook my head as I typed my information into the boxes.

Hair color: Blonde

Eye color: Green

Age: 26

Height: 5'6"

Weight: _____

I frowned. Did they really expect people to fill that in?

I stared at my blinking cursor. I'd just weighed myself this morning, so I knew that I was 121.4 pounds. But did I really want to put that out there for the world? Or a potential mate?

A girl liked to keep some things a mystery, you know?

Maybe I'm not cut out for this online dating thing.

I mean, sure, anyone who saw me in real life would be able to see that I'd finally lost the little pooch I'd had from my pregnancies. But I was more than just a number on the scale, wasn't I?

I looked at the screen again.

I was also a woman in desperate need of a date.

And based on the way I'd teared up tonight, I needed to find someone fast so I could stop feeling sad over the things I missed about Vincent. So, I typed in the number and scrolled down to the next item on the list.

Hobbies.

Did watching Korean Dramas in my pajamas while I ate Pad Thai with chopsticks count? That was the activity I'd looked most forward to last weekend, anyway.

The only other thing I did these days when Jaxon wasn't home was work. And counting work as a hobby probably wasn't going to make me look good. Most guys on this website probably weren't looking for a workaholic or a lazy Netflix binger.

I need to come up with something cool-sounding. Something that would make me appear like I actually had a life.

I used to enjoy hiking and going on vacations back when Vincent and I were together. Even if I didn't make time for those things these days, I could still count them, right?

Deciding that was probably as good as I was going to come up with at this time of night, I put them in. I could update my profile later if this version of me wasn't interesting enough to guys.

I filled in a few more things and then uploaded one

of the photos I'd taken right before Vincent startled me and another he'd taken of me when we were in Mexico two years ago.

Using a photo your ex had taken on a couple's vacation probably wasn't the best idea, but it was one of the best photos I had of myself. I was glowing in that photo —bursting with happiness since I'd just found out that morning that we were expecting baby number two after trying for two years to get pregnant.

I studied the photo when it finished uploading onto my screen. I really had been on top of the world that day. Everything in my life was going just the way I'd wanted. I had an amazing husband, a wonderful son, a thriving career, a beautiful home. And finding that the infertility treatment had finally worked had been the icing on top of the cake.

I sighed and ran my fingers over the image on my screen. That girl had no idea that her happiness would be so short-lived.

My heart hurt in my chest as I remembered the heartbreaking miscarriage that followed two months later, and then the death of her marriage six months after.

But even though this past year had been a nightmare, I had made it through. The doctor may have said that I probably wouldn't be able to have any more children after that pregnancy had failed, but I was still alive.

And while I hadn't been on a date in over a year, I hoped that at least was about to change.

With the magic of the Internet and a shiny new profile, I'd find my next dream guy soon. He had to be out there somewhere, just waiting for me to get the nerve to sign up for online dating.

So with my heart racing only a little, I scanned my profile once more. And after making sure all the words in the "About Me" section were spelled correctly, I hit publish.

Hopefully I'd have a new man to show off to everyone in no time.

———

"WHAT ARE YOU LOOKING AT?" Kira asked when she came into my office the next morning, a cup of coffee in each hand.

I held up my phone for her to see. "I signed up for online dating last night and am just checking to see if I matched with anyone."

"Oooh, that sounds fun." She came to my desk, handed me my coffee, and then took the seat across from me.

"We'll see how fun it is soon." I took a sip of my coffee—the Oreo creamer she'd put in making it just sweet enough for my sugar tooth. "It's been about ten hours since I signed up so it's likely no one even saw my profile yet."

"I doubt that." She snickered. "You have no idea how many hours a day some guys spend on those apps."

"I guess I'll see."

With my heart in my throat I clicked on the dating app and waited to see what it had for me this morning.

When I saw the notifications icons on the top right hand corner, it told me I had matched with eight of the guys whose profiles I'd liked before going to bed, *and* I had three messages waiting for me to read.

"That was faster than I expected." I looked across my desk to my friend.

"Maybe online dating is better than you thought?" She raised an eyebrow as she took a sip from her coffee.

"Maybe."

I'd put it off for so long because I assumed it would be hard to find a guy interested in Vincent Lake's castaway, but either the guys in the Denver area were just really thirsty right now, or they didn't care or know about my link to the famous quarterback.

"Are you going to just read your messages to yourself, or are you going to share with a friend?" Kira said impatiently.

"You want to hear them?" I gave her a doubtful look.

"Yes," she said. "This is the kind of stuff I live for."

I smiled at her enthusiasm. And it was true. Kira

was such a hopeless romantic. She would eat, breathe, and drink romance novels if she could get paid for it.

"Okay." I cleared my throat, getting ready to read the message from what my app told me was a thirty-one-year-old guy with short, strawberry-blond hair. "The first guy's name is Dave," I said. "And his profile says he's into long-distance running."

"So he's athletic," Kira said in an interested tone. "That's something you like."

I nodded. I did like a man who wasn't afraid to break a sweat.

"It also says he's a lawyer in Denver with a two-year-old daughter."

"Well, that's kind of perfect," she said. "You'd definitely have something to talk about."

We would.

"So, what did he say?"

I looked down at what he'd sent me. "He says, 'Hi Emerson. How has your week been going?'"

Kira's expression was unreadable.

"Is that good or bad?"

"Eh." She tilted her head to the side and scrunched up her nose. "I mean, it's okay. But not super interesting."

It seemed fine to me. But what did I know? I hadn't ever dated like this before.

"Should I say something back?"

"If you want. I mean, you might as well if you think he seems interesting enough."

He was cute. And we did have some things in common...

I quickly typed in my response that I'd just won a court case the day before so it was going pretty well, and then closed that chat and went on to the next message.

"Next is from a guy named Chris," I told Kira.

"What does he look like?" she asked.

I tapped on my phone and showed her the photo of a twenty-eight-year-old guy with a man-bun. I didn't usually go for guys with longer hair, but he had the jawline of a Greek god so I'd swiped right the night before.

"He's cute," she said.

"Yeah." I looked at the screen again and went back to see what he'd said to me.

My usual type hadn't worked out so well the first time, so maybe going for a different type of guy this time around would turn out to be a good thing.

But when I opened the message, he'd left a variety of fruit and veggie emojis.

I frowned and showed the screen to Kira. "Do you think he's trying to invite me to a vegan restaurant?"

I mean, I usually used words when I talked to people, but Kira seemed to think having an interesting opener was important, so maybe this was this guy's go-to move.

At least...that was what I thought before Kira burst out laughing.

"A vegan restaurant!" She slapped her leg and laughed like I was hilarious or something. "You're so innocent sometimes, Emerson."

I squinted at the message to see if I could understand it.

Was this like some sort of code?

Did eggplants mean one word? And peaches mean another?

"You really don't get it?" she asked.

I shook my head. "Apparently, I've been living under a rock."

So Kira went on to explain that the guy had basically asked me to hook up with him.

"What?" I asked. "He doesn't even know me!"

Kira shrugged. "Welcome to online dating, honey. Not everyone is looking for the same thing."

I shook my head. "Well, I guess I'm going to have to just tell him no thanks then."

"Good choice."

I quickly typed my response and then tapped the block button on the screen. I might be desperate to find a date to a wedding in a few weeks, but I was not interested in a relationship that started off like that. I was a relationship girl and would be in a serious relationship before I let things get too physical.

"Any other ones?" Kira asked after my cheeks had finally cooled from the embarrassing message.

"Just one more," I said, opening the last message from a guy with blond hair and super cute dimples named Ricky. "His profile says he's a year younger than me. But he's *really* cute and six-foot-five." An inch taller than Vincent. "So he could be just what I need."

I read his message.

Ricky: *Are you Emerson Lake? As in Vincent Lake's ex? My buddies and I have all been trying to get tickets to this Sunday's game. Think you could hook a brother up?*

I sighed and clicked out of the app, setting my phone on my desk and picking up my coffee cup again. "So much for online guys not knowing about my past."

"What did he say?" Kira's black eyebrows knitted together in concern.

I told her what it said and then sighed. "I know our divorce was all over the tabloids, but I kind of hoped none of these guys would recognize me for it."

But I should have known something like this would happen.

Vincent and my divorce had been everywhere when the news first broke last year. I'd shut down my social media profiles and made myself into a hermit in our small town, barely doing anything besides work and running errands. For some reason I'd assumed that by hiding out for the last twelve months, the Dragons' fans would have forgotten about my tie to my famous ex-husband.

But it looked like, at least in this fan's case, I was more memorable than I wanted to be.

"Just ignore it," Kira said, sitting up straighter. "You're doing this to move on. You don't owe any of Vincent's fans anything."

I nodded, letting the heat from the coffee cup warm my hands. "I guess 'boring opener Dave' turned out to be the most promising of the three."

"For now," she said, pushing herself onto her feet and getting ready to go back to her desk. "But this is just day one. Who knows what will happen next?"

"I guess," I said, trying to sound more enthusiastic than I really felt about all of this. "Maybe I'll swipe through some more guys on my lunch break."

"That's my girl." She smiled. "At least you're likely to see a few hot men that way." She winked. "And just remember, if worse comes to worst, Marty will be excited to see you again."

I shook my head and laughed. "I think you keep bringing him up because you're trying to blackmail me into keeping my chin up."

She laughed and winked. "Maybe."

I tossed a paperclip at her. "Thanks for the pep talk."

"Anytime."

She left my office, and I opened the file for the case I was working on today. I had a case to win in a couple of weeks. I would just have to worry about my dating life later.

4

VINCENT

"WHAT KIND of pizza do you want?" I asked my buddy, Cole, who was sitting on the couch in my living room, looking at his phone. It was Friday night and we'd had a long day at practice. It had been a long week actually, as we'd done everything we could to prepare for this Sunday's playoff game. I was definitely in need of a chill evening where we did everything but talk about the possibility of the Dragons making it to the Super Bowl for the first time since I'd joined the team seven years ago.

I didn't need to think about all the pressure that was resting on my shoulders as the quarterback.

Cole's dark brown eyes slid away from his phone screen for a second. "I like that wood-fired pizza you guys have on main street."

"The Pizza Cart?" I asked.

"Yeah, they make the best Hawaiian barbecue pizza."

"I don't know why you like ruining your pizza with pineapple, but I'll write it down," I said.

Cole's family had moved from Hawaii to Colorado when he was in high school so he could have a better chance at getting scouted for college football teams. And that guy ruined all kinds of perfectly good foods by putting pineapple on top: burgers, pizza, chicken. Nothing was safe from that tropical fruit.

"Don't knock it til you've tried it," Cole said, pulling his curly black hair into a ponytail.

"That's okay," I said. "I'll leave all the pineapple for you." I scribbled his order down on a piece of paper. "And what about you, Jaxon?" I looked to where he played on the floor with the giant Dinosaur puzzle I'd bought him for Christmas. "What kind of pizza do you want?"

"Cheese pizza," he yelled over his shoulder.

I should have known. Kids have the blandest palettes.

I didn't really feel like cooking again tomorrow, so when I called to place our orders I added a Margherita and Calabrese & Sausage pizza for myself, along with their raspberry pecan salad so I could have leftovers.

After ordering, I joined Cole on the couch.

"What are you looking at?" I asked, when I noticed him swiping his finger across the screen one direction and then the other. "Playing that jungle game again?"

But when I leaned closer to see, he angled his phone away from my view before making the screen go dark.

"Not a game then?" I narrowed my gaze.

Did he have a secret girlfriend he hadn't told me about?

"I—uh." He put his phone on his knee. "It's not what you're thinking."

I leaned away and lifted my hands in the air so he would know I wasn't judging. "What you do in your private time isn't any of my business."

He shook his head. "No, really. It's not that..." He sighed and picked up his phone. "Promise you won't tell the guys if I show you?"

I studied his face for a moment, having no idea what he was so anxious about. "Sure."

He better not show me weird photos of himself.

He unlocked the screen and showed it to me. "It's a dating app."

I pulled my head back, surprised. "You signed up for online dating?"

He shrugged, his cheeks coloring. "Arianna was giving me a hard time last week about never going out with girls even though I'm this *big star receiver*." He did air quotes when he said the last three words. "So I decided to sign up for this to prove a point."

"Arianna got you to sign up for this?" I asked. Arianna was my baby sister who was also Cole's best friend.

"Yeah."

"But aren't you worried women will just fill up your inbox because you're the wide receiver for the Dragons?" That was enough to keep me off online dating.

He shook his head. "Not yet. I'm using my middle name Tyler instead of Cole, and I haven't posted any photos of my face."

I furrowed my brow. "You can do that?"

He shrugged. "No one stopped me."

Then to demonstrate, he tapped his screen a few times to bring up what I guessed was his dating profile.

There was a photo of him with a hat on taken from behind, sitting on his fishing boat. And another of him holding the bonnethead shark that he'd caught on his big fishing trip to Florida last spring—his face blocked out enough by the huge fish that you'd only know it was him if someone told you.

He scrolled down the page so I could see what he'd said about his interests and hobbies and what he was looking for in a woman.

"Everything in my profile is all the real me," he said. "I just didn't talk about my job or show my face."

"And it's working?" Because if I was ever going to try dating again, it *would* be nice to find someone interested in me as a human and not just me as the famous football player.

He lifted a shoulder. "It's going all right. I haven't been trying too hard to set up actual dates or anything since the season is still busy and I want to focus on that," he said. "But I've matched with a few women."

"So how does it work?" I asked.

It was probably ridiculous that I was a thirty-one-year-old man with no idea how online dating even worked these days, but I hadn't had to know about it before since I'd found Emerson so long ago.

"Well," Cole said, tapping on his screen a few more times. "On this particular app, you have to match with someone before you can message them. And to do that, the app presents you with a photo of the person, their name, and age."

I watched as he brought up a photo of a girl with black hair named Ashanti who was twenty-three and lived in the Denver area.

"So you decide whether to match with them based only on the photo, name, and age?"

"No, if you want to see more before swiping, you can check out their profile."

He tapped the screen a couple of times and brought

up Ashanti's profile so we could see that she was into snowboarding and football.

"And if you like what you see, you swipe right?" I asked, remembering some of what I'd heard the single guys on the teams talk about.

"Yeah, and if you aren't interested, you swipe left," Cole said.

He must have liked what he'd seen in that girl's profile because he swiped right.

"That's efficient," I said when a photo of another woman with blonde hair and blue eyes showed up on his screen.

"When I first heard about this app, I thought it was shallow." He shrugged and swiped left. "But most people go off looks in the first place so it's pretty realistic, I guess."

"So can you message that girl you swiped right on a moment ago?" I asked.

"Only if she matches with me," he said, swiping left on another girl. "Meaning that she will have to swipe right on my photo as well."

"I see," I said.

He swiped right on another girl. "But if a girl has already seen my photo and swiped right on it, and if I did the same with hers, then a little box will pop up to tell me we've matched, and I can message her right away if I want."

"And you said you're still getting matches even without showing your face?"

"I'm sure I'd get more if they saw my face, since we all know how irresistible the ladies find this handsome Polynesian mug of mine, but I do okay." He shot me a smirk.

I laughed. "And it's been how long since you've been on a date?"

"Not as long as you," he shot back.

I rolled my shoulders back. "Yeah, yeah."

He put the phone down on his knee. "Yes, in all seriousness I probably would match with more women if I did have my face on there, so that is a drawback of trying to keep my identity under wraps. But enough women don't seem to care about it."

"I guess those workouts we did before your fishing trip last year paid off then, huh?"

The guy worked hard on the field during the season, but I was pretty sure he would have just laid around a good chunk of last spring if I hadn't been on his case about working out together.

He shrugged. "I would have still worked out. It just wouldn't have been at eight in the morning."

"So you're saying we should work out at ten instead once this season is over."

"Sure."

Hopefully that wouldn't be for another few weeks.

ABOUT TWENTY MINUTES LATER, I carried our food into the kitchen. "Pizza's here," I called out to Jaxon and Cole. I still hadn't gotten around to buying a kitchen table, so I set the pizza boxes and salad on the kitchen island and pulled out a stool for Jaxon to climb onto.

My therapist told me the reason why I was still in this small apartment and unable to bring myself to fully furnish it was because I was resisting facing the truth of my new reality.

But what did he know?

I'd been busy. I'd find a more permanent home eventually. This place was working just fine for Jaxon and me—for now.

"Did you get me cheese pizza?" Jaxon asked as he climbed onto his stool.

"I sure did." I set a plate in front of him and opened the box so he could see it.

His brown eyes went wide, as if in awe that he would get the whole thing to himself. But I really didn't know why he'd be that surprised. I always did things like this.

Sure, I probably should have hired a cook or learned to cook myself now that I was a bachelor again, but ordering enough food so I could have leftovers or having a personal shopper stock my freezer with frozen dinners was working just fine at the moment, so why fix what wasn't broken?

I wasn't living in denial that things were really over with Emerson.

Really.

"Found any more matches?" I asked Cole when he joined Jaxon and me at the island. Cole had his phone out again and was swiping left and right.

He shrugged. "A few."

He set his phone down and opened his pizza box. He rubbed his hands together as he looked at all the pineapple and Canadian bacon covering his pizza. He pulled out a piece and took a bite. "You don't know what you're missing."

"I'm fine with my choice." I put a slice from each of my pizzas on my plate and dished out a big serving of the salad.

I was about to dig in when Cole said, "You got the girliest salad they have there. What's wrong with you?"

I frowned and looked at the salad with raspberries, feta cheese, candied pecans and various greens.

"Are you saying raspberries are girly?" I asked. Because the last time I checked, guys could eat fruit.

"No, it's just..." He paused and stared at me like I was missing something vital. "No guy goes to a restaurant and orders a salad with pink vinaigrette. I mean, I didn't even know they served salad at The Pizza Cart."

"That's because it doesn't have pineapple in it."

"Or because it's something you order when you're eating with a girl."

"Which you obviously never do," I said. "Hence the dating app."

He scowled and took another bite of his pizza. "Not for long."

He picked up his phone to swipe through his dating app again and I picked up my fork to eat my *girly* salad.

And as the tangy taste of the vinaigrette hit my taste buds, I realized something.

Cole was right. I hadn't thought about it until then, but I had totally just ordered Emerson's favorite salad.

Man, my subconscious mind really did work over-time sometimes.

I looked at the two pizzas in front of me. I'd even ordered her favorite Margherita pizza.

I might as well just invite Emerson to eat with us while I was at it.

Oh well, as long as I didn't tell Cole what I'd just done, no one would have to know.

I stuck my fork into my salad and glanced over at Cole's phone to see what kinds of girls were looking for dates in the Denver area. There were girls of all sizes and colors—something to fit all the different tastes a guy might have.

I swallowed a bite of my salad. "She's cute," I said when a girl with dark brown hair and brown eyes came onto the screen.

His thumb seemed to hover over the image, as if he was deciding whether to swipe right or not.

"She actually looks a lot like my sister, now that I think about it," I said when he didn't do anything.

He pursed his lips as if my bringing up Arianna had struck some sort of nerve. After a short pause he said, "Yes, she does."

And he swiped right.

Interesting.

He and Arianna had been best friends since she moved to Denver with my mom, but was it possible there was more to their friendship than either of them had ever told me?

I was about to stand up to refill my glass with water when a new image came up on his phone that made my heart stop.

What?

I immediately zeroed in on the woman's green eyes and shoulder-length blonde hair. Then I took in the navy-blue dress that I'd seen just a few days earlier.

"Is that Emerson?" Cole asked, mirroring my thoughts. "Because dang, she looks hot!"

"I'm sitting right next to you, bro." I shoved him in the side. "Don't you know you don't say things like that in front of me?"

"I'm sorry, but—" He put the screen in front of me. "—any heterosexual man would say the same."

I sighed and studied the image of Emerson looking up at me with her big turquoise eyes.

Cole was right. She looked gorgeous.

"Did you know she was dating again?" he asked, taking another look at my ex-wife.

"She said she had a date for Derek's wedding, but..." I shook my head. "I didn't think she'd be on a dating app."

An app where she probably had all sorts of guys swiping right if Cole's reaction was anything to go by.

"Can I see what her profile says?" I held my hand out for his phone.

He handed it to me, but before I could bring up the rest of her profile, Jaxon suddenly yelled, "Mommy!" from beside me.

And before I knew what was happening, Jaxon leaned closer and swiped a greasy pizza finger across the screen like he thought it would show more photos of his mom.

"No!" I said too late.

And in the next instant, a message popped up on the screen saying, **You have a match!**

5

VINCENT

"IS THERE A WAY TO UNDO THAT?" I showed Cole the screen, my heart racing in my chest over the fact that one of my closest buddies had just matched with Emerson.

Over the fact that she had seen something in his profile that had made her swipe right in the first place.

Did she swipe right on lots of guys?

Or did she just like Cole's profile because he was muscular and brown and caught huge fish?

She had always loved our beach vacations. Was she looking for someone new to explore the beaches of the world with?

"Wait." Cole's brown eyes went wide after he got a better look at his phone, his bushy eyebrows raising like he hadn't noticed what Jaxon had done until now. "Did Jaxon just match me with your ex-wife?"

I nodded, panic rising in me. "I think he was trying to swipe through more photos of her like he does in my photo app."

Cole took his phone back from me and seemed to study the image that had Emerson's face next to the one of him on his boat and the button beneath that asked if he wanted to message her.

"You know what this means, right?" He turned his gaze on me.

"That I need to be more careful with your phone?" I asked, unsure what he was trying to say.

He shook his head, and I was surprised to see a slow smile replace the look of shock on his face before. "It means that Emerson thinks I look hot."

I shoved his shoulder. "She can't even see your face in those photos."

He shrugged like it didn't matter. "Well, she obviously likes what she can see." He held up his arm and flexed. "And guns like these are exactly what she's looking for in a guy."

"Whatever," I said. "It's probably more like she was looking at your photo with Jaxon beside her and he wanted to see another photo of the shark."

Cole leaned over the counter, watching Jaxon who

was currently dipping his pizza in the glass of milk I'd gotten him.

"Is that true, Jaxon? Have you seen this photo of me before?"

Jaxon looked up from the mess he was making and his blond eyebrows knitted together as he studied the tiny photo. "A shark!"

Cole nodded. "Yes, buddy, it's a cool shark."

"Have you seen this photo of Cole and his shark before?" I asked, hoping that somehow my guess had been correct and that this whole matching thing was just my son's doing.

But Jaxon shook his head and said, "No. Do you still have the shark?"

Cole shook his head. "No. Sorry, buddy."

But Jaxon didn't seem to really care because he just pulled his pizza out of his milk and took a bite off the end.

My son wouldn't touch the mac and cheese I made him last week, but he'd purposely eat soggy pizza.

Kids have the weirdest taste buds.

"Do you want to see what she put on her profile?" Cole asked.

I turned my attention back to him and saw that he had already brought up Emerson's full profile. The photo of her in the navy-blue dress was front and center.

She still looked amazing in it, but that wasn't what caught my attention this time.

Instead, my eye caught on the bottom right corner of the photo where I noticed the bottom of the gray joggers I'd worn to her house on Tuesday night and the top of my foot in my black socks.

So this photo really was from that night?

Did that mean she had only been pretending to have a guy to send those photos to? And that she'd set up this dating profile *after* I'd left her house?

Was she, like me, only pretending to have a date for Derek and Kira's wedding?

It was probably farfetched for something like that to be true, but the thought of her not having actually moved on with someone else yet did ignite a few sparks of hope in my chest.

"What other photos does she have on there?" I asked.

But when Cole swiped to bring up the next photo, my stomach clenched. It was the one I'd taken of her on our vacation to Mexico a couple of years ago.

The photo of her in her pink sundress on the beach where she was smiling into the camera like she had the secret ingredient to my happiness.

The photo that I had framed after that trip and was currently sitting in the drawer of my nightstand for the nights I wanted to torture myself by looking at it and remembering what I was missing out on.

"How did you let her get away?" Cole looked sideways at me, clearly noticing how beautiful Emerson was.

"Because I'm an idiot." I grunted. "Let's see the other ones."

And either he had caught onto my sudden mood, or was just interested in seeing other photos of Emerson, because he immediately brought up an image of Emerson wearing a backpack and white hat as she stood on a bridge that led to a volcano during our hike on our last trip to Hawaii.

Another photo that I'd taken.

Was using photos that I'd personally been there for some part of her plan? Did she think the universe would direct her to Mr. Right as long as a piece of my ripped-out heart was part of the process?

"Are there any more?" I asked.

But when he tried swiping, it just went back to the first one again.

Well, at least she hadn't used a photo that she'd cropped me out of.

"Do you want to read the rest of her profile? Or are you kind of done with this?" Cole asked.

I sighed. "Let me just read it over real quick."

It couldn't make me feel much worse than I was

already feeling, right? Plus, I was really curious about what kind of guy she'd say she was looking for.

But as I read over what she'd written, it did indeed make me feel worse. Not because she said anything bad necessarily, but because she sounded like she was planning to take this online dating thing seriously and was actually ready to date again.

How was it possible that I could be so far from ready to not only move on from the past but even go on a single date, while Emerson was actively putting herself out there?

"You gotta hand it to the girl," Cole said after he'd read through her profile as well. "She knows what to say to get a guy to swipe right. She sounds witty and fun. And with photos like that..." He raised his eyebrows.

"Are you trying to tell me that if I wasn't sitting here right now, you'd be messaging her?"

"If I was a jerk who hit on his buddies' ex-wives, then yeah, I'd definitely be messaging her right now."

I ran a hand through my hair and leaned back in my stool. "Which means she's probably matching with all kinds of guys right now."

"Probably."

I sighed and pushed my plate away from me, suddenly not feeling so hungry anymore.

"I'm supposed to be focusing on winning our game this weekend," I said. "I don't need this in my head."

Cole pushed a button, making the screen go dark so I couldn't see the photo of Emerson smiling coyly up at me anymore.

"Just don't think about it." He set his phone on the counter and picked up a piece of his pizza. "You tried to make amends, but she wasn't interested in fixing things."

"I cheated on her. Can you really blame her for not wanting to trust me again?"

He lifted a shoulder. "Not really." He took a bite of his pizza. After he swallowed, he said, "But you need to stop beating yourself up over it. You can't change the past. You can only do your best to be better from now on. And if that means you have to watch your ex-wife fall in love with another guy, just try not to look too closely."

"Says the guy who spent the last three years watching Arianna date a guy everyone knows is all wrong for her."

He narrowed his eyes at me. "What are you trying to say?"

I picked up my empty glass from the counter then stood to take it to the fridge. "That I think I've finally figured out why you don't date any of the girls throwing themselves at you."

"Hey." He pointed to his phone. "I signed up for online dating."

"And didn't you say you only did that because

Arianna was making fun of you?" I raised an eyebrow at my friend as I walked around the kitchen island. "Because if you were really serious about dating, you'd be at a club with the other guys tonight instead of hanging out with an old divorced guy and his kid."

I glanced at Jaxon just as a big piece of his pizza broke off and landed in his cup of milk with a plop.

"Here, let me get you some new milk, buddy," I said, taking the cup with who knew how many pizza floaties in it and dumped its contents in the sink.

"Just so you know," Cole said as I grabbed a new cup for Jaxon from the cupboard and filled it with milk. "I signed up for online dating because Arianna offered to be my dating coach."

"Your what?" I lifted my gaze to him after setting the cup of milk in front of my son who immediately started dunking his pizza in it again.

Cole shrugged. "I pretend like I suck at dating and she teaches me how to win a girl over." He took a sip from his water and set it back on the counter. "Sure, it's not exactly dating her, but until she sees that Chad is a jerk, I can be her special project and she will be forced to look more closely at me and maybe see how dateable I really am."

"You're not delusional enough to think she's going to teach you kissing techniques, are you?" I pushed my cup against the filtered water dispenser in the fridge.

"I wouldn't stop her if she tried."

I shook my head and took a sip of my water. "Let me know how that works out for you, bud."

He shrugged. "It's part of the long game, my friend. It's not like I can just tell her I've been in love with her since we first met and hope she'll still want to be my friend."

"Yeah, I get that." I leaned over the island and pulled my pizza over to me. "But in the meantime, don't accidentally message Emerson when you're trying to find a date. I don't care if these coaching lessons from Arianna are the only part of the dating process that you care about."

"Of course I'm not going to message her. Emerson may be hot, but she's not even my type."

But apparently, my sister was.

"Good." I picked up a piece of pizza and took a bite. As I chewed, I tried not to think about how if I could just figure out a way to keep all the other guys out there from hitting on Emerson I might be able to concentrate on the biggest game of my career so far this weekend.

6

EMERSON

"I SAW in your profile that you enjoy traveling," my date Dave said after the waitress brought our entrees to the table Friday night. "So my question for you is, if you could only travel to one place for the rest of your life, where would you go?"

Dave and I had been messaging off and on all week, and the conversations had been interesting enough. So when he asked me to meet him at my favorite new restaurant in Sutton Creek, Element 47, I had said yes and hoped it would go well.

I was a little jittery with nerves and not sure how much dinner I'd actually be able to eat because of them, but so far, for my first date since Vincent, it was actually going all right. Dave turned out to be a better conversationalist than I would have guessed from his initial message and was asking lots of interesting questions. While he wasn't exactly the tall, dark, and handsome football-playing type that I'd gone for in the past, he was still good-looking. And I liked that his blue eyes were even more vibrant than they'd been in his profile photos.

"I guess it depends on the time of year I'd be going." I cut into my salmon. I really loved seeing new places all over the world and had yet to go back to the same place more than once. "Like, would I be going there the same time every year? Or would it be a place I'd need to be okay traveling to in both the summer and the winter?"

"How about this." He pursed his lips and stabbed his zucchini with his fork. "You can choose a place to visit in the warmer months and another place to visit in the colder months."

"Then that's easy." I shrugged. "I'd go to Glacier National Park in the summer and in the winter I'd head to Hawaii."

A slow smile spread across his lips, and I liked the way it lit up his ocean-blue eyes. "Sounds like we'd be great traveling companions."

"Why?" I asked.

"Because those are two of my favorite places as well."

"You've been to Glacier?" I asked, somewhat surprised. I myself had never even heard about it until Vincent's parents planned a family reunion there three years ago, the summer before his dad died of a brain aneurysm.

"I grew up in Montana actually, so I went there all the time as a kid."

"That's cool. It's so beautiful there."

My mind conjured up images of the beautiful lakes surrounded by tall mountains with spots of snow that stayed even through the summer. I had grown up watching the movie *Heidi*—the one where a girl lived with her grandfather in the Swiss Alps—and so when we'd gone on the hike in Logan Pass I couldn't help but feel like I was in a place just like that.

"It really is Montana's hidden treasure." Dave poured a little more red wine into his wine glass. "So many people I talk to are all about leaving the country to see new scenery, but just in the U.S. we have so many different climates worth exploring."

"It's so true," I said.

He set the bottle back on the table and picked up his fork again. "So you said you have a son, is that right?"

"I do," I said, a nervous flutter going through my stomach. Starting to talk about our kids might lead to talking about future plans for more kids, and I knew it could be a dealbreaker given my particular issues. But I put on a smile because I loved bragging about my son, and said, "His name is Jaxon. He's four years old and my favorite person in the whole world."

"Four?" He raised his eyebrows. "You don't look old enough to have a four-year-old."

I furrowed my brow, not sure if I should be offended or not. "I don't?"

He shook his head and picked up his wine glass. "I don't mean that in a bad way or anything. I just..." He seemed to think for a moment. "I just assumed that with all you've accomplished so far in your life, getting your law degree and already practicing for two years, that it would have been impossible to do with a baby as well." He took a sip of wine and set his glass back on the table. "I mean, I could barely take care of myself and keep up with my studies when I was in my early twenties, let alone be married and take care of a baby."

So he was impressed?

Deciding to take it that way, I lifted a shoulder, poked at my food, and said, "My mom and ex-husband were really supportive of me accomplishing my goals at the time, so we were able to make it work." My mom was excited to have a grand baby to dote on, and so instead of putting Jaxon in childcare while I finished my last year of law school, she had taken care of him during the day and Vincent was a big help in the evenings when I needed to focus on my homework.

"That's good you had that kind of support," he said.

"What about you? You have a daughter, right?"

"Yes, her name is Callie." His smile broadened at

the mention of his daughter. "She turns three at the end of March, so I'm a little further behind you in that arena."

"So you just have the one daughter?"

"Yes. My ex-wife and I waited until we were both settled in our careers before we started trying for kids."

"That's smart." Having Jaxon so young had definitely made me grow up fast.

But even though balancing everything had been tricky, having him at twenty-two had turned out to be a big blessing. Because if Vincent and I hadn't accidentally gotten pregnant, who knows if we'd have been able to have any kids at all, thanks to my body deciding to break on me.

"And are you hoping to have any more kids in the future?" I asked, trying to get a gauge on Dave's goals for a family. The date had been going well so far, so it would probably be a good idea to know this before I got my hopes up too much.

But when he answered, I almost wished I hadn't asked.

"I'd love to have a whole basketball team of them." He grinned. "So as soon as I find the right woman for me, I'll have to get to work on that again." He winked.

And I knew he was just being light-hearted and possibly flirtatious, but the thought of the guys I went on dates with expecting to have lots of children someday wasn't as easy for me to think about.

"And what about you?" he asked when I didn't say anything. "How many kids would you like to have?"

I pretended to think about it, like I hadn't thought about the answer to that question thousands of times over the past few years.

Then I lifted a shoulder and tried to seem as neutral as I could about the whole thing and said, "I don't know. When I was little, I always wanted to have a boy and a girl, but since life turned out differently than I expected, just having Jaxon here safe and sound is enough for me."

"Do you mean things turned out differently because you got divorced?" he asked.

Sure, we could go with that for now.

"Yeah, I don't think many people plan to get divorced when they get married."

"Sorry, dumb question." He chuckled awkwardly. "But you're only twenty-six, right? And beautiful and smart. I'm sure you'll get that little girl before you know it."

I felt my smile faltering, but I forced it to stay. "We'll see."

He must not have caught on to my discomfort because he winked and said, "This may be jumping the gun a little, but who knows, if things work out between us, you might be able to help me with that basketball team of mine."

I looked down at my plate, feeling a burning sensation fill my cheeks.

Yeah, this probably wasn't going to work out after all.

It took all my willpower not to look around for the waitress and ask her to box up my food so I could run out of the restaurant and hide.

But Dave must have seen something in my expression because he reached across the table and covered my hand with his. "Sorry, that was way too soon," he said. "I think I may have had too much wine to drink tonight. I was just talking hypothetically. I know this is only our first date. "

"No, that's fine." His hands were softer than I expected. And having been used to Vincent's rough and calloused hands, I didn't like how it felt. So I slipped my hand out from under his, picking up my napkin to pat my face so he wouldn't know I was resisting his touch on purpose. "I-it's just my first date since the divorce, so I guess I didn't expect to start talking about settling down and having kids quite yet."

"Obviously I'm a little rusty at this as well." He flexed his fingers like he had indeed caught onto what I'd just done before picking up his fork again. "I've only just started dating again and am a little nervous."

I was just trying to think of a less awkward topic to

talk about when the corner of my eye caught on a flash of blond curly hair running down the restaurant aisle toward me.

"Mommy!" The flash slowed, and before I knew what was happening, Jaxon was throwing his arms around my waist and hugging me.

"Jaxon?" I returned his hug and ran my fingers through his curls. "What are you doing here?"

I pulled away, and that was when I saw a flustered-looking Vincent slipping out of a booth several tables down. He wore the gray ball cap that he always wore when he was trying to blend in in public, his dark hair curling around his ears. He turned his head over his shoulder looking for where Jaxon had disappeared to. His best friend Cole was sitting across from him and seemed to be helping with the search by pointing in my direction.

Vincent seemed to spot Jaxon quickly enough, but when his brown eyes met mine, his step faltered—almost like he hadn't really expected the woman Jaxon had jumped out of their booth to see was going to be me.

And as he got closer, his gaze slid to Dave and a look of surprise and something else flashed across his face.

Disappointment?

Frustration?

"Daddy is getting us dessert." Jaxon bounced up and

down, bringing my attention back to him. "He said if I ate salad I could have some."

"Well, that sounds fun," I said, wondering what I should do next.

What was the proper etiquette for bumping into your ex-husband and your son when you were on a first date?

Was I supposed to introduce Dave to Vincent? That wouldn't be awkward or anything.

Should I just quickly send Jaxon back to his dad and pretend like we hadn't bumped into each other at all?

Or maybe I should pretend this date was going better than it really was and hopefully make Vincent jealous. I had told my friend Ivy a while back that I wanted to get all dressed up and do something like that.

I *was* all dressed up.

But before I could figure out what to do, Jaxon turned to Dave with a big smile on his face and said, "Hi. I'm Jaxon."

I looked across the table to Dave to see his reaction to all of this. He smiled at Jaxon and held out his hand. "Hi, Jaxon. My name is Dave."

Instead of giving Dave a handshake like he had probably expected, my son slapped his hand and gave him a high five instead.

Dave seemed to catch on quickly enough, though,

and followed it up with an exploding-knuckles gesture, which brought a bigger smile to my son's face.

"Okay, buddy," I said, noticing Vincent was only a couple of feet away now. "It's probably time for you to go back to dessert with your daddy and Cole."

I gave him a little nudge, but instead of moving, his shoulders slumped and he pulled on my arm and whined, "But I want to be with you."

I bent closer to Jaxon's ear, desperate to avoid a scene, and whispered, "We can have dessert together tomorrow, okay?"

He pouted his lips into a frown and breathed out of his nose loudly, but a moment later, he nodded his head slowly and said, "Okay."

I gave him one more hug and kissed the top of his head. "Have fun with your daddy."

Vincent had reached us by this point, and when our eyes caught, he mouthed, "I'm sorry."

"Let's leave mommy to finish her dinner with her friend." He grabbed Jaxon's hand, his cheeks slightly pink from what I could only guess might be embarrassment over having to chase his son through a restaurant. His gaze briefly caught mine again before he nodded to Dave and said, "Sorry to interrupt your meal."

And as Vincent and Jaxon walked back to their table, I looked at Dave to see what he thought of all this. Then I saw recognition dawning on his face.

His mouth dropped open. "Your ex-husband is Vincent Lake?"

I pressed my lips together and nodded. "Yes."

He blinked his eyes a few times and craned his neck over his shoulder to watch Vincent and Jaxon slipping back into their booth. "I saw something in the news a while back about him splitting up with his wife, but..." He turned back to me with wide eyes and shook his head.

"Yes?" My heart was beating rapidly in my chest as I waited for whatever he had to say about it.

Did he believe the rumors that had been spread about me? How I had had a mental breakdown and was now practicing witchcraft in my back yard at midnight?

Or the one where I had slept with multiple team-mates of his and he'd caught me in the act?

Or maybe the one where I had become addicted to plastic surgery and Vincent refused to foot the bill for any more?

Vincent and I had never gone public with the real reasons behind our divorce, mostly because it wasn't any of their business.

But also partly because even though I hated what he'd done to us, I still cared about him enough that I didn't want to have a part in the media raking him over the coals. He was still my son's father.

Having my name dragged through the mud was just a fun side effect of not addressing it.

I looked down at my plate as I waited for Dave to show me in real time just how any future dating prospects would respond to discovering who I had once been married to.

"I-I'm suddenly..." He cleared his throat. "I'm suddenly not so sure I'm the best fit for you." He set his fork and knife down on the table, like he was ready to just end the meal right then. "I have a feeling you might be used to a lifestyle I would never be able to provide."

So he must have read the tabloid article about how I had demanded ten million dollars a year in child support and alimony.

Oh well. I supposed I'd already figured things wouldn't work out after hearing he wanted a basketball team of children. Maybe this was for the best.

Sure, I could tell him that I hadn't asked for anything more than the house and my car, because I was a grown woman with a career and could take care of myself, thank you very much. But I didn't need to defend myself to him.

For a lawyer, he was awfully quick to believe the first story he'd come across.

So I said, "I understand."

"You do?" A bewildered expression crossed his face. Like he truly thought I must be crazy.

Maybe he'd read more gossip articles than I thought.

"Of course," I said. "Dating is all about trying to find a good fit for you, and it's okay if I'm not it for you."

"Well, that's very understanding of you."

I nodded. Yes, I could be grown up about this.

But since it would be extremely awkward to finish this meal together now, and I really did want to eat every last bite of the salmon and Greek salad sitting on my plate, I decided to have a little fun while I was at it. "I actually wasn't sure it would work out, either." I picked up my glass of water and took a sip, hoping to appear as unbothered as I could.

He furrowed his brow. "Why weren't you sure?"

I set my glass back on the table and picked up my fork and knife again to cut into my food. "I was hoping to find someone to come to the séance I'm having this weekend to talk to my grandmother who died last year, but I didn't really get the vibe that you're as in touch with your mystical side as much as I am."

His eyes went even wider, and I had to work hard to keep a straight face.

"Oh that's..." He shook his head and pulled his wallet out of his back pocket. "I actually think I should get going." He plopped enough cash to pay for both our entrees and a tip on the table. "It was interesting to meet you, Emerson."

"It was great to meet you, too." I smiled up sweetly at him.

He gathered his coat from beside him and quickly slid out of his seat. "Have a good rest of your night. I, uh, hope you find what you're looking for."

I nodded. "I hope you do, too." I took another bite of my juicy salmon and enjoyed the tangy taste of the lemon glaze as it filled my mouth.

Dave might go to the gossip sites and confirm that I was indeed into dark magic, but this food was totally worth it.

And without another glance my way, Dave left the restaurant and left me to finish what was left of my dinner alone.

Hooray for starting off dating with a bang.

7

VINCENT

"HEY, will you take Jaxon to the truck for me?" I asked Cole after we had finished our dessert and were walking toward the parking lot behind the restaurant. "I need to tell Emerson something real quick about Sunday."

Emerson had looked like she was getting ready to leave just as we were walking out of the restaurant, so I figured I could just hang behind for a minute and catch her before she left in her car.

"Sure." Cole shrugged, and then turned to Jaxon who was having fun making footprints in the snow that had fallen outside. "Want to race me to your dad's truck?"

Jaxon's face lit up with delight and he yelled, "Yes!"

And they were running off a second later.

"Watch out for ice," I called after them.

I didn't know if they heard me, but Cole did reach out for Jaxon's hand, ready to catch him in case they did happen upon some ice.

As I waited by the side of the building for Emerson, I pressed the button on my key fob to start my truck so it could be warming up while they waited.

A moment later, I heard the soft tap of high heels on the snow-dusted pavement, and when I turned to see who it was, I found my ex-wife walking toward me wearing the white wool coat I'd bought her for her birthday two years ago. I hadn't seen her wear that coat since before the divorce. Should I take that as a sign that her anger toward me had lessened, at least enough that she could now wear something that tied her to me in a small way?

I knew the second she noticed me because her footsteps stuttered and she placed a hand to her chest.

"Oh Vincent!" she said. "What on earth are you doing hiding behind the restaurant?"

"I wasn't trying to scare you, if that's what you're thinking." I couldn't help but give her a half smile. "I noticed that you were getting ready to leave and figured I'd wait for you here."

"So you were watching me finish my dinner alone?" she asked, and it looked like her cheeks were slightly flushed more pink than they already were from the cold.

"I wasn't watching, I just *noticed* you," I clarified.

"And did you send my date a thumbs-up on his way out for his good sense in dodging this bullet?"

"No." I furrowed my brow. "I wouldn't do that." Yes, maybe I had peeked over in her direction several times once I knew she was sitting in the same section of the restaurant as us. But did she really think I'd rejoice because a guy walked out on her?

"Sure." She started heading toward the parking lot again.

I jogged to catch up. "I don't know why the guy had to leave early, but if it was because he's a jerk, I hope you know me well enough to know that I wouldn't be happy about that."

She stopped walking and turned to look at me with a sigh. "Okay. So what did you need to talk to me about?"

I was about to tell her about my mom's text when out of nowhere, a car appeared at the entrance of the parking lot, going much faster than it should have considering the compact space and snowy conditions.

"Watch out!" I yelled when it looked like it was going to hit Emerson. But she was slow to respond, so I grabbed her arm and yanked her out of the way.

"What are you..." She squealed, bumping against my chest with the momentum.

And all I could mumble was "Car," because the dangerous circumstances and having her body suddenly pressed against mine after a year of zero physical contact had temporarily overwhelmed my senses.

We both wore thick coats, so it wasn't even that intimate of a position, but one whiff of her shampoo and I found my stomach muscles clenching.

I had missed the way she smelled.

She recovered her footing a second later and pushed herself away, putting a good two feet between us. And all I wanted to do was pull her back against me once more, because for those few seconds, I had been happy again.

"I guess I need to pay better attention to my surroundings." She tucked a lock of her blonde hair behind her ear, her green eyes dark in the moonlight. "Thanks for saving me."

"No problem." My voice came out lower than usual, so I cleared my throat and willed my heart to resume its normal rate.

"So what were you trying to say again?" She blinked, like she was still recovering from the near accident.

"Umm." I shook my head, trying to remember what I'd wanted to talk to her about before her breathtaking beauty made me lose my train of thought. Then it came to me. "I got a text from my mom earlier this evening about her plans for the game on Sunday. She said she would like to pick Jaxon up around one-thirty, if that's okay. Traffic will be crazy that day, so she wants to leave plenty of time to get to the stadium."

"Sure, that should be fine," she said.

I nodded, debating on whether to refer the other part of my mom's message to her. The part where she said I should tell Emerson that my mom and Arianna would love to have Emerson join them at the game.

Deciding to risk it, I added, "She also wanted me to tell you there's a spot in the stadium suite for you if you want to come." I swallowed. "She, uh, says that she misses sitting with you at the games."

Emerson's expression went from comfortable to suddenly wary.

"She invited me?" She said it like she didn't quite believe me—like she suspected I was the one behind the invitation and not my mom.

"Yes," was all I said. It was the truth.

But it was also true that I wanted her there, too.

After all the years we'd dreamed of the Dragons making it this far in the postseason, it only seemed right that she should be there.

I wouldn't have made it this long with the Dragons without her support.

So even if we weren't married anymore, she should have a spot at the game...if she wanted it.

I watched her face go through a range of expressions: from surprise, to confusion, to worry.

Her eyes seemed to search mine for some hidden motives, so I tried to appear neutral about the whole thing so she wouldn't know how much I hoped she'd say yes.

Finally, after she seemed to have an internal debate with herself, she said, "I don't know if that's such a good idea, Vincent."

And my heart, which had inflated with hope over the past few seconds, shriveled back to its regular size. "You don't?"

She mulled it over for another second before nodding solemnly and saying, "The suite is for close family and friends. I don't belong there anymore."

"Okay." I studied her face for a moment before I nodded and said, "I guess I can understand that."

Even though I didn't love her answer, I wasn't about to beg her to come if she didn't want to. I'd done enough begging for her to take me back to know that once Emerson made up her mind about something, it was almost impossible to change.

She pulled her coat closer to ward off the cold and forced a smile. "Tell your mom and Arianna thanks for thinking of me, though, and that I'll make sure to have Jaxon ready on time so they won't be late."

"I'll tell her." I pushed my hands into the pockets of my coat. I knew I should probably say goodbye and head to my truck since it was only ten degrees outside and Jaxon and Cole were waiting for me, except I couldn't help but ask, "Was that guy you were out with tonight the guy you're bringing to Derek and Kira's wedding?"

The guy she'd said those photos from the online dating website were for.

She looked down at her feet for a second before meeting my gaze. Then she shrugged and said, "I may have exaggerated a little when I said I already had a date."

"You did?" I asked, my heart bumping against my ribcage. "Why?"

She turned her head to the side, as if my question made her uncomfortable. "Because I knew you were bringing someone, and I didn't want you to know that I still hadn't gone on a date yet."

Wait. What?

"Tonight was your first date?" I blinked, not sure I'd heard her right.

I thought I was the only one having a hard time getting back out there. Her online profile had definitely made it seem like she knew what she was doing, anyway.

She furrowed her brow like I'd hurt her feelings with my question. "Not everyone has legions of people throwing themselves at them."

"If you're trying to say that I do," I said, "you'd probably be interested to know that I haven't started dating yet, either."

Confusion covered her face. "But Kira said..."

I shook my head. "Kira was misinformed. I don't have a date yet."

She seemed to let that soak in for a moment and it almost looked like she was relieved in a way.

But was she relieved because she was just glad she'd been able to move on first? Or relieved because the thought of me dating someone else bothered her as much as seeing her on a date with that red-headed dude had bothered me?

"Well, looks like we're both trying to appear cooler than we really are," she said. "And if tonight is a sign of how the dating world is, I'm going to need to work on some things."

I wanted to tell her she was perfect just the way she was and that she didn't need to change herself in any way—that any guy would be lucky to go on a date with her. But I knew I was a big reason why she was doubting herself in the first place. I'd broken her confidence. Marriage was supposed to mean security. And I'd ruined it.

So I could only say, "I'm sorry that dude had to leave early." I swallowed. "I hope it didn't have anything to do with Jaxon and me interrupting."

She lifted a shoulder. "It was pretty much doomed

from the moment he said he wanted five kids and I knew I couldn't give him even one."

She said it lightly, but I knew her well enough to see the pain etched behind her eyes.

And I hated that. I knew how much she wanted another baby.

"I'm sorry," I said in a low voice that I hoped conveyed how I too felt that pain with her. I would have loved to have given her that baby girl.

"No worries." She wiped at her eye and looked away for a second before meeting my gaze again. "Anyway, when he figured out that you were my ex, he seemed to remember all those rumors about Vincent Lake's ex-wife last year and was happy to split."

She laughed like it was comical, but I didn't see anything funny about it. Not only had I ruined the future we'd dreamed about together, but because of who I was to the rest of the world, other people had misinformed opinions about my wife.

Or rather, my *ex*-wife.

I should have just come clean to the press and lived with the consequences.

"I'm sorry I ruined your date," I said lamely.

"It's okay," she said with a shrug. "It can only get better from here on out."

I clenched my jaw before realizing what I was doing and tried to relax my face so she wouldn't know just how much the thought of her meeting and dating lots of men bothered me.

And since I didn't have it in me to wish her luck with other men, I glanced toward my truck and said, "Jaxon and Cole are waiting for me. I better get back to them."

She nodded. "I better get home, too."

"Have a good night, Emerson." I dipped my head forward. And unable to help myself, I added, "You look really great tonight, by the way."

"Thank you," she said, a sad sort of smile lifting her lips. "You look good, too."

When her gaze scanned me from head to toe, I couldn't help but wish that the attraction we still had for one another was enough to fix everything I'd broken.

I took a step back. "I'll see you tomorrow."

She nodded. "Good night, Vincent."

And all I could think of as I walked back to my truck was that I was the stupidest man in the world to throw away something as good as we once had.

Sometimes I really hated myself.

8

EMERSON

I WAS tired when I got home after my failed date and short conversation with Vincent, but instead of going to bed like I probably should have, I drew myself a bath and decided to see if I had matched with any other guys since I'd last checked the dating app.

While I may have found out that Vincent too had embellished his date status for Derek and Kira's wedding, it didn't change anything for me. If anything, after having Vincent see my date with Dave crash and burn firsthand, I was even more determined to find a date.

Sure, Vincent had been sweet enough about the whole thing and said Dave was dumb to leave, but I had my pride. I would not show up alone and only cement even further in everyone's mind that I was less worthy than my football star ex.

So if it meant messaging every guy I had matched with and swiping through another hundred photos before I went to bed tonight, so be it.

Heck, with how I was feeling right now, I might even add going clubbing to my to-do list.

When I opened my app, I had a few messages to respond to, so I quickly sent my replies before checking to see who else I had matched with.

You have six new matches.

The words showed at the top of my screen. I was about to check out which guys had liked my profile when Ivy Evans's face showed up on my screen. My best friend from high school.

She was requesting to FaceTime with me, but since I was currently in my bathtub I declined the video call and only had the audio come through.

"Hey Ivy," I said, putting my phone to my ear.

"Hey," she said. "Is now a good time to talk?"

"Sure," I said. "I was just about to message some more guys. But this is more fun."

"Oh," she said, sounding disappointed. "So I'm guessing the date with Dave was a bust?"

"Yup."

When I didn't expound further, she said, "What happened?"

"Well, it was going okay at first," I said, remembering back to the first part of the night. "Dinner was good and the conversation was engaging."

"Yeah?"

I ran my fingers through the bubbles in the water. "But when he started talking about wanting to have enough kids to build his own basketball team, I pretty much knew it wasn't going to work out from there."

He and I both only had one kid each, so it would take at least three more.

"Oh." Ivy's voice was soft. "I'm sorry."

I nodded even though she couldn't see me and swallowed the emotion bubbling in my throat. When I felt I could speak again, I said, "So anyway, that was the first sign that we weren't going to work out."

"The first sign?" she asked. "So there was more?"

"Yep," I said. "After the whole kids thing came up, Jaxon suddenly showed up at my side."

"What?" Ivy asked, her tone surprised. "How? Did he and Vincent follow you there? Was Vincent trying to sabotage your date?"

"I don't think so." I shook my head and laughed. Ivy used to have her own gossip blog so of course she'd think of something like that. "Apparently, it was just a weird coincidence. I think they wanted some of that chocolate lava cake they serve there, and they just happened to want it the same night I was there."

"It is a great cake," Ivy said. "That's the cake I ate the night Hazel thought I was secretly dating you."

"It is?" I laughed, remembering Ivy's story. She'd run into Miss Hazel, her grandmother figure, who was having dinner with the guy she was crushing on before —who was now her boyfriend. But back then, Ivy had pretended to be on a dinner date with a fake boyfriend when it was really me she was eating dinner with. And since the universe can't let any lie go unpunished, when Ivy tried to come clean about the fake boyfriend thing, Miss Hazel misunderstood and somehow interpreted it to mean that Ivy and I were romantically involved.

So to prove she was into men and not girls, Ivy ended up kissing Justin right there in the restaurant for all the customers to witness.

"Sounds like Element 47 is quite the exhilarating place to go on a date for both of us," I said.

"Or fake date," she interrupted with a laugh.

I had to smile. "Yep. It has turned out pretty hazardous for both you and me."

"I don't know," she said thoughtfully after her laughter had died down. "I did end up with the guy I kissed that night."

"I guess that's true," I said.

"Maybe the restaurant's real magic isn't necessarily in matching you with the person you went to dinner with, but the person you felt the most sparks with while you were there?" she said. "Was there a hot waiter? Or some other guy sitting at another table who piqued your interest?"

I thought about it. But I couldn't remember anyone that I'd felt any sort of spark with while I was there.

In fact, I hadn't even felt anything when Dave touched my hand at dinner.

If I were to be honest with myself, the moment that had caused my body to react the most to someone tonight was those few seconds when I'd been in Vincent's arms after he saved me from that car in the parking lot.

Yep, my body was really stupid sometimes.

I sighed. "If the restaurant has any sort of magic, it must be dark magic because the guy I felt the most sparks with was Vincent. And I'm pretty sure that's not happening again."

Yes, we still had amazing chemistry. And yes, there had been a few times over the past year when he'd done something sweet with Jaxon or looked at me the same way he had on our wedding day, which had made me wish I could forgive and trust him again.

But going back to someone just because they still made your heart flutter was not a smart way to go about life. Marriage took so much more than attraction and a few tender moments. It took hard work and trust.

And as much as Vincent told me the night with

Victoria was a mistake and meant nothing to him, I couldn't get over the fact that he had slept with her instead of coming straight home to me.

While I knew no one was perfect, and we all make mistakes we wish we could undo, there were just some things that you can't overlook. My mom had forgiven my dad for cheating on her so many times, only to have him leave her in the end to be with a woman twenty years younger than him. I refused to turn a blind eye and forgive and forget like she did. I wasn't going to repeat the pattern that I'd grown up with. Butterflies in my stomach or not.

Ivy must have known something was going on in my head because she said, "It must be so complicated to be around Vincent all the time."

"Way more complicated than I thought." I let out a long sigh. "When we got divorced, I naively thought it meant I would be done with him for good. I somehow didn't think about how I'd still have to see him a few times a week when we exchanged Jaxon."

Yes, I was glad that Vincent and I had a son and that he was still a great dad to him, but divorce was so much more complicated when you had a kid in the mix. You couldn't just make a clean break and never see each other again.

"Oh well." I sighed again and popped a few bubbles

with my pointer finger. "He knows I'm still looking for a date to the wedding, so I'm determined to make that happen."

"Did you match with any more cute guys?" she asked.

"I was just about to check them out when you called. I had six matches at least. Hopefully a couple of them are cute and okay with not adding more children into the mix."

"I'm sure you'll find a guy soon."

Afterwards, Ivy caught me up on everything going on in her life. She was getting settled in her apartment in California. She had moved there to be closer to her movie star boyfriend Justin, and also just because she really loved it.

"Justin is filming in Texas right now," she said. "So I've been filling my time with working at the magazine, which has been good. And I'm excited to fly out to be with him next weekend."

"Sounds like things are going really well for you," I said. "I'm so glad things are working out. You deserve it."

Ivy had been through so much already in her life. It was good to see her getting the things that she had always wanted.

"Thank you," she said. I heard the smile in her voice. "I'm really happy right now."

I smiled. "You sound happy."

"So when are you and Jaxon going to come visit?"

"I'm still not sure," I said. "I was hoping to take some time off in May. Jaxon is getting to the age where I think he'd really enjoy going to Disneyland and the San Diego Zoo, so I really want to take him before the weather gets too hot there."

"And of course you're going to take him to the beach, right?" she asked.

"Of course."

Vincent and I had always talked about renting a big house on the beach for a couple of weeks and just enjoying the ocean and everything along the coast.

I may not have Vincent to do that with anymore, but I could still do it on my own. And it sounded like Ivy might be up for tagging along as well.

"I'll have to look at my schedule a little closer and make sure I have a few weeks without court dates, and then I'll let you know."

"Sounds good," she said.

The water was only lukewarm at this point, the bubbles all but gone, so I knew I'd need to hurry and lather up before it got much colder.

"Anyway," I said. "I better get going now. I'll let you know if I get another date set up."

"Yes, make sure you do."

We said our goodbyes, and then I quickly did my

thing and got out. After dressing in my tank top and shorts for bed, I messaged a few of the guys I'd matched with and went to bed.

Hopefully, I'd be one step closer to finding my Prince Charming when I woke up in the morning.

9

VINCENT

"UM, I THINK WE HAVE A PROBLEM," Cole said in a low voice when I let him into my hotel room Saturday evening.

It was the night before our big game, and I had just been going over my notes for the game tomorrow when his knock interrupted me.

"What?" I asked, feeling my heart rate pick up. "Did Tony sneak his girlfriend into his hotel room again?"

To keep the team in the best mindset before the games, we always stayed in a hotel the night before. That way we were free from outside distractions and able to really prepare ourselves for the next day.

But some of the guys weren't so great about sticking to Coach Anderson's rules.

"No, it has nothing to do with Tony," Cole said.

"Did Bryce get drunk again?" I asked.

"No." Cole gestured for me to sit on the chair in the corner while he pulled the chair out from under my desk, turned it around, and sat down facing me. "It has to do with this."

He held his phone out for me to take.

I furrowed my brow, confused at what could be causing him this much stress.

Had someone written an article about one of us? The press always seemed to have something up their sleeve.

But when I looked at the screen, I saw something entirely different. The logo for the dating app he'd been showing me yesterday was at the top of the screen next to Emerson's profile photo. And below it was a message bubble with the words, **Hey Tyler. Weekend priorities: fishing, Netflix, or trying something new?**

My jaw dropped, and I looked back at Cole as I realized what this meant. "Emerson messaged you?"

He nodded, an uncomfortable expression on his face. "Yeah, apparently she messaged me last night, but I didn't see it until a few minutes ago."

The timestamp did indeed say that it had been sent last night at around ten.

"What should I do? Just ignore it?" Cole asked. "I can't exactly tell her it's me, that would just be weird.

How would I explain swiping right on my best friend's ex-wife?"

"I don't know." I ran a hand through my hair, my palms sweating as I glanced at the words Emerson had written to my friend. "What do people usually do in this kind of situation?"

"I have no idea," Cole said. "I usually type a quick response to see if a conversation starts, but I'm pretty sure I should just leave her hanging."

He probably should.

But was it crazy that I almost wanted to respond for him?

I probably would have started with a boring "What's up?" or some other lame conversation starter. But this quick message, though not intrusive, gave the other person an opportunity to share something about themselves in a non-invasive way.

Emerson had told me last night was her first date since the divorce, but was it possible she had lots of conversations going on like this with multiple guys?

I was about to hand Cole his phone back when I saw the conversation dots appear under her initial message.

"It looks like she's typing something," I said.

"What?" Cole swiveled his chair closer to me and looked over at the screen.

And within a few seconds, a second message came through.

Emerson: **Uh oh—Radio Silence. Should I get my cape and tights and come rescue you?**

And right after that message, a gif of a female super-hero appeared.

Cole and I turned to each other with wide eyes.

I swallowed. "Seems like she's pretty interested in talking to you."

He seemed to swallow hard as well and held his hand out for his phone. "I'd better tell her it's me. This is just weird."

He was just typing in a message explaining that it was him and that he'd accidentally swiped right the night before when something popped into my head.

"Hold on." I snatched the phone from him.

"What are you doing?" He reached out to take it back, but I stood and walked to the other side of the room.

"Let's think this through first."

"What?" he asked. "What's there to think through? I'm not going to try to date Emerson."

"I know. I don't want you to date her but..." I sighed. "I'm probably crazy for saying this, but I just wonder if this is some sort of gift from the universe or something."

"A gift from the universe?" He was eyeing me like I was crazy.

I shrugged. "I don't know. I guess, for a year I've been trying to figure out how to get her to forgive me, how to get her to let her walls down so we can actually have a real conversation with each other, but it hasn't worked. So it just seems like, maybe this is the universe's way of letting me do that."

Cole's black eyebrows squished together. "But dude. She's messaging *me*. Not you."

"I know." I sighed again. "But she doesn't know it's you. I mean, all she knows about you is what you have on your profile. Your photos don't even show your face. All she knows is that you like fishing and have a similar body type as mine."

"So you're saying she only swiped right on me because she thought I looked like you?" He tilted his head to the side. "Because if she was looking for you, she could have just told you that this morning when you dropped off Jaxon."

"I don't mean it like that," I said, trying to sort through my own thoughts that were going about a mile a minute. "I guess what I'm hoping happened was that she did it subconsciously."

"But you don't fish."

"You're being too literal," I said. Then I shook my head. "I don't know. Maybe I'm trying to make something out of nothing just because I hate the thought of her moving on when I can't."

Cole leaned back in his chair and crossed his arms. "So you're saying you want me to message her back and use some sort of voodoo magic and somehow inspire her to realize she really wants to get back with you?"

"No." I looked back at his phone and the messages she had already sent and tried to figure out what I was actually trying to say. "I just want a second chance so bad that I want to somehow use this situation to win her back."

"As in, you want to use my profile to chat with your ex-wife?" Cole offered. "Kind of like that old Tom Hanks movie my mom used to love?"

"*You've Got Mail?*" I asked. That was one of Emerson's favorite movies, too, and she had picked that at least once a year for us to watch for a date night in.

"Yeah, that's the one," he said.

"I guess it would be kind of like that." I pursed my lips and thought about it.

The characters in that movie had never been married and divorced, but they were rivals. And when the Tom Hanks character found out who he'd fallen in love with through email, he had used the situation to his advantage to help Meg Ryan's character to move past the issues they had and fall in love with him.

If I could pull off something similar and not make Emerson really mad at me for doing it, it would be a miracle.

Because nothing else I'd tried had worked.

Maybe this opportunity really was the miracle I was looking for.

"I just want to send her a few messages and see what happens," I said.

"I should probably recommend some sort of intervention or call your therapist to talk you out of doing this." Cole shook his head like he still couldn't believe what I was suggesting. "But go ahead and respond to her." He gestured to his phone.

So I made myself as comfortable as I could be, given the sudden swirl of nerves in my stomach, and tried to figure out a good response.

10

EMERSON

MY HEART JOLTED in my chest when a message came through from Tyler.

It was Saturday night, and Jaxon and I were watching *The Croods* for about the hundredth time this winter. So while the caveman dad started to tell his stories where everyone inevitably died, I had decided to check back on the guys I'd messaged last night.

A couple had responded earlier, and we'd messaged back and forth this afternoon, but Tyler—the buff-looking fisherman—had left his message unread all day.

Until now when he'd apparently seen my second message that had teased him about his lack of response.

Tyler: **Thanks for swooping in and saving me with that cape. And out of those three**

options you gave me, I'd probably pick trying something new.

I'd thought he might pick fishing, because of the photo with a huge fish and the other with him watching the sunset on a boat, but since he had chosen the "doing something new" option, it told me that maybe boating and fishing were just some of the "new things" he had tried one weekend and weren't necessarily hobbies.

I was about to ask him what kind of new things he'd like to try when he followed up his response with a question.

Tyler: **What about you? Would you prefer fishing, Netflix, or trying something new?**

I thought about it.

If I was going to choose the answer that would give him the best insight into my real life, I should probably say Netflix, since it *was* the weekend and I was currently watching a movie with my son.

Plus, it would probably be a good idea to get the whole having a kid thing out in the open just in case he hadn't looked too closely at my profile.

So I said, **Since I'm currently watching The Croods with my son, I should probably pick Netflix.**

Then, just so he didn't think I was a boring single mom, I hurried and added, **Though you really can't go wrong with any of those choices.**

I held my breath and waited to see what Tyler thought about my responses.

Would he run the other direction now that I'd talked about having another man in my life?

Thankfully, I didn't have to wait long for him to say, **You have a son? How old is he?**

I smiled, happy that he hadn't just ghosted me at the mention of Jaxon.

Me: **He's four and pretty much the cutest thing in the world.**

The conversation dots showed on the screen for a moment, but then they disappeared. Maybe he was ghosting me now...

So I quickly shot him another message.

Me: **Do you like kids?**

The conversation dots showed again. His response came back a few seconds later.

Tyler: **I love them. I actually have a son of my own.**

I released the breath I hadn't realized I'd been holding.

He was a parent, too.

So even though he liked trying new things, he would understand how you couldn't always just up and do whatever you wanted all the time when you had other people relying on you.

But the relief only lasted for about a second when I

remembered how Dave had also loved kids...enough that he wanted five. Before things went any further with this conversation, I decided to nip the topic in the bud.

Me: **You love kids? Does that mean you want to have a bunch of them? Hypothetically speaking...**

His response came back quick.

Tyler: **I don't know if I'd go that far. ;) I do love my son and would be open to having more if the opportunity presented itself, but I don't "need" more.**

My chest lightened and a smile slipped on my lips as I read his response. Already this short messaging session was turning out to be more promising than last night's date.

Maybe there were some guys out there who wouldn't be completely turned off when they found out the chances of me having another baby were very slim.

Maybe I should let this guy know who my ex-husband was while we were at it and see if he'd heard and believed any of those rumors about me like Dave had.

But Tyler sent me another message before I could respond to his.

Tyler: **What about you? Do you want more kids?**

I momentarily had the thought about how weird it

was to talk about how many kids we wanted in our futures when we knew next to nothing about the other. But I pushed the thought away because it was important for him to know up front that having more kids most likely wouldn't be part of *my* future.

I only had four weeks to find a date. I might as well find out where Tyler and I would stand when he found out sooner than later.

So I said, **I would love to have more kids, but my baby maker is apparently broken.**

Now if that wasn't laying all my cards out there, I didn't know what was.

When he didn't respond for a few minutes and the read receipt showed he'd seen it right after I'd sent it, I knew I'd said too much.

Way to go, Emerson. You're never going to get a guy if you just say stuff like that.

I quickly typed, **Sorry. TMI.** And then I covered my face with one of the throw pillows and screamed into it.

What kind of girl says stuff like that to a stranger and still hopes to continue to have a conversation?

I'm an idiot!

I shook my head into the pillow, wishing it could somehow erase the humiliating moment. I had only told a handful of people about our infertility issues in real life, and yet, here I was just blabbing about it to Tyler.

I really should have taken some sort of online-dating-for-dummies course. They probably would have warned me about saying things like that.

"Are you scared, Mommy?" Jaxon asked, his voice full of concern.

I pulled the pillow away from my face and looked at him on the cushion next to me. His brown eyes were wide with compassion.

I reached over and patted his leg. "I'm not scared. I was just being weird."

Really weird.

He gave me a warm smile that showed all of his baby teeth. "It's okay. I'll keep you safe." And when he scooted closer and wrapped his little arms around my torso to give me a hug, my heart completely melted.

Jaxon really was the best.

I leaned over and kissed the top of his head. "Thank you for keeping me safe, Jaxon. I love you."

"I love you too, Mom." And then he pulled his arms away and turned so his back was resting against my side, all cuddled up next to me.

We continued to watch the movie like this for another few minutes when my phone finally vibrated and a message from Tyler showed up on my screen again.

11

VINCENT

IT TOOK me a few minutes to convince Cole to let me keep his phone while he went back to his room to read and meditate, but he eventually said I could have it for the next hour, as long as I didn't do anything with it besides message Emerson.

So once I was back to being alone in my room, I read over the last few messages Emerson and I had sent each other, my heart going back to the same racing beat it had been at ever since I sent her the first message.

And as I read through them, I couldn't help but wonder if she said all these things to every guy she matched with.

Or if I, aka Tyler, was the only guy she had told about her struggle to get pregnant and maintain it after Jaxon was born.

Our inability to do that.

At least, when there had been an *us*.

I assumed she hadn't tried to get pregnant with anyone else in the past year. Not if what she'd said about her date from last night being her first since the divorce was true, anyway.

I swallowed as I tried to think of how to respond to her last message. Her apology for TMI told me she was self-conscious about putting it all out there, so I didn't want to say the wrong thing.

Heaven knows I'd said the wrong thing in the past when I was just trying to comfort her about not being able to have a baby.

I chewed on my lip, my thumbs hovering over the keypad on Cole's phone. Then I typed out, **I'm sorry to hear about that. That has to be difficult.**

It was the best I could come up with at the moment.

If I knew Emerson, she was probably already freaking out over the fact that "Tyler" was taking so long to respond, so I pushed send and hoped she'd still want to keep the conversation going with me. Because even though we'd seen each other several times each week for the past year as we exchanged Jaxon, this was the most vulnerable she'd been with me in a long time.

And I didn't want it to stop.

I wanted to get as much out of the next hour as I

could because I didn't know if I'd ever get this opportunity again.

Another message came back.

Emerson: **It is what it is.**

I waited, hoping she'd say something else, but she didn't.

Think, Vincent, think.

I needed to think of something to keep her talking. I didn't want to lose this moment and have her start messaging with some other guy because the topic was hard or awkward. But I also didn't want to change the subject outright, or she might think she'd made *me* uncomfortable.

I rubbed my hands over my thighs.

Should I tell her that I had experienced the same thing? Just from the man's side of it.

Tell her that it had killed me to see her feel so empty and broken and not be able to fix it for her?

Or would that seem like too big of a coincidence and somehow clue her into who she was talking to? I'd already mentioned having a son.

How many single guys in the Denver area fit that demographic?

Probably more than I would think, but I didn't want to risk outing myself yet.

Thankfully, the universe, or whatever force was working with me to make this conversation happen, must have decided to intervene again because Emerson sent another message and saved me from coming up with anything.

Emerson: **Anyway, enough about that. Let's talk about other stuff. You said you had a son. Does that mean you're divorced?**

Me: **Yes.**

Emerson: **Me too. And if you can tell from the way I blabbed all my secrets to you it's probably obvious that I haven't really dated since then.**

I was surprised she was being so honest.

Was she so open with everyone now? Because those last six months of our marriage I didn't think she had even been this open with me.

But instead of allowing myself to be hurt over it, I responded, **I actually really appreciate the transparency. It's refreshing. And if we're both being transparent here, I haven't been on a date since my divorce either.**

I hadn't even had any interest in it. Not when I knew I was still in love with my ex-wife.

Emerson: **How long ago was that?**

Me: **Just over a year. You?**

I only asked that last question because "Tyler" *should* be curious about that.

Emerson: **Same.**

Me: **Looks like we're on about the same time frame as the other.**

Exactly the same time frame.

Emerson: **Sounds like it.**

The conversation continued for the next hour but moved to much more lighthearted topics. We talked about what we liked to do in our free time, our favorite movies, and our most embarrassing moments. And even though I thought I knew Emerson after being married to her for four years and knowing her for six, I realized through our conversation that there were a lot of things I hadn't ever asked or taken notice of.

She still sounded like the same woman; she was just more open and didn't have the walls up.

Maybe it was because of the low-risk nature of just chatting with some random guy on an online dating app that put her at ease, but I found myself letting my walls down as well and not worrying so much about saying things the right or wrong way and feeling like I was walking on eggshells like I had so often this past year.

When Cole knocked on my door to ask for his phone back, I quickly messaged Emerson one more question.

Me: **I have a big day tomorrow and need to call it a night, but it's been great chatting**

with you tonight. Is it okay if I message you again soon?

And after it had gone through, I held my breath. The phone vibrated in my hand a second later.

Emerson: **I'd love to chat with you again soon. Have a good night, Tyler.**

I smiled.

Me: **You too, Emerson.**

And when I handed Cole's phone back to him, I felt lighter than I had in a very long time.

Cole glanced at his phone before slipping it into the pocket of his sweatpants.

"I'm guessing your conversation went well?" He raised a dark eyebrow and seemed to study me.

I nodded, knowing I probably had one of those goofy smiles you normally saw on a teenager's face instead of that of a supposedly tough NFL quarterback. "It did."

"And I'm also guessing she has no idea she's messaging you?"

A twinge of guilt worked its way into my heart. I sighed and said, "No."

"So what are your plans for this?" He leaned against the metal door frame and folded his arms across his broad chest. "I don't want to burst your bubble or anything, but what will you do if she decides she wants to meet for a date? Because this conversation *is* happening because of a dating app. What will you tell her?"

I ran a hand through my hair and shrugged. "I haven't really thought that far." I had just been living in the moment and reveling in the fact that I was even talking to her. "I guess I'll just see how it goes."

"Well," he said, reaching out and patting me on the shoulder. "Just be careful. I don't want you to get your hopes up too much. It might be fun to pretend like you two are just two strangers chatting for the first time and don't have any baggage. But if you want anything to work in the real world, you're probably going to need to also work it out in the real world."

I sighed again. Even though I didn't like hearing it, I knew what Cole was saying was true. Because if Emerson had known it was me that she was talking to tonight, she probably wouldn't have said half of that stuff.

I pursed my lips together and thought about what I could do. But like what happened ever since I'd confessed my biggest regret, I still had no idea how I could fix things.

I leaned back against the wallpapered wall. "I guess I have some things to figure out, don't I?"

"Just try not to worry too much about it tonight, okay?" Cole nodded and stood to his full height. "We still have a big game to win tomorrow."

"I guess I better hit the sack then," I said, knowing I would have to figure this out after tomorrow's game.

He moved to leave, but before he could walk into his room across the hall, I said, "You're not going to go back in there and read through everything Emerson and I just chatted about, are you?"

"Nah, man." He scrunched up his nose and waved a hand at me. "I have my own lady issues to worry about. I don't need to get any more involved in yours."

And with that, I shut the door to my hotel room and tried to do my best to clear my mind of any worries or hopes I had for the future.

I had a game to win tomorrow and I needed to focus on that if we were going to do well.

12

EMERSON

"I'M READY FOR BREAKFAST," Jaxon's voice sounded at the side of my bed Sunday morning, waking me up way earlier than my body was ready for. "I want pancakes."

"You woke up too early." I rolled over to my side, wishing I could just have a few more minutes of sleep before I had to get up for the day.

But Jaxon grabbed my arm and pulled on it. "Get me pancakes now, Mom."

I sighed and rolled back over to face him. He had his mind on pancakes, and I knew my son well enough to know that once he decided he wanted pancakes for breakfast, he wouldn't give up on them until I let him help me make them.

"Okay, just give me a minute." I sat up in bed,

adjusting my shorts that had ridden up in my sleep. "Let Mommy go to the bathroom, and then I'll meet you downstairs in the kitchen."

That seemed to do the trick because he got a big, wide smile on his face and he scampered out of my room, his feet making a soft thumping sound in his footie pajamas.

I dragged myself into the bathroom. I knew once I got myself going I'd wake up a bit more.

It had taken me a while to fall asleep after my chatting session with Tyler. I had chatted with a few other guys during the day and had even scheduled to meet a guy named Andy for drinks on Monday after work, but for some reason, it was my conversation with Tyler that had me unable to fall asleep until the wee hours of the morning.

There had been something about it that just seemed different from my other conversations this week. Not only had we been able to touch on a few difficult topics right from the start, but we'd also been able to just talk about random stuff.

And I'd loved it.

It was the kind of conversation I'd been missing. Deep one minute, lighthearted and flirty the next.

He'd told me that he too had been divorced for about a year, and while I didn't know any of the particulars that had led to that yet, I couldn't help but feel that his ex-wife's loss was every single woman in the Denver area's gain.

Maybe *my* gain.

I shook my head.

Now I was being ridiculous. I hadn't even met him in person, and yet, I was already running off with thoughts like that.

Heck, I didn't even know what he looked like. Not really. His face was covered or hidden from all of the photos he'd shared.

And believe me, after I'd put Jaxon to bed last night, I'd definitely inspected his profile photos again to see if I could zoom in on that fishing photo and get any insight into how cute he might be.

Because he just had to be cute, right?

But he wore a hat and big sunglasses and everything from the eyes down was blocked by a huge fish, so I had no idea what the rest of his face looked like.

Once I was done in the bathroom and had switched my messy braid into a high ponytail and put on my robe, I grabbed my phone from my nightstand and headed downstairs.

Jaxon was already standing at the kitchen island on his special stool when I got to the kitchen, wearing the dinosaur apron my mom had sewed for him.

"Looks like you're all ready to go," I said before

opening the pantry and grabbing the box with the pancake mix.

I mixed the pancake batter in a bowl and then he helped me pour it onto a warm cast iron skillet. While we waited for it to get to where he could help me flip the pancake over, I checked my phone to see if I had any messages in my dating app.

But when I looked at my screen, I saw a notification from the security system that said motion had been detected at our front door at 3:37 this morning. I frowned and swiped my finger across the notification, wondering what it could have been.

When the infrared video came up onto my screen, I saw someone wearing a black hoodie and a gorilla Halloween mask walking onto my front porch with something under his arm.

My eyebrows squished together and my heart raced as I watched the unfamiliar figure bend over and put whatever he'd been holding down on my porch and then run off.

What the heck?

I slid a shaky finger across the video feed to rewind it and watch it again.

"The pancake's ready to flip," Jaxon said, startling me.

I jumped and dropped my phone onto the counter.

"Oops, Mommy." Jaxon laughed, apparently

thinking it was funny. "You dropped your phone. You're silly."

"I need to be more careful, huh?" I forced a smile and quickly helped him flip the pancake over. Then I went back to watching the video again.

Who was that? I wondered as I watched the dark figure repeat what I'd just seen.

The person didn't seem too tall, maybe an inch or two taller than me, but it did look like a male physique under the baggy sweater. His shoulders weren't that broad though, so maybe it was a high schooler playing a prank?

"I'm going to go check something at the front door real quick," I told Jaxon after grabbing him a plate for his pancake. "I'll be right back."

When I opened the door, I instantly jumped back, because lying right there on the welcome mat was a creepy-looking porcelain doll with a note attached with a rubber band to its chest, which said, "You ruined my life. I'm going to ruin yours."

13

EMERSON

"WHAT'S GOING ON HERE?" Janet Lake, Vincent's mother, asked when she stormed into my house two hours after I found the doll on my doorstep.

As soon as I'd realized what I was looking at and what it might mean, I had immediately locked my front door, ran through the whole house like a madwoman and made sure all of the doors and windows were locked. Then I called the police.

Three police cars were at my house ten minutes later and a search of the property and security footage was done. I'd had the foresight to tuck Jaxon away in my bedroom to watch Netflix and eat his breakfast before the police showed up, so thankfully, he didn't realize that I was in panic mode.

I had just finished answering all of the police officers' questions when my ex-mother-in-law and Vincent's sister Arianna stepped into the kitchen.

"Why are the police here?" Arianna asked me when I didn't answer her mother's question. "Is Jaxon hurt? Are you okay?"

I drew in a deep breath and looked at the women who I used to call family. Janet was in her fifties, her hair in a pixie cut and as dark as Vincent's. Arianna was just a year younger than me and she had long dark hair, perfect cheekbones, and ultra-long legs that made her look like she belonged on the runway at a fashion show.

"We're okay," I told them. "Jaxon is watching a movie in my room."

"Then what the heck is going on?" Janet asked.

"Someone dropped off a creepy doll and a threatening note on my doorstep last night, so I called the police to tell them about it."

Since Sutton Creek was such a small town, with rarely anything exciting going on, all three of the on-duty cops had shown up to help me out.

"What?" Janet and Arianna shouted at the same time.

"Someone left a doll and a note on your door?" Arianna asked.

I nodded and creepy chills raced down my spine as the image of the doll popped into my mind again.

Thank goodness the police had taken that disturbing thing with them.

"Do you know who left it?" Janet asked. "Did you catch them on that fancy doorbell camera you have?"

I shook my head. "The perpetrator was wearing a gorilla mask in the video. So we don't have much to go on. For all I know it could just be bored high school kids trying to stir up some trouble for fun."

I really had no idea.

Yes, I was a lawyer and had investigated weird situations before, but nothing like this had ever happened to me.

When we bought this house, we hadn't thought that we needed to put in the huge security gates, because this was Sutton Creek. It was my hometown, and everyone knew everyone. The police literally did sit around drinking coffee most of the time because dangerous things just didn't happen here.

But could that be changing?

"Are the police going to do anything about this?" Arianna asked.

"They'll do some more investigating, see if anything else was reported in the area. And then they said they'd keep an eye on my house for the next few days to make sure no one else comes poking around."

"That's good," she said, seeming to be somewhat comforted. "But you're not planning on staying here, are you? Because it's not safe for you to be here alone."

"I'll probably be fine. I mean, it was just a doll and a note. It's not like they tried breaking in or have damaged anything."

"Yet," Arianna said, her face showing she was unconvinced that I was safe.

And even though I was trying to appear like things would be just fine on the outside, on the inside I was agreeing with her.

I didn't want to be here alone. Not for even a minute.

I mean, right before they had shown up I had considered packing up a suitcase with enough clothes for the week and then heading to my mom's house. Until I realized my mom had gone to visit my brother and sister-in-law in Nebraska for the week.

Janet shook her head and made a tsking sound. "Sorry, but even though you and Vincent aren't together anymore, you're always going to be like a daughter to me and I just can't allow you to stay here by yourself. Not until we know more."

"I agree," Arianna said. "So I'm pretty sure you're coming with us."

"To the game?" My voice raised an octave with my surprise. "But I already told Vincent I didn't belong there."

I'd just had some wacko threaten my life, I didn't need to add possibly running into the Dragon Ladies to my to-do list for the day.

"But you do belong there. You belong there just as much as any one of us," Janet said. "Plus, I already know that your mom is out of town and the rest of your friends are going to already be at the game. So, sorry honey, but you're going to be coming with us whether you like it or not."

"But I don't..." I looked down at my feet, trying to think of a good excuse to go anywhere besides the game. I still had my slippers, pajamas, and robe on. Vincent had already said his mom was worried about beating traffic and getting to the game in time. She wouldn't want to wait for me to shower and get ready. So I said, "I still have to get Jaxon dressed to go with you. And there's no way I'm going looking like this."

"I'll get Jaxon ready," Arianna said. "You go take a shower. You can put your makeup on in the car."

"But..." I was about to protest, to tell them that I really was fine on my own. But then I remembered the guy in the gorilla mask and decided that I really didn't want to spend the next several hours here all by myself. Everyone I knew was going to the game. I needed to be around people right now.

Even if some of those people were the Dragon Ladies.

I let out a long sigh and said, "Fine."

WE ARRIVED at the Dragons stadium an hour before kickoff, so once we were past the crowds and safely inside the luxury suite Vincent had reserved for the season, I tried to relax and make myself at home after the crazy morning. I really needed a break from the real world after the intense past few hours.

The suite was like a mini hotel room, with a huge window on one end with seats that overlooked the stadium. Couches and chairs sat in a small lounging area with a TV for special video footage of the game. And in the corner, there was a little toy area for Jaxon to play in when he got bored with the game.

I set my purse on the granite counter and took in my surroundings. The food for the game was already out—hot food sitting in their warmers, chilled food sitting on ice.

Vincent and I had opted not to have a full staff at our house—just a cleaning crew that came in once a week to keep things tidy—so I'd always loved coming here and feeling pampered with the food already laid out when we arrived.

And until I stepped back in here and remembered the luxury of it all, I hadn't realized how much I'd missed this. I still made a good income as a lawyer and had been able to maintain a housekeeper so I could focus on Jaxon and work when I needed, but being married to a high performing NFL quarterback had definitely had its perks. I certainly wasn't eating at fancy restaurants and traveling as much as I used to.

"I'm sure you remember your way around." Janet set her black-and-white checkered purse on one of the chairs and started removing her thick coat. "Go ahead and make yourself at home."

"Thanks," I said, feeling somewhat awkward. The last time I'd been in this box, I had been the hostess instead of her, so it was a strange feeling to be back here but as an outsider instead of the wife of the football star.

But I tried to push the awkwardness away and went to see what kind of beverages they kept stocked in the fridge these days.

When I opened the fridge, I saw they had the usual diet Coke, diet Cherry Dr. Pepper, and Root-beer that Janet, Arianna, and Jaxon loved, respectively. But also, along one side was a row of my personal favorite flavors of La Croix.

I pulled out a can—Passionfruit essence—and studied it with narrowed eyes. "Is one of you finally trying to kick your diet soda habit?" I asked, glancing at my ex-mother-in-law and sister-in-law.

"As if." Arianna wrinkled her nose. "That stuff is still super gross." And as if to prove her point, she joined me at the fridge and pulled out her diet Cherry Dr. Pepper.

"So, is it for you then, Janet?" I asked.

But Janet just shook her head and said, "No, honey. Sadly, if I was to get a blood test right now, it would most likely come back with a high concentration of diet Coke."

"Then who drinks it now?" I asked. Was it for Janet's sisters and their husbands who had flown in from Alabama to watch the game and would be here soon?

"Well," Janet said, setting her coat over the arm of a chair. "I think Vincent asked the caterers to keep those in there for you."

"He did?" My eyebrows knitted together. "But I told him I couldn't make it today."

Had he not heard me right on Friday?

But Janet just gave me a sad sort of smile and said, "I think that son of mine hasn't quite come to terms with everything yet."

Was she saying Vincent had been hoping I'd come to a game for a while then?

"Are you saying these are here each game?" I asked. "Not just today?"

Janet nodded, her expression careful. "He told them

at the beginning of the season to keep everything the way you liked it."

"H-he did?" I stuttered, my body feeling tingly with those words.

Janet just looked at me with sad eyes. "He probably wouldn't like me saying this, since he's supposed to be this big, tough guy on the field, but I think he's still having a hard time accepting that he's divorced."

Oh.

I looked down at the can of sparkling water in my hand and willed my heart to go back to its regular speed.

Vincent was still having a hard time with everything?

I knew he'd said he still hadn't started dating yet, but I thought that was just because he was busy with football and Jaxon.

"I know what he did was nearly unforgivable and that he hurt you terribly, Emerson." Janet stepped closer and rubbed my back with her hand. "But I guess maybe all of us wish things could have turned out differently."

"Yeah." I bit my lip and ran my finger along the rim of the aluminum can, not able to meet Janet's eyes in that moment because I didn't want her to know how many times I had wanted things to be different over the past year.

It took a minute to regain control of my emotions,

but I was able to meet her gaze again and said, "I wish things had gone differently, too."

Because even though Vincent had broken my heart, I still missed him sometimes. And when I was being truly honest with myself, I knew there was a part of me that would always love him.

He'd been my first love. And though we'd had our struggles, especially during those few months leading up to when he cheated, most of our marriage had been good. We were best friends. Possibly even soulmates.

Soulmates that turned out were only meant to be married for four years.

I opened my can of La Croix and took a sip, suddenly wishing it was red wine instead.

Janet must have picked up on my mood, like she always did, because she put her arm around my shoulders and pulled me closer. "It's okay to miss what you had." She gave me a squeeze. "And even if you aren't Vincent's wife anymore, you're still one of my favorite daughters. So how about we celebrate being together today instead of dwelling on the past or worrying about anything else?"

I rested my head against her shoulder momentarily and sighed. "I think I'd like that."

Heaven knows I already had enough to think about at the moment—online dating, a creepy doll with a note.

I really didn't need to worry about the dynamics between me and my ex.

So instead of thinking about my worries, I forced my mind to live in the present moment where I was hanging out in a beautiful suite with my adorable son and two women who still felt like family, and cheering on the team that was still my favorite in the NFL.

14

VINCENT

"THANKS FOR A GREAT SEASON, COACH," I told our head coach, Steve Anderson, on my way out of the locker room.

We had lost the game.

We were ahead by six points at the half against the 49ers. I wasn't able to do much with our offense but luckily, our defense shut them down until the end of the fourth quarter. We were first and ten on the 49ers twenty-five-yard line with a minute thirty left on the clock. I took the snap, read the defense wrong, and handed the ball to the fullback on an option play instead of keeping it. He was almost immediately smashed by the middle linebacker, and the ball popped out and was recovered by the defense on the 49ers thirty-yard line.

They executed some great run plays and got to our thirty-yard line.

We had used up all of our timeouts and there were eight seconds left on the clock when they sent four receivers down field. The 49ers quarterback threw a Hail Mary pass into the end zone. Eight bodies jumped into the air—it was anyone's ball, but when all was said and done, the other team came down with the ball and won the game.

It sucked that we lost after being so close to advancing closer to the Super Bowl, but I was trying to focus on the positives at the moment.

We had made it to the playoffs for the first time since I'd been on the team, and we were in a good place to do well next year.

"I'll see you tomorrow, Vincent. You go have a nice night with your family," Coach Anderson called, looking up from his phone.

"Thanks, Coach. You too. Tell Coleen and the kids I said hi."

Even though the season was technically over, I still had to come back over the next week to clean out my locker and do a few exit interviews. And though I wished we still had two more games in the lineup, it would be nice to take a few months off. This season had been demanding as I'd worked to prove that I was as good as ever after my injury last year. It would be nice to take it easy for a bit, and maybe I could finally take Jaxon to that dinosaur museum in Utah he'd been talking about.

I checked my phone to see where my mom had decided we should meet up for dinner.

Mom: **Just come to the house when you're done. I'm going to order food in to avoid the crowds.**

I tucked my phone in my pocket and headed to the team parking lot to find my truck.

My mom's house was on the west end of Denver, so I worked my way through traffic and hoped my food wouldn't be too cold by the time I got there.

After my dad died of an aneurysm about three years ago, my mom and Arianna had left my hometown of Auburn, Alabama to be closer to me. She worked as a nurse at the Rose Medical Center and had been there for me more than anyone over the past year as I tried to figure out how to look forward to a future that Emerson wasn't a part of.

The porch lights were on when I pulled up to her ranch-style house. Arianna's car was still parked on the left side of the driveway, which meant she hadn't run off to hang out with her boyfriend Chad as soon as the game was over. The rental car my aunt and uncle were driving was parked in front of the house. I pulled to a stop behind it and parked.

I opened the door of my truck and climbed out, my muscles already giving me some insight into how sore I was going to be tomorrow. And when I walked up the path, I could hear the sound of Jaxon's new favorite song "Immortals" from the movie *Big Hero 6*.

That kid.

He was something amazing.

Without him, I don't know how I would have pulled myself through this past year.

I opened the front door, and when I stepped into the living room where Jaxon was currently showing off his new ninja moves, I saw the last person I expected to ever see at my mom's house.

Emerson.

My breath caught in my throat, and it took a moment for my heart to remember it was supposed to beat again.

What was she doing here?

"Daddy!" Jaxon stopped mid-kick and bounded toward me, jumping into my arms.

I hugged him tight, all the while looking over his shoulder to watch Emerson who had slipped off the brown microfiber couch to stand a few feet in front of us. She wore a Dragons black-and-gold baseball cap and a plain white T-shirt and jeans. And when our eyes locked, I couldn't help but think that she was the most beautiful woman I'd ever seen.

"You did a good job at your game," Jaxon said, bringing my attention back to him.

"Thank you, buddy," I said, setting him down and standing up straight again.

"Watch my new trick," Jaxon said, already ready to move on to the next topic. "I just taught myself."

And without another moment's hesitation, he went right back to what he'd been doing when I came in. He did a few kicks and spins, followed up with a donkey kick with the support of a couch cushion.

"That's so cool," I said. And as he continued to do more of the same, I let my gaze drift back to Emerson.

"I guess you're probably wondering why I'm here." She tucked a stray strand of hair behind her ear, seeming to read my thoughts.

"Just a little curious," I admitted.

"So it's actually a long story." She pressed her lips together. "But I, uh, ended up going to the game with everyone after all, and your mom insisted that I stay to eat dinner with you guys."

"You were at the game?" My eyes widened.

She'd come?

She looked to the side like she was uncomfortable

then lifted a slender shoulder and said, "Yeah, things just worked out so I could come."

"I'm sorry we couldn't win it for you," I said, wishing we could have won the one game she'd attended this season.

"You guys did great." She smiled, like she didn't want me to be disappointed on her account. "It was a close game. I was just happy to be there again."

Jaxon's song ended and he stopped his ninja dance long enough to say, "Guess what, Dad?"

"What?" I asked.

He stepped closer, his face full of some sort of excitement. "Someone left a scary doll at our house today. Mommy called the police."

"Wait. What?" I scrunched up my face in confusion, not sure I had heard Jaxon right.

And when I glanced at Emerson, I saw her giving Jaxon a stern expression that made it seem like she hadn't wanted Jaxon to say that.

"What's he talking about?" I asked, watching Emerson's face for her reaction. "You called the police today?"

"Hey, Jaxon, buddy," Emerson said to Jaxon who had started turning around in circles on the carpet. "How about you go help Grandma finish setting the table, okay?"

"Okay." He stopped his spinning, wobbling a little like he was dizzy, then he ran out of the room toward the kitchen without another word.

Once Jaxon was gone, I crossed my arms over my chest and studied Emerson. "What's going on?"

She chewed on her lip for a moment before shrugging. "I guess someone visited our house last night and decided to leave us a little gift."

"A gift?"

She nodded and then went on to tell me about how the security camera had caught someone with a gorilla mask putting a porcelain doll on the front porch, and how when she'd checked this morning she found a threatening note attached to it.

Then she told me about the police coming right over and searching the yard for anything else that seemed suspicious. And the more she talked, and the more I thought about the kind of danger they could be in, the more upset I became.

"Do they have any idea of who it could be?" I asked, my whole body feeling rigid.

She shook her head. "We're guessing it might just be some bored high schoolers trying to pull a prank on us, but we really have no idea."

"And what's going to happen in the meantime?" I asked.

She just shrugged and said, "I guess we just have to wait and see if anything else happens."

She looked like she was trying to pretend there was nothing to worry about, but from the way her hand was shaking when she smoothed the front of her shirt down, I knew she was scared.

15

EMERSON

"YOU'LL WAIT and see what happens?" Vincent's eyebrows knitted together, his brown eyes showing a fire in them that I hadn't seen since I'd given him the divorce papers.

Before he could get more upset, I hurried to say, "The police are planning to watch the house for the next few days to make sure nothing else happens."

"And that's supposed to make me feel better about you and Jaxon staying there tonight?" He shook his head. "Come on, Emerson. You deal with criminals all the time at work. You have to know that staying at your house isn't a good idea."

"I know..." I said. "It's not exactly my first choice, either. But since my mom is out of town and all the hotels are booked because of the playoff game, I don't exactly have anywhere else to go."

"You could stay here," he suggested. "I'm sure my mom would love to have you."

"She invited me, but I already said no since I don't want to be more trouble." Arianna was already sleeping on the couch as it was since her room was taken by Janet's sister.

He seemed to think for a minute.

"I'm sure we'll be okay," I said, hoping I sounded more confident than I felt so he wouldn't feel like he needed to fix this for me. "It was just a doll and a piece of paper."

But he shook his head. "The note said they wanted to ruin your life. That, to me, says they have much more planned than a creepy doll."

And when he said it, icy chills raced down my spine.

What was this person planning to do to me?

And why?

Vincent must have sensed the fear creeping over me because he stepped closer. And for a minute it looked like he wanted to pull me in his arms the way he used to when I was scared. But then he seemed to think better of it because he stepped back again.

And I didn't realize until he retreated just how much I wanted someone to hold me right now and make me feel safe again.

He cleared his throat and swallowed, looking at me with careful eyes. "Just stay at my place tonight." His words came out so quietly that I wasn't sure I'd heard him right.

"What?"

He cleared his throat again. "I'm going to be taking Jaxon home with me tonight to keep him safe. I can't control what you do, but you're his mother and it matters to Jaxon that you're safe. So please, for his peace of mind, just come stay with me tonight."

Was it wrong to want Vincent to want me with them tonight for his own peace of mind, too?

I thought about his offer for a moment.

Aside from the hour I'd spent at his place on Christmas when Jaxon invited me to come see the presents Santa had brought him, I'd only been in Vincent's house for no more than a few minutes at a time.

Would it be weird?

"It's just for tonight," he said, anticipating my hesitation. "If you want to stay in a hotel tomorrow when they have more openings, I can get you one."

"I can pay for my own hotel." I straightened my shoulders.

It was probably stupid of me to insist on doing that since he was loaded, but I didn't want to feel like I owed him any favors. I could provide for myself.

"If you insist on it." There was a hint of a smile on his lips that made me wonder if he actually liked this new feisty side of me.

I pretended to think about his offer for another second, just because I didn't want to seem like I *needed* him to save the day. But since I really wasn't stupid and didn't want to put myself back in danger, I said, "Fine, I'll stay at your place for one night."

"Thank you," he said. "I'm sure that will make Jaxon feel a lot better."

Just Jaxon? Seemed like he relaxed his stance just a little, too.

"I'll have to stop by my house in the morning so I can get ready for work and get my car."

"I think I can handle that," he said. "I'll be going to the stadium in the morning, anyway."

After we settled the particulars, we went to join everyone in the dining room for the late dinner.

But even though Vincent had seemed to relax a lot more when I said I'd come to his house, I was somehow even more amped up than I'd been before.

Because I was going to be staying at Vincent's apartment tonight.

IT WAS ALMOST ten o'clock by the time we left Janet's house. It had been a long day and I was exhausted. And when we got on the road in Vincent's truck, it only took a few minutes for Jaxon to zonk out in his booster seat in the back. Which left Vincent and me a twenty-minute drive to fill with small talk.

It had been a long time since I'd been in his truck, but it was still basically the same as it had been when we'd been married. It was clean, with just his football bag on the seat next to Jaxon. His black lava stone mala hung from the rearview mirror. And the light scent of his cologne filled the air.

That man had his faults, but coming home after practice or a game smelling like sweat was definitely not one of them. He always smelled so good. I allowed myself a moment to settle into the heated leather seat and just breathe it in.

Even though this day had been long, I had to admit sitting in his truck right now was nice. Like for the next twenty minutes I could just sit here and not worry about anything.

I'd always loved his truck. There was just something about a big, muscular guy driving a big truck that had always been so attractive to me. Like the primal need I had as a female in our species to be protected from danger was instantly set at ease by this.

"What are you thinking about?" Vincent asked as he

pulled onto I-70. "I don't think you've been this quiet around me for a long time, and I can't tell if you're lost in thought or just tired."

A slight smile lifted my lips at his question. He was always curious about what was going through my mind. Even when we'd fought in the past, he always wanted to know exactly what I was thinking so he could figure out a way to make things better.

But since I couldn't come out and tell him that I was thinking about how amazing he smelled and how the primitive side of me missed being in his truck, I said, "I was thinking about how nice it is to just close my eyes in a car and still be going somewhere."

"Yeah?"

I nodded and lazily turned my gaze toward him, with my head still resting against the headrest. "I didn't even think about it until just now, but since I do all the driving wherever I go these days, I forgot how much I used to love closing my eyes and dozing off whenever we took long drives."

He nodded slowly, his gaze still on the road. "I guess I never thought about things like that."

"Yeah," I said, looking through the windshield at the moonlit road surrounded by snow-covered spruce trees. "It's just interesting to think about the things I used to take for granted."

Like how I'd always had someone there to help carry the load when things got crazy.

Or how I always had someone to talk big decisions out with before I made them.

I mean, my mom, Ivy, and Kira were great to listen to me, but having someone with an actual vested interest had been nice. Vincent had always helped me see things from different angles.

And I didn't have that anymore. The only other person directly affected by my choices these days was Jaxon. Since he was only four and a half, he didn't exactly have the same insights an adult would.

Which was definitely something I missed about being married.

But I guess, in a way, Vincent was still showing up for me.

I was the type of person who hated asking for help and Vincent knew it. So he'd offered it anyway—almost demanded it—because he knew me well enough to know that I needed him to be that forceful to accept the help.

I didn't think I'd thanked him for it yet. And the least I could do was tell him thank you.

So I looked back to him again, swallowed some of my independent woman pride, and said, "I don't think I mentioned it earlier, but thank you for helping me out tonight. I know having your ex-wife stay at your bachelor pad probably isn't your first choice for your Sunday evening after a long game, so I really appreciate it."

He glanced sideways at me for a second. "Of course I'd help you out." He gave me one of his meaningful smiles. "Even though we're not married anymore, I still care about your well-being."

I nodded and shifted in my seat. "Well, you're a much bigger person than I am sometimes."

"So..." His smile widened and his eyes lit up in the way they always did when he was about to tease me. "Are you saying that if the tables were turned, you'd be telling me to go ahead and stay at the house and hope the gorilla guy got me?"

I couldn't help but laugh. "If it happened a year ago, I wouldn't put it past me," I said. "But thankfully, for your sake, my beast-mode has calmed down a little more in the past few months."

The anger phase of my grief cycle had definitely been strong in the first six months after the divorce. I was easily triggered and definitely had Vincent walking on eggshells every time we exchanged Jaxon.

But things were getting a lot better now that my emotions had calmed down a bit.

He raised an eyebrow. "Does that mean you don't throw darts at my NFL photo anymore?"

I gasped. "How did you know I did that?"

Had Ivy snitched on me?

He chuckled as he turned the wheel to take the curve in the road. "You had the dart board sitting in the coat closet one night when I brought Jaxon back home. The photo was still pinned to it, with about a hundred holes poking my face."

I covered my face with my hands, so embarrassed that he had seen that. "I promise I only did that once," I said, daring a glance back at him. "And it involved a late night with Ivy and lots of wine."

Probably a whole bottle, in fact.

"You have nothing to feel bad about," he said, surprising me at how chill he was about the whole thing. "In fact, I wouldn't blame you if you did it every night. I deserved it after what I did to you."

And when he looked at me with his eyes all soft and pleading, I really did believe him. He'd done nothing but apologize since the moment he told me everything.

I just hadn't been in a place where I could hear or accept his apologies before. But I was getting closer. A little less angry at him every day. Which told me I was moving closer to the acceptance part of the grief cycle.

I said, "For what it's worth, I don't hate you as much as I did."

And as I watched him for his reaction, I saw his Adam's apple bob, like my admission was bringing on some strong emotion he was trying to repress.

It seemed to take him a moment, but when he was

able to speak again, he said, "I appreciate you telling me that." He swallowed again, and when he spoke his next words, his voice was thicker than it had been before. "I hope someday you'll be able to forgive me."

With his words and the sincere way he said them, a mix of emotions swirled through me: hope that something like that was possible and a wish that there had never been a need for forgiveness in the first place.

Oh how I wished we could go back in time and fix things before they started going downhill. Because even though I was finally getting to a better place and had picked up the pieces of my life, I'd give anything to have my little family put back together.

But since I couldn't go back in time and fix everything before it happened, I tried to think about the possibility of what he wanted. And even though I knew I still wasn't there yet, I said, "I hope I can forgive you someday, too."

16

VINCENT

"I SEE you haven't bought any furniture since the last time I was in here," Emerson said to me when I came back to my living room after putting Jaxon in his bed. "Is it too much to hope that you have an extra bed for guests in that third bedroom of yours?"

"Um, not exactly." I scratched the back of my neck. "I don't really have a lot of extra space in there with all my gym equipment."

I guess I probably should have considered where she would sleep before insisting she stay over. I'd just been so determined to have her not stay at her house that my thought process hadn't gone that far.

"Okay." She said the word slowly as she looked around my small living room that had a single couch—a very worn and not super comfortable couch from my pre-Emerson days that I'd been meaning to upgrade. "I guess I can just sleep on the couch then. You have extra blankets, right?"

Yeah, having extra blankets would have been good too.

"I might have one somewhere..." I said, not sure if I'd ended up switching the laundry from the washing machine to the dryer yet. Jaxon had insisted we have a picnic inside on Thursday night and accidentally spilled his cup of milk all over my only extra blanket. "I think I started to wash my extra blanket but with the big game on my mind, I may have forgotten to switch the load."

"Do you want to check?" She raised her eyebrows, looking hopeful.

"Sure," I said. "I'll be right back."

I hurried down the hall to the closet where my washer and dryer were. And sure enough, when I opened the lid, I found the blanket.

And of course it smelled like it had been left in there a few too many days. So I added some more detergent to the washing machine and started it again.

I went back to Emerson.

"No blanket?" she asked.

I shook my head. "No."

"Well, I guess I can just wear my coat if I get cold."

Sleep in her coat?

Now if having my ex-wife sleep on my dumpy

couch wearing a coat to stay warm when she stayed the night at my place wasn't a sign that I was the worst host in the world, I didn't know what was.

"You can just sleep in my bed," I said, realizing I should have offered in the first place. "I can sleep on the couch."

She gave me a skeptical look. "But you just got tackled by a bunch of three-hundred-pound guys," she said. "I can't take your bed from you when you're already being so nice to let me stay here."

"No, really. I can take the couch. It's no problem."

She looked back at my couch and seemed to inspect it. It had definitely seen better days, and there was a spot in the middle that had sunk in.

But it wasn't *that* bad. I could handle one night of bad sleep. It wasn't like I had a game to play tomorrow.

"You know better than I do how important rest is for you after these games." She turned her gaze back to me and studied me from head to toe. "Plus, you're six-four and sleep on a California king-sized bed. There's no way you'd even fit on that couch lying down."

"So I'll curl up a bit," I said. And to prove my point, I walked past her and lay myself down on the couch. Sure, it was lumpier than I remembered, but my body was exhausted enough that I was bound to fall asleep anyway. I waved a hand in her direction. "I'll be fine out here. Go ahead and take my bed. I can't have my mom finding out that I'm not a gentleman."

Emerson just stared at me with a smile that told me I looked ridiculous. "How about we both just sleep in your bed?" she said. "I mean, it's not like we haven't done it before. It doesn't have to be weird."

"What?" I bolted upright, not sure I was hearing what I thought I was hearing.

She nodded and gave me an uneasy look. "We can be adults about this, right?"

Sleep in the same bed as Emerson?

I knew we'd done it hundreds of times before, but for some reason, the thought of her sleeping just a foot or two away from me made my heart race.

But if she was okay with it, I could be okay with it.

So I said, "I guess that could be okay. It is a big bed."

"Right," she said, seeming a little more comfortable with the idea. "And as long as we promise to stay on our own sides of the bed it will be almost like sleeping in separate beds."

Except that when we used to share a bed, we'd always both end up in the middle by the morning—even when we'd gone to bed angry and had clung to our sides when we'd first fallen asleep.

But I wouldn't mention that right now, because the prospect of sleeping on this terrible couch was feeling less and less appealing the longer I sat here. So before either of us could see reason and change our minds, I stood and said, "I guess we should probably get to bed then."

A little apprehension formed behind her eyes, as if she wasn't quite sure it was a good idea to sleep in the same bed as me after all. But then she nodded and said, "Yeah. Let's go to bed." Then she quickly shook her head, her face flushing. "I mean, let's go to your bedroom." She shook her head again. "To sleep. Only to sleep." Her cheeks darkened further. "You know what I mean."

I laughed, loving the way the color on her cheeks made her look. And also loving that even though we weren't together, she could still blush around me.

"I know what you meant," I said.

Her shoulders relaxed and she released a sigh. "Good."

And without another word, I led her down the hall toward my room. But from the butterflies that swarmed in my stomach a little harder with each step I took, I had a feeling that I probably would have gotten more sleep on the couch tonight.

Because I was definitely not tired anymore.

17

EMERSON

WELL, this night just got more interesting, I thought as I followed Vincent down the hall to a part of his apartment that I had never been to before.

And as I followed, I allowed myself to take in his muscular torso.

He really was the epitome of a male specimen. Broad shoulders. Amazing triceps. Perfect forearms with just the right amount of vein poppage going on. His torso was lean, but even though I couldn't see through his shirt, I knew he had a natural eight pack that most of his teammates had to do lots of core workouts to achieve. His athletic butt deserved to have its own Instagram fan account dedicated to it. And his legs, yeah, they were amazing, too.

Pretty much my ex-husband was God's gift to the universe and a huge reason why the Dragons' female fan population had risen over the past few years.

I shook my head.

Why was I even thinking about this? Thinking about how hot he is was not something I needed to do right before I was going to sleep in his bed.

Yes, he was still the most attractive man I'd ever laid eyes on. But it didn't mean I needed to remind myself of all the reasons why.

Especially if I was going to keep my hands to myself when we were sleeping just a foot or two apart.

And I would keep my hands to myself.

Because even if it had been a year since I'd kissed or been held by a man, I was an evolved being. I was an independent woman who didn't need a man to fill any carnal needs.

I wasn't an animal.

Plus, kissing and cuddling were totally overrated anyway. The only person I needed hugs from these days was my adorable sweet four-year-old.

Yep.

I was practically invincible to temptation.

But when I allowed myself one more look at the man who had always been my Achilles' heel, I had a feeling I'd need a little more than pure self-restraint to keep me from accidentally bumping up against him in the night.

I might just need a mountain of pillows.

Hopefully he had more pillows in his apartment than he had blankets.

"So this is my room," Vincent said, breaking me from my nonsensical thoughts when we made it to the first door at the end of the hall. He switched the light on and gestured for me to step inside.

I furrowed my brow as I took in the room. It was practically empty.

"You only have a bed and a nightstand in here?" I turned to look up at him. "Where is the rest of your stuff?"

There were no pictures on the wall. No football gear stashed in the corner. There wasn't even a TV or a dresser in here.

What happened to all the stuff I'd had the movers pack up for him when he was at an away-game one weekend?

He shrugged his broad shoulders, the fabric on his black T-shirt stretching tight against his muscular chest. "I keep everything else in my closet."

Well, his closet must be jam-packed then, because now that I thought about it, the rest of his apartment was pretty bare as well. The kitchen counters were always clear. His living room only had that dumpy couch, a small chair, and a TV that hung on the wall.

And aside from a photo of him and Jaxon that I'd seen on his fridge, there were no other decorations anywhere.

"If the rest of your house is this empty, I think I need to see this closet of yours." It had to be stacked with boxes.

He gave me an amused look but didn't say anything. Instead, he led me into his master bathroom that was similarly tidy and mostly empty and opened a door across from the sink. He turned on the light to his small walk-in closet and my eyebrows squished even closer together when I saw it also had barely anything in it, too.

Had his truckload of things gotten lost in transit?

Because in front of me there were about five suits hanging on the rod, two tuxedos, a few dress shirts and slacks, and the dresser that was the twin to the one in my bedroom which I guessed held his T-shirts, jeans, and workout clothes.

I turned to him with a confused expression. "Are you, like, a minimalist now?"

He shrugged and leaned against the doorframe, his towering height making me feel small and petite. "I guess. At least that's what I'm working toward."

Which would explain why he only had one extra blanket and hardly anything else in the whole house.

"How long have you been one?" I asked, my interest piqued. Because even though he'd always been tidy and very conscious of his spending when we were married, he had definitely had more things than this.

"Not too long." He rubbed the back of his tanned neck, drawing my eyes to his big, rugged hands that had expertly thrown a football earlier today. "I, uh, read a few books on minimalism last summer during training camp after my therapist got me hooked on personal development books."

Wait, he had a therapist?

Had I heard him right? Maybe he'd said something else...a thera___. Well, I couldn't exactly think of another word that resembled *therapist* at the moment. So I moved on to the next surprising thing in that sentence.

Vincent was reading.

And not just the children's books Jaxon begged us to read, but actual personal development books.

That was new.

Why did the thought of him reading in his room at night suddenly make me even more attracted to him than I'd been earlier?

Deciding to ask about the less charged topic of the two, I asked, "What got you interested in reading?"

When we were married, he was the guy who joked about waiting for the movie version of a book to come out instead of reading it since he hated reading so much. And now he was actually reading? Of his own free will and choice?

He stood straighter and walked out of the closet area. "I started for a couple of reasons." He leaned against the bathroom counter, supporting himself with his hands in a way that made his forearm muscles flex. "First, because I needed to work on some things." He looked at me through his lashes, telling me his therapy had something to do with the divorce and everything leading up to it.

"And then I just wanted to get better at reading." He cleared his throat. "I've always used my dyslexia as an excuse not to read before, since it took me so much longer than everyone else to make sense of it all. But my therapist helped me realize that some of the insecurities I had in the past came from my embarrassment about being dyslexic and having trouble reading. So he suggested I start reading aloud to myself. The personal development books were the smallest ones in the book-store, so I kind of got on this personal development and minimalism kick and became a better reader all at the same time."

"I never knew you were embarrassed about being dyslexic," I said, seeing a different side to him that he hadn't let me see before.

He shrugged and looked off to the side for a second.

"I didn't exactly like to bring it up," he said. "I mean, you are this genius lawyer who graduated from college two years early. And I'm just an athlete who barely made the grades to not get kicked off the team. I didn't exactly want to remind you that you could have married someone smarter."

And when he met my gaze again, there was a vulnerability there that I had never seen before. It was like he was opening the darkest corners of himself up to me and just hoping I wouldn't reject him.

As I realized how much he was trusting me in this moment, the intense feeling that burned in my chest left me feeling weak.

I leaned against his closet door for support and just took him in. Here was this giant of a man who was in the top one percent of all the athletes in the whole world, and he had been ashamed of a reading disability he was born with?

Enough that he hadn't even felt safe talking about it with his wife?

Had I really been that hard to talk to back then?

I just watched him for a moment.

"I'm sorry if I ever made you feel less than for not being into the same things as me," I said, searching his eyes so he'd understand that I meant what I was saying. "I always thought you would wake up one day and realize I didn't belong in your world of football and fame. That you'd see me for what I was. Just a nerdy girl who you felt you had to marry because we slipped up and I got pregnant."

18

VINCENT

I BLINKED my eyes a few times as Emerson's confession hit me.

She thought I'd only married her because we'd gotten pregnant with Jaxon?

"How could you think that?" I asked. Because until this exact moment, the thought had never crossed my mind.

Not one single time.

Sure, we had hurried to Vegas and gotten married quicker than I'd originally planned, but marrying her had always been part of my endgame. I had just been waiting for the right moment to ask her and hadn't found it before she took the pregnancy test.

"I don't know." She shrugged and looked down at her feet. "Just the way you wanted to rush through everything made it seem like you cared more about maintaining your good-boy public image than the actual marriage vows."

And when she put it like that, I guess I could see how she had seen it that way.

And I may not be able to fix everything between us, but I could try to at least fix this.

So I stepped closer and lifted her chin with my fingers and said, "I'm sorry I made you feel that way." I paused, looking into her beautiful green eyes and willing her to understand me. "I shouldn't have reacted like I did back then. It was wrong of me to rush the wedding like that. It had to feel pretty crappy to have the day you probably thought about since you were a little girl be turned into a spur-of-the-moment weekend trip."

I dropped my hands and stepped away again. Wishing I could go back in time and tell myself not to be such an idiot.

"It's not all your fault," she said in a quiet voice I could barely hear.

I looked back to her face.

She swallowed and stepped closer, close enough that if I reached out I'd be able to pull her against me.

"I could have told you to wait if I had really wanted to," she continued.

"Yeah?" I asked.

"But I guess I figured it was my one chance to nab

you and make sure you were mine, so I'd gone ahead and done it."

My throat constricted, an ache forming at the back of my throat over the thought that at one time, she had thought I was worth calling hers.

It took a moment, but once I could trust my voice not to crack, I said, "I hope you know that even though I made a million mistakes, one thing never changed."

Her green eyes widened, as if she was almost afraid of what I might say next.

Like it might hurt her.

But I had to say it.

"I never regretted marrying you, Emerson." I reached out and took her hands in mine, running my thumbs along her knuckles. "And even now that we're not together, I still don't regret it, because you gave me some of the happiest years of my life. You gave me Jaxon. And even if we don't always see eye to eye on everything, I feel lucky that I still get to be involved in your life even if it's just because we share a son."

She sniffled, and that was when I noticed her eyes were more watery than they'd been before. So I did something I hadn't dared do in over a year: I tugged her closer to me and invited her into my arms.

At first she seemed to hesitate, like she was afraid of getting close, but then she sighed and closed the distance between us. When she rested her head against my chest and slipped her arms behind my waist, it filled my soul in a way it hadn't been filled since we'd broken up.

We fit together.

Her body next to mine still felt right after all this time.

"You're an amazing woman," I whispered, resting my chin on the top of her head. And even though it ripped out my heart to say it, I said, "And even if things couldn't work out between you and me, I hope the next guy you give your heart to appreciates and understands what he has. Because you deserve the best, Emerson. You deserve the world."

A world where I would be the supporting side character instead of the lead.

In that moment I knew that I would always love Emerson. It was just one of those irrefutable truths that would always be.

But maybe truly loving her now and wanting the best for her meant being there for her as she moved on.

I could only hope that someday I'd be able to move on, too.

19

EMERSON

I DON'T KNOW how long Vincent and I stood there in each other's arms. How many heartbeats had passed as I rested my head against his strong chest? How many breaths we each took as the minutes ticked by?

But even though I knew I should let him go and head for bed because I had work early in the morning, I couldn't seem to pull myself away. I didn't want to ruin this tender moment we were having, because I knew once we stepped away, I'd likely never have a reason to be in his arms again.

And the thought of never being held by him again hurt more today than it had in a long time.

We had come to a resolution that we'd been missing over this past year. We had both hurt each other a lot— said things we didn't mean. But something was apparent in all of this: we had both cared deeply for one another for a period of our life.

We had simply let our insecurities cause a divide and leave us vulnerable to the outside forces that would inevitably break us.

Even though I was still processing everything we'd said tonight—because there was a lot—the steady beat of his heart next to my ear reassured me that we would come away from this okay. And maybe, just maybe, full healing was closer than I had ever imagined before.

He would support me as I worked to move on and rebuild my life with someone else.

And he—

Well, I had a feeling he might be one step closer to being able to switch up the drink selection in his luxury suite next year.

We could be each other's cheerleaders from now on. Maybe we could even be friends.

Vincent's chest expanded as he drew in a deep breath. And when he started rubbing my back with his hands, I relaxed against him even more.

When was the last time we'd done this? I knew it hadn't happened since the night he told me everything.

I hadn't allowed him to touch me after that.

Had it happened the Saturday before? When he'd left with his weekend bag to fly to an out-of-town game?

Or had we just exchanged a quick goodbye peck on the lips before he left the house that morning?

I couldn't remember.

I couldn't even remember our last kiss.

And for some reason, this realization made my chest hurt a little.

If I'd known it would be our last, I would have savored it more—let it be one to remember.

It only seemed right that the last kiss you had with someone be as embedded in your mind as much as your first.

"What are you thinking about?" Vincent asked, his voice quiet next to my ear.

Of course he'd ask that question right when I was thinking about the very last thing I wanted him to know I was thinking about.

Kissing him.

"Nothing," I hurried to say.

Why did my voice have to come out sounding all breathy?

He stopped the movement of his hands on my back.

"Nothing?" he asked in his deep voice that reverberated in his chest. "Really?"

"Uh huh." I nodded and pulled away to look at the V-neck of his T-shirt, working hard to keep my face from giving my thoughts away.

"Then why won't you look at me?" he whispered, a suspicious tone in his voice.

"I am looking at you." Maybe not his face, but the skin below his neck was still a part of him.

He chuckled lightly, the deep sound causing more goosebumps to race across my skin. "I thought this whole conversation we've been having was all about being open and honest with each other. Why are you lying to me now?"

Because if I told him I was thinking about kissing him, he'd probably think I was interpreting his kindness in letting me stay here and the moment we were sharing as something more than it was.

And I wasn't.

I knew the Emerson-and-Vincent train had crashed and burned long ago. And there was no way to get a train back on the rails that was burnt to a crisp.

But even though I knew all that, it didn't mean I couldn't still wish to remember certain "lasts" with him.

Like the last time we laughed so hard together that we couldn't stand up straight.

Or the last time we stayed up late talking because we didn't want to stop.

"Were you thinking about what happened at your house this morning?" he asked when I didn't say anything, his tone serious.

"No," I said. Somehow I'd been able to push that to the recesses of my mind this past hour.

"Then are you thinking about work?" he asked. "Do you have another big case coming up?"

Was he seriously just going to guess until he figured it out?

I already knew the answer to that question.

Yes. Yes, he would. Because this was Vincent Lake and he was one of the most persistent people I knew.

So I lifted my gaze up to his face and said, "I wasn't thinking about work." But at this angle, with us standing so close to each other and with our arms still around each other's waists, I was right back to thinking about kissing him again.

His gaze flicked down to my lips for a split second before returning to my eyes.

Had he just thought about kissing me, too?

That couldn't be good.

Could it?

He cleared his throat. "I can keep guessing all night if you want me to."

I bet he could.

I focused on his Adam's apple and said, "Don't take this in a weird way or anything, but I was trying to remember the last time we kissed." I let my eyes flicker up to meet his. "Because I can't remember it."

His eyes widened, and I knew I'd caught him

by surprise. But he seemed to recover quickly enough and said, "Why are you thinking about that?"

"I don't know." I lifted a shoulder, my cheeks blooming with heat. "It just came to my mind."

"Well..." He frowned and seemed to mull over it. "It might have been when I first got home from that last game before you kicked me out."

"See, and I wondered if it was before you left."

"It's probably one of those." He shrugged.

I nodded. "But isn't that kind of sad? That we can't even remember it?" I asked. "Almost four years of marriage and we can't remember."

He pursed his lips together. "I think it's pretty normal." His thumbs traced a line along the center of my back. "You just get in the routine of things and don't think as much about them."

I guess. But if I was going to never kiss again the first guy I'd ever given my heart and soul to, I wanted to at least end with something memorable.

"You're thinking about something again," he said, as if he could read my mind. "What's going through that genius mind of yours?"

"Promise you won't make fun of me or get all weirded out?"

"I promise."

"Okay." I sighed. "I was just thinking about how

lame it is to end things the way we did and how I want a redo."

He pulled his head back and sputtered, as if my words had made him choke on something.

And that was when I realized how I had sounded. "I didn't mean I wanted a redo right now." I shook my head. "Like, I don't think we should kiss right now or anything. I just meant that I wish I could go back in time or something and redo our last kiss, and somehow let myself know ahead of time that it would be the last so I would remember it better."

Just stop talking, Emerson!

I thought that explaining it would make me sound less like a weirdo, but the more I continued, the more I knew I was just embarrassing myself more.

But to my amazement, Vincent didn't push me away from him and run. Instead, he got a contemplative look on his face. "I guess that makes sense."

It did?

I swallowed. "It does?"

His thumb ran along my spine again. "I mean, everyone always talks about their first kisses being memorable. Why shouldn't last kisses be the same?"

"See?" I nodded. "That's what I was thinking, too."

"It's not like it has to be weird or anything. I mean, it's just a kiss."

"Yeah," I said, relieved that he didn't seem to think I

was crazy for bringing it up. "We've kissed tons of times. This would just be the bookend to our story."

"It started with a first kiss under the tree at your dorm room. It could end here at my place."

He said it like it was completely fine and normal, but when I searched his eyes, there was a hint of sadness in them. Like he too understood the finality of this moment.

And I almost wanted to run from it, because I suddenly realized why we didn't always remember the lasts in our life: because lasts were sad.

Saying goodbye was hard, so it was easier to just not think about them.

"So should we just do it right here, then?" He nodded to his small bathroom. "Is this where it should happen?"

I looked around at our surroundings. It wasn't nearly as big and high end as the bathroom we'd once shared at our house. It was still tidy, and he had taken good care of it—whether that was with the help of a cleaning company I still didn't know. But it was very *Vincent*. Masculine and clean with the faint scent of his body wash still clinging to the air from when he'd last showered.

I'd forgotten how much I loved the smell of him.

But instead of letting my mind go down that rabbit hole, I made myself focus back on the present and said, "This is probably as good a place as any."

It wouldn't be like one of those romantic movie scenes, where the couple was standing outside under a streetlamp while snow softly fell around them. But those kinds of scenes were for first kisses.

This was a last kiss. A plain old bathroom was probably perfect.

"So should we just—" He tilted his head to the side and shrugged. "—go for it then?"

I smiled. He wasn't Shakespeare, but his straightforwardness was definitely all him.

"Yeah, we probably should."

He pushed away from the counter and stood to his full height, the movement making me step back and straighten up as well.

I looked up at his face, having to crane my neck because he was so much taller than me.

"Why do I suddenly feel like I'm in middle school and trying to figure out how to kiss the pretty girl at the dance?" he asked with a half-smile on his lips.

"I don't know," I said, my stomach feeling like it had a flock of hummingbirds flapping around inside. "I mean, I feel like I'm at least sixteen."

His smile broadened at my attempt of a joke. "You always were the mature one."

I couldn't help but smile back. "What can I say, I'm an old soul."

He stepped closer and ran his thumb along my cheek in a caress that made a trail of fire follow it. "So, are you ready?"

I didn't know if I could ever really be ready for this. But I said, "I'm telling my mind that it needs to remember this last one this time."

"Me too," he said.

We looked at each other for another long moment, and then, before I could lose my nerve, I placed my hands on his shoulders, stood on my tiptoes, and pressed my lips to his.

And just like I remembered, his lips were soft and warm and tasted of his minty Chapstick.

I was just getting used to the sensation of my lips sparking to life against his after so long when he pulled away. I held still, not opening my eyes, hoping he'd come back again.

But he didn't.

That was it?

Had he really only been humoring me and a few seconds was all he could take?

My ego a little bruised, I lowered myself back down to my heels and looked at him with searching eyes.

"Was it really that horrible, then?" I asked, my face burning with humiliation. Because if he could barely stand to kiss me for two seconds, it was no wonder that we hadn't worked out.

But to my surprise, his brow knitted together as if he was confused by my question. He said, "No. Did *you* think it was horrible?"

"No. I thought it was okay," I said, relief beginning to pulse through me. And feeling a little more confident that he wasn't about to scrub my kiss off his lips with soap and water, I ventured to say, "But you pulled away really fast, so now I'm worried that you equate kissing me on the same level as kissing your great aunt Mazie."

"Kissing great aunt Mazie?" He wrinkled his nose. "Definitely not like that at all."

I frowned. "Then why did you pull away so soon? I thought we were going for a memorable last kiss here. Not another forgettable one."

"Yeah, we were..." He rubbed his hand along the back of his neck. "I guess I'm just a little rusty and maybe a little nervous."

He was nervous?

Why did that alone make me feel about a million times better?

"Well," I said. "If you're rusty, then so am I since it's been the same length of time for me as it's been for you." At least, according to what he'd told me, it didn't sound like he'd kissed anyone else since our divorce.

"I promise I wasn't trying to make you feel bad with

the brevity of that kiss." He let his hand drop to his side. "Do you think we should give it another try? Now that we've gotten the first one out of the way?"

"Yeah." I licked my lips as anticipation filled me again. "For memory's sake, I think we probably should."

"Okay," he said. "Just go easy on my ego, okay? Every athlete needs time to warm up first."

I nodded, but any response I had to his last sentence got lost on its way from my brain to my lips when he stepped closer, slipped an arm behind my waist, and slowly ran his thumb across my lips.

Ok, wow. Maybe all he really did need was that warm-up. Because this was definitely more like what I remembered from him.

My heart thumped hard against my ribs. I tried to tell my heart to calm down, because he was only turning up the charm to make this memorable and not because he had actual feelings for me, but my heart didn't want to listen. It wanted this to be real for some stupid reason that I didn't understand.

"Are you ready to make a memory?" he whispered, his warm breath caressing my lips.

If I hadn't caught the slight shake in his voice I never would have guessed that he was nervous about this, too.

It really was like being sixteen again, wasn't it? Sixteen and about to kiss the hot guy at school who everyone knew was way out of my league.

"I'm ready." And before I could think another thought, Vincent closed the distance between our lips.

I gasped, somewhat caught off guard. But his hand cupped my neck, steadying me and pulling me closer as he coaxed my lips to move slowly with his. And even though it was much the same as the kiss before, it was also different. He kissed me gently, his lips lingering and coaxing mine to move with his. And when he finished one kiss, he came right back and kissed me again.

He kissed me as if I was fragile and he didn't want to break me. Whatever rustiness he'd claimed to have earlier must have worn off in the first few seconds, because this man clearly remembered how to kiss me the way I liked to be kissed. And the slowness of the kiss made my stomach twist and shake with pleasure I hadn't felt in such a long time.

I could barely draw in a decent breath as his warm lips caused crackles of electricity that sparked mine to life again. And suddenly, I never wanted this last kiss to stop. It felt much too good to be so close to Vincent with his lips capturing mine between his.

So before he could get any ideas of ending our final kiss before I'd had enough, I let my hands trace their way up his arms to rest behind his neck. He was so tall that he was almost bent in half to kiss me. I raised myself up on my toes to help him out, and he reacted by pulling me closer and wrapping his arms tightly around me.

"You think you'll have any trouble remembering this?" he asked, breaking the lock his soft lips had on mine.

"I think I might need a little longer...." I sighed, trying to catch my breath, but it was coming in short little bursts. "To fully cement it in my mind, that is."

Okay, I was probably being totally obvious in how much I was enjoying this last kiss with him, but at the moment, I didn't really care. My mind had gone to that foggy, detached place where it didn't care about anything besides getting more of this. More of Vincent's lips on mine. More time with his arms wrapped around me. More us.

And as I let my logical mind take a backseat for once and had the rest of me just live in the moment, a realization came to my mind that I had only noticed small glimmers of before.

Maybe I didn't want this to be our last.

But a thought like that was too big to consider when my mind was so caught up in the feeling of everything, so I pushed it back to the recesses of my brain and told myself not to worry about it.

I didn't need to worry about little thoughts like that. And when his lips trailed away from my mouth to kiss the sensitive skin at the nape of my neck, I stopped thinking altogether.

"I've missed this," he whispered, his voice husky and warm.

"You have?" I asked, not sure I'd heard him right.

He nodded and trailed kisses up my neck, along my chin, and back to my mouth. He gripped my waist, and before I knew what was happening, he turned us around and lifted me in the air. He set me down on his bathroom counter, and somehow, pulled me even closer until there was no space between his muscular body and mine.

Man, he felt good.

I let my hands slip along his broad shoulders, along the contours of his chest and down the length of his torso.

He was a work of art, really. The epitome of the perfect man that I still saw in my daydreams.

And I wanted more.

I slid my fingers along the hem of his shirt and let them linger on the warm skin above his hips. I imagined what he might do if I was to take off his shirt. Would he let me?

"What are you doing?" he mumbled against my lips. "This is just a kiss, right?"

It was supposed to be. But there was another last I suddenly wanted to experience with him.

"Emerson?" The word was almost a plea. But a plea for what?

I smoothed my palms along his lower back, trying to decide what I should do. Except my reasoning skills were almost non-existent at this point.

His hands traced their way down my sides. "We probably shouldn't," he said. "Right?"

And there must have been something about him saying something *shouldn't* happen that triggered something from the past, because that was when an image of him kissing a woman with dark hair pushed its way into my mind.

Him and Victoria.

"Stop!" I gasped, pulling my lips and hands away from him like he had burned me.

He did as I said, lifting his hands from my hips and taking a step back as if he was being held at gunpoint.

"What's wrong?" His eyes searched mine. "Did I do something wrong?"

I shook my head, feeling a sob work its way into the back of my throat. "I can't do this."

I put my hand to my chest, feeling my heart rip apart inside of me.

I couldn't breathe.

I literally couldn't breathe right now.

Vincent's eyes filled with concern. "What's wrong, Emerson? What's going on?"

He tried to put his hands on my shoulders, but I

pushed him away. "Don't." I slipped off the counter and onto the tile floor. "Please don't touch me."

His eyebrows knitted together, his brown eyes wide and full of so much confusion and hurt. "What did I do?"

I looked around the tiny bathroom, with its white walls that seemed to be closing in on me.

I had to get out of here. I needed air.

I pushed past Vincent and ran to the sliding glass door on the other side of his bed that I knew led to a balcony. I opened the door and practically flung myself onto the balcony, rushing to the guardrail and leaning over with hopes that the cold night air would make it easier to breathe again.

Breathe, Emerson. Just breathe, I told myself. *In through your nose and out through the mouth. In through the nose and out through the mouth.*

I closed my eyes and focused on the breathing techniques I'd learned when I'd taken up meditation last year—did my best to push away the image of the man I had loved giving what should have been meant only for me to another woman. And after about thirty seconds, as I focused on my breathing, I was able to replace that image with a mental picture of the sandy beach in Hawaii, the aqua blue ocean waves lapping at its shore.

And after a minute or two, my heartbeat slowed down to where it was only racing a little, and the tears that had sprung to my eyes the moment the cold air had hit me disappeared as well.

I turned to go back inside and found Vincent standing in the door with so much worry and fear in his eyes.

"Sorry," I said, hugging myself to ward off the cold.

He stepped backward to let me in. Once I was inside, he shut and locked the balcony door then pulled the curtains closed.

He turned back to look at me, his eyes haunted.

"What's happened?" he asked. "Did I take things too far?"

"No." I shook my head and wiped at the moisture at the corner of my eye. "I just—" I sighed. "It just brought back bad memories."

20

VINCENT

IF I THOUGHT I hated myself before, it had nothing on how I felt after Emerson explained what had happened in my bathroom. And if I had been delusional enough to think for a few fleeting seconds as we'd kissed that we might have a chance of working things out after all, those thoughts were dashed as soon as she said what she did.

Nothing had changed. Absolutely nothing.

Every time I thought things were possibly going to get better, every time I thought there was a flicker of a chance for us to get back together, that stupid night would always be there between us.

No matter how much I wanted it to just disappear, it never would. It would always be right there, waiting on the sidelines for the perfect moment to come back and torture me. To torture her.

"So I hope you can understand why we shouldn't try that again," Emerson said, referring to the kiss in the bathroom.

The kiss that had been everything to me...until it stabbed us both in the back.

"I'm really sorry, Emerson," I said from my spot on the floor across from her, my back against the wall. "I'm so sorry for all the pain I've caused you." I lifted my gaze to where she sat on the edge of my bed, hugging a pillow to her chest, and I wished she could understand just how badly I meant those words.

"I know." She nodded and looked to the side. "I think there's just some things you can't come back from. And apparently, this is it for us."

Her words scraped at me like sandpaper on my heart. But even though the finality of her words hurt like nothing I'd ever felt before, I said, "Do you want me to go sleep on the couch now?"

I wouldn't want to sleep in the same bed as me if I was her. But she surprised me by shaking her head and saying, "No. I think it'll still be okay. Your bed looks big enough to fit you, me, and all our baggage."

Her lips lifted into a slight smile, and I couldn't help but admire her all the more for her strength.

"I have a T-shirt and gym shorts you can wear if you

want something more comfortable to sleep in," I offered, taking in the T-shirt and jeans she still wore.

She set the pillow back on the bed beside her and stood. "That would be nice. I'm pretty beat now."

The feeling was mutual. Over the past twenty minutes, we'd talked and she'd cried, and I had done my best not to cry because I wasn't the person who deserved to cry about this situation, not when I was the one who caused it. And now, all my energy had completely drained from me.

But I managed to find the strength to stand and dug through my dresser until I found a gray T-shirt and black gym shorts for Emerson.

"Here you go," I said when I stepped back into my bedroom with the clothes in hand. "You can change in here. I'm going to check on Jaxon and a few things before heading to bed."

"Thank you." She looked up at me, her eyes appearing turquoise from the tears she'd shed.

After she walked into the bathroom and locked the door behind her, I went down the hall to poke my head in Jaxon's room.

He was sleeping with his arms wrapped around his stuffed cat. I walked into his room and sat on the edge of his bed. Then gently running my fingers through his short blond curls, I whispered, "I love you, buddy. Sleep well." Like I did every night. Bending over closer, I kissed him softly on the cheek and said, "Sorry I couldn't get our family put back together for you."

And that was when the tears I'd been fighting for the past twenty minutes poured out, refusing to be held in any longer.

I ENDED up falling asleep next to Jaxon and woke the next morning to the sounds of him and Emerson chatting happily in the kitchen. I rubbed my neck as I sat up, already regretting falling asleep there. And when I moved again, I was reminded of the beating I'd taken on the field the day before.

Get-Right Day at the stadium was going to be fun today.

But I guess it was fitting. I was emotionally spent from last night. Might as well match it with the soreness in my body.

After a trip to the bathroom, I made my way back down the hall to the kitchen where I found Emerson standing at the stove with her hair pulled up into a high ponytail, my oversized gym shorts cinched about as tight as they could go to fit around her slender waist, and the bottom of my oversized shirt tied in a knot so it didn't drown her.

She looked up when she noticed me, giving me a

tentative smile. "We decided to go ahead and make breakfast burritos," she said. "I hope that's okay with you."

"Yeah, it's just fine," I said. "I feel like a bad host not cooking for you."

She stirred the scrambled eggs with peppers and onions. "It's no problem. Your body needed the rest."

Apparently.

But to make it look like I wasn't a completely inept host, I went to the cupboard and pulled out three plates and cups for us, setting them on the kitchen island where Jaxon was already sitting.

"I haven't gotten around to buying a table yet, so we'll have to eat here."

"That's fine." She glanced over her shoulder. "I figured that since you're a minimalist you just didn't feel like you needed one."

That was a better excuse than the real reason. So I decided not to correct her.

"Did you know Daddy slept in my bed last night?" Jaxon said excitedly to Emerson.

"I did notice that," she said, her eyes briefly meeting mine. "You must have a really comfy bed."

"The comfiest." Jaxon's face lit up. Then he turned to look at me with so much concern etched in his brown eyes. "Is that why you were crying? Was you sad your bed isn't soft like mine?"

Alarm bells went off in my brain.

Had Jaxon just outed me?

"I thought you were sleeping," I said, noticing how Emerson stopped her stirring when Jaxon mentioned my emotional breakdown from last night that I had hoped to keep private.

Jaxon shrugged. "You waked me up."

I hadn't been crying that loudly, had I?

"I'm sorry I woke you up," I said since there was obviously no saving myself now. "I was just having a hard time last night."

"But you is all better today, right?" He looked hopeful.

Emerson seemed to busy herself with seasoning the egg mixture with salt and pepper, and I suddenly wished my four-year-old wasn't quite so observant.

But even though a big part of me was embarrassed that Emerson now knew I had left her to go cry like a baby in our son's bed last night, I dug deep to salvage what was left of my dignity and said, "Yes, I think I'll be okay. Thanks for asking."

"That's good." Jaxon smiled, content with my answer. Then he looked at Emerson. "Is breakfast almost done? I's starving."

"Almost," she said. "How about you go wash your hands in your bathroom and then it should be ready."

"Okay," he said. And in a few seconds he had disappeared down the hall.

I was tempted to follow after him, just to avoid the awkwardness that clung in the air, but Emerson looked like she had something to say. Hopefully it didn't have anything to do with me bawling like a baby. Because if she'd heard me too I might just need to hand in my man-card.

But she surprised me by saying, "While he's gone, I just wanted to tell you that the police called me this morning."

"They did?" I sat up straighter.

"Yes." She pulled the tortillas out of the microwave and set them on the counter. "They said they caught the guy who left the doll last night."

"Really?" I asked, feeling some of the tension release from my body. "Who was it?"

She turned off the stove and set the skillet on the granite countertop. "Apparently, it was the teenage son of the guy I prosecuted last week."

"It was?"

She nodded. "Yeah. I guess he blamed me for his dad going to jail and forcing him into the foster care system. So he decided that playing a few pranks on me was warranted."

"Do you know what he was doing last night when they caught him?"

"The police said he had another doll, this time with its head cut off."

"What?" My eyes nearly bulged out of their sockets. "That's sick and twisted."

"Yeah, it is." She shrugged. "But they have him in custody now and are trying to figure out what to do with him."

"So do they think it's safe for you to go back home?"

"They said they'll still keep an eye on things for a few days just to make sure there was no one else involved, but they think I can sleep there tonight without any worries."

"I can get you a hotel if you're worried about it." I offered, still not sure I was ready for her to go back home.

"That's nice of you to offer." She looked at me through her lashes. "But I think I'll be okay."

"Are you sure?"

"Yes. I appreciate you helping me out last night, but I think I've got it from here."

Which was Emerson code for: Sorry if I got your hopes up, but I don't need you in my life anymore.

21

EMERSON

"HOW DID YOUR DATE GO?" Kira asked when she dropped by my office Monday afternoon. I had gotten in later than usual since my schedule was off after staying at Vincent's.

"My date?" I scrunched up my nose, trying to remember what she was talking about.

"Yeah..." She returned the confused expression. "Didn't you have a date with a guy on Friday night? Dinner at Element 47?"

Oh yeah. With everything that had happened yesterday, I'd completely forgotten the first half of my weekend.

"Sorry, it's been a *really* eventful weekend." I stacked a pile of manila folders together on the top corner of my desk for her to file.

She raised an eyebrow, her interest piqued. "What does that mean? Did your date turn into a weekend together?"

"What? No." I sat up straighter. "Of course not."

"Oh." Her expression fell. "Then what happened?"

I told her all about my date with Dave and how it had failed miserably once I knew he wanted kids and he found out I was Vincent Lake's ex-wife. Then I told her about messaging a couple of guys on Saturday—which I'd somehow completely forgotten about until then, too. And then I told her about the creepy doll on my doorstep and how I ended up going to the game on Sunday.

"How was the game?" she asked.

I lifted a shoulder. "It was fun. A little weird to be watching it in the luxury suite with Vincent's family, but the game was exciting and gave me a few hours without thinking about everything else going on, so that was nice."

"That's good."

"Yeah." I tucked some hair behind my ear. "And then Vincent insisted I stay at his place that night instead of going home. So that was interesting, to say the least."

"You slept at his apartment?" She pulled her head back, her dark eyebrows shooting up.

I nodded, still not sure how I really felt about the whole weekend.

"And did anything happen?"

Of course she would ask that.

"Probably not what you're thinking," I said before she could get any crazy ideas in her head. "But we did talk about a few things that needed talking about, and... we may have kissed."

I said those last four words quickly, hoping she might not catch on to them.

But when her mouth dropped open, I knew she'd heard.

"You and Vincent kissed?" She quickly shut the door to my office, as if to keep anyone else from overhearing our conversation, then took the seat on the other side of my desk. She scooted as close as she could then leaned over my desk and whispered, "Tell me *everything*."

I bit my lip as the memory of the kiss passed through my mind. Even though it hadn't exactly ended well, I couldn't deny that for those few moments when I'd been wrapped up in Vincent's arms, I had felt amazing. Euphoric even.

Euphoric enough that I'd been tempted to take things further for a minute there.

"I'm dying here," Kira said, interrupting my thoughts. "What the heck happened?"

"It was supposed to be our last kiss—you know, the one we would remember since I couldn't remember the last one before it." I sighed and leaned back in my chair. "But then I suddenly started thinking about him being with Victoria and everything went down the drain after that."

I hadn't imagined that scenario for a long time, him and the *other woman*, but even though time had passed, it hadn't weakened the power it had over me. I'd had a visceral reaction, the force of which I hadn't been ready for.

Kira's brown eyes filled with sympathy. "Oh, I'm so sorry, honey."

"It's okay." I drew in a deep breath. "It's probably for the best since I wasn't exactly thinking clearly at the moment and might have just kept things going until I did something I would later regret."

Even though I'd always told myself that I needed to be in a committed relationship before I had sex again, kissing a man I had amazing chemistry with and had already experienced a physical relationship with had a way of blurring the lines.

But I had stopped it, so that was all that mattered.

"And how did Vincent handle everything?" she asked. "Because I asked Derek about Vincent's plus-one for the wedding and he said I must have remembered wrong because he doesn't think Vincent was bringing anyone."

"Yeah, he told me he didn't have a date, either," I said.

"Do you think he's still in love with you?" she asked.

My chest tightened and it took a moment for me to breathe again. But instead of answering her, I said, "When I explained why I freaked out, he seemed to understand and looked like he felt really bad." I rubbed at a smudge on my desk, remembering the tortured and regretful expression on his face as we'd talked after my breakdown.

"So did you leave his house after that?"

"No." I shook my head. "I still stayed. But he ended up sleeping in Jaxon's room, which was probably for the best."

Knowing that that big man had sobbed himself to sleep next to my son had nearly gutted me when I'd found out about it this morning. It just seemed like we should have already met the quota of pain we caused each other by now.

"Anyway," I continued. "The police called this morning and said I should be safe to stay at home tonight. So I'm going to just try to put this weekend behind me and try harder to move on."

"That's all we can do sometimes." Kira nodded. "Move on."

And as if the universe was trying to send me some sort of signal, my phone dinged. It was a message from a guy named Andy.

I shifted through my memory, trying to remember who Andy was. Then it came to me—he was one of the guys I'd messaged on Saturday afternoon before Tyler.

I swiped my finger across the screen.

Andy: **Hey Emerson! Are we still on for drinks at Roco's tonight at 7?**

"What is it?" Kira asked, probably noticing the apprehension on my face. "Is it the police? Or Vincent?"

I shook my head and showed her the message from the dating app. "It's a guy I set up a date with before all the crap hit the fan this weekend."

She narrowed her eyes, seeming to study his photo. "He looks cute."

"Yeah, I guess." I shrugged and glanced at the image of a guy with bleached blond hair and the shoulders of someone who lifted a lot of weights. "I'm just not sure I'm really in the mood to make small talk with a stranger tonight."

"I get that," she said. "You can cancel if you want. I'm sure he would understand if you explained your weekend."

I did have a pretty good excuse.

"Plus, if you don't have a date for my wedding, I can still hook you up with Marty."

"Are you trying to use some sort of reverse psychology to get me to keep my date with Andy?" I narrowed my eyes.

"What? Me?" She put her hand to her chest in an innocent gesture, but her lips spread into a guilty grin.

"You are pure evil sometimes," I said.

She laughed. "I just think you deserve to let loose once in a while and drinks with a cute guy seems like the perfect way to do that."

I thought about it.

I did need to move on, and I still needed a date for the wedding. I might as well go and see how it went. I was going to be without Jaxon tonight anyway, I might as well have some company.

So I typed in a response. **I'm looking forward to it. See you at seven.**

And then, just because his message had reminded me of Tyler, I decided I might as well message him, too.

22

VINCENT

"WHAT'S GOT YOU DOWN TODAY?" Cole asked when I walked into the locker room to pack up for the day. "Still bummed about yesterday's game?"

We had finished our day at the stadium, getting massages and all the fun physical therapy they did to help our bodies repair from the beating we took during our game the day before.

"It's a little of that." I pulled a clean shirt over my head, the thin fabric stretching as I brought it down. "But most of it has to do with Emerson."

"Yeah?" he asked. "Did she find out it was you who was messaging her?"

"No. It's not that." I sighed and sat down on the bench. "She had some weird stuff happen at her house this weekend, so she ended up staying at my place last night."

Cole's thick eyebrows raised. "What?"

"I slept in Jaxon's bed," I hurried to say before he got his hopes up.

"Oh." He relaxed again. "So, what's going on then?"

I tried to decide how much I wanted to tell him. We didn't exactly talk a lot about our *feelings* with each other very often. I'd saved talks like that for my therapist over the past year.

But my therapist couldn't fit me in his schedule until tomorrow, so I rubbed the back of my neck and said, "Some stuff just happened that made me realize that even though I've been hanging on to the hope that she might give me a second chance someday, it's probably not possible." The image of Emerson running to my balcony flashed through my mind again. "I broke us irreparably."

I really had traumatized her with what I'd done.

"I'm sorry to hear that."

"Yeah." I rubbed my hands along my thighs.

Cole gave me a hesitant look, like he had something to tell me but wasn't sure he should.

"What is it?" I asked, my chest tight.

He lifted a shoulder then pulled his phone out from his locker, and after a few taps on the screen, he showed it to me.

"Emerson sent me this message a little while ago."

I furrowed my brow and took the phone from his hands. Emerson had messaged the profile I'd used to chat with her last Saturday.

Man, that seemed like a lifetime ago.

Emerson: **How was the rest of your weekend? Mine was interesting. I'd love to chat about it over dinner sometime.**

The words blurred for a moment as I read them again. I didn't know what I expected her to do after last night and this morning, but for some reason, I hadn't expected her to throw herself back into online dating the same day.

Maybe she really did feel nothing for me.

Maybe that kiss last night had only been for memory's sake, after all.

I'd thought for a minute that things might have turned into something more, that she might have had some residual feelings for me, but apparently, it had all been in my head.

She had shut the door to the possibility of us when she'd drawn up the divorce papers. And it was only me who had been confused over the past year.

I blinked my eyes a few times, pushing down the surge of emotion that came with the realization that I never had a chance of getting Emerson back and that I'd just been fooling myself.

I handed Cole his phone. "You should probably just delete those messages," I said.

He took the phone back, confusion in his eyes. "You're not going to respond?"

I shook my head and stood, needing to get out of the locker room. "If she knew it was me she'd chatted with on Saturday, she wouldn't be interested in having dinner."

"Are you sure?" Cole slipped his phone into the pocket of his sweatpants. "She's trying to set something up, so I'd say she's interested."

"Because she thinks it's a guy named Tyler. A guy who didn't cheat on her. A guy she could start out with on a fresh clean slate." I looked down at my feet. "She would walk right out the door if she saw me waiting for her at a table." I turned to Cole. "Maybe even run."

"So you're just going to leave her hanging then? Just ghost her?"

I nodded. "It's for the best."

He gave me a look that told me he wasn't so sure, but after studying me for a moment, he nodded. "Okay."

"Thanks."

"And if she tries messaging again, what do you want me to do?"

"Just ignore her." I stood and shut my locker. "She'll get over Tyler and find someone else in no time."

And maybe it was time for me to really try to move on, too.

23

EMERSON

MY DATE with Andy ended up being a bust.

As were my dates with Trever, Milo, Gavin, Robert, Julio, Gabriel, Ross, and Doug over the next month.

And you know what was even more of a bust?

Tyler.

The guy I had felt so connected to before the dumb doll showed up on my porch and led me to staying the night at Vincent's house...well, he seemed to have dropped off the face of the earth because I hadn't heard a single word from him.

I had been tempted to ask him if I really did need to come and save him with my cape and superhero powers, but after three messages had gone unanswered, I gave up.

I tried dating the other guys who actually responded

to me. But sadly, none of those had wowed me in person as much as Tyler had through the phone.

"You sure you aren't trying to find Vincent 2.0?" Ivy asked me one evening after I'd finished lamenting over the fact that it was the night of Kira and Derek's rehearsal dinner and I still didn't have a date.

"Vincent 2.0?" I held my mascara wand in the air. "What do you mean by that?"

We were FaceTiming so I could have company as I got ready. If I was going to survive this weekend without a date to protect me from all the gossip I was expecting, I needed to at least look fabulous.

The line was silent for a second before she spoke in a cautious tone, saying, "Are you sure none of these guys can measure up because you have a very specific measuring stick? One that is nearly identical to Vincent?"

My jaw dropped and I looked at her face framed by her dark hair. "What makes you say that?"

I heard her sigh through my iPad. "How about I give you a rundown of what you've said about each of the guys you've been on dates with recently, and then maybe you can decide if my question is off-base."

"Okay." I put my mascara wand back in the tube and then set my hands on my hips like I was preparing for a brawl. "Go ahead and try to prove your point."

Because I *so* was not comparing every guy to Vincent. I didn't want Vincent.

I wanted the *opposite* of Vincent.

Mostly...

Ivy turned her back to the camera for a moment, like she was grabbing something off the end table beside her.

"Did you take notes?" I asked.

"Maybe," she said before a rustling sound came through the earpiece. When she turned back to me, the top of a piece of lined paper was visible through the screen.

Should that surprise me?

Probably not.

Ivy *had* run a gossip blog for years. Of course she'd keep detailed notes about my failing dating life.

"Okay," she said. "This is what you've told me so far."

I looked up at the ceiling and shook my head.

"Is there something on your ceiling?" she asked.

"I'm listening." I ignored her question, impatient for her to get on with it so I could tell her that she was ridiculous to think I was sabotaging all my dates on purpose.

"Okay good." She cleared her throat. "So first on my list is Andy: the blond-haired, blue-eyed scientist who just moved here from Australia." She glanced at her paper momentarily. "When you got back from your date at Roco's, you claimed it was an okay date and the conversation was interesting enough, but ultimately, his hair was too light and his hands weren't manly enough."

"He had girly hands!" I gasped, shocked that she'd actually written all of that down. "They were practically the same size as mine."

"With Trevor," she said, ignoring me. "You said he was well traveled and had a cute Southern accent but wasn't tall enough for you to wear heels around. And he didn't know anything about football, which you said was a crime."

Well, when you lived in the same town as the Dragons, it kind of was a crime.

She continued reading from her list. "And Milo's eyes weren't a dark enough color of brown. Gavin's voice wasn't deep enough. Robert dressed too metro and said he would never lounge around in athletic clothes. Julio wasn't muscular enough. Gabriel liked the wrong kind of music. And Ross wouldn't eat sushi with you."

I waited for her to say more, but that seemed to be the end of her list.

"So what if I have a type?" I said. "I like a tall, dark, and handsome guy who is at least six inches taller than me, likes sports, and is adventurous with his food choices. Lots of women go for that."

"Then what about Doug?"

"What about him?"

"You said, and I quote: 'He checked pretty much every box, but when he walked you to your car, he stood on the right side of you instead of the side closest to traffic. So you couldn't give him a second date.'"

"Is it so wrong that I want a guy who follows proper etiquette and tries to keep me safe when we're walking somewhere?" No. It wasn't. "Vincent always walked on the outside, closest to traffic." It was a tiny gesture, but when we first started dating, it had told me that he was a gentleman. And I wanted to date and marry a gentleman.

Ivy was quiet for moment, and that was when I realized what I'd just said.

I'd just compared Doug to Vincent.

I closed my eyes and sighed. Then picking up my iPad to have a better view of my friend, I said, "So maybe you might have the teensiest point."

Her blue eyes totally had an "I told you so" gleam about them. "They do say the first step to recovery is admitting you have a problem."

"Yeah, yeah." I leaned my iPad against the wall in front of me again and picked up my mascara to give my lashes one more coat. "So if you're so smart, what do you suggest I do?"

"As I see it, you have a couple of options," she said.

"And they are?"

"Well, as you know, I too have a little experience with holding grudges against the man I won't let myself admit I still have feelings for."

"Justin stood you up for our high school prom," I said. "Vincent cheated on me when we were married. I'm not sure those are on the same level."

"I know," she said. "Just hear me out."

I finished swiping the mascara on my lashes and picked up my long-wear, shimmery pink lipstick.

"You told me at Christmas that you still miss him sometimes," she said. "And that there were times when you wondered if you divorced him too quickly."

"It was the holidays and I was going to have my first Christmas alone." I paused from applying my lipstick to look at her. "Of course I was feeling sad about things."

She didn't seem to care about my excuse, though, because she said, "I know what he did was horrible and that there's still a lot of pain and heartache there, but I wonder if you don't owe it to yourself to explore things with him a little more. You don't have to kiss him again or anything, since you might not be ready for that yet. But you guys were a great couple for a long time. I think that maybe instead of trying to find a Vincent 2.0, you might owe it to yourself to feel things out with Vincent 1.0 before you shut the door on him completely."

And even though I knew it was completely irrational, my stomach decided to flutter with hope as I took in what she was saying.

But my stomach told me to do lots of stupid things all the time: like eating that entire roll of Oreos last night and getting that extra helping of pasta today at lunch even though I wasn't hungry anymore. So really, my stomach couldn't be trusted.

Logic was much better to rely on.

Except, even logic was really confusing sometimes. Because as she spoke, logic was telling me that maybe my actions were proving that deep down I really did want to get back with my ex.

"He sounds like he's been doing everything right," she said. "He cut off all contact with Victoria immediately after he sobered up that night. He went to therapy. He's given you space and respected every boundary and request you've ever given him. He made the divorce as clean and easy as he could, giving you everything you wanted out of it. Plus, he's a great dad to Jaxon. Yes, he got drunk and made a huge mistake one night, and you are completely just in having your reservations. But I know you. And I just think that deep down, you do want your family to be put back together."

I wiped at my eye, a sudden wave of emotion coming over me as my best friend said all the things I hadn't wanted to admit to myself.

"I know you're scared of getting hurt again," she said gently, like she could tell her words were making me emotional. "But sometimes, people do change and are worth giving a second chance."

I wiped at my eye again. "Are you trying to make me ruin my makeup before I have to see him at the wedding rehearsal?"

"No." She gave me an understanding smile. "I'm just returning the favor you gave me in December. You helped give me the courage to put myself out there with Justin, and I've never been so happy before. I just want you to be happy again."

But did I dare try again?

Could I really get over the betrayal enough that it wouldn't catch me off guard again? Or would I continue to be triggered whenever we got close?

I didn't know.

Plus, wasn't I getting way ahead of myself?

First off, I wasn't even sure I really wanted to try to be with him again. I hadn't ever consciously thought about it until just now.

And secondly, I didn't even know if Vincent would be interested in rekindling our romance, either.

Sure, Derek had told Kira that Vincent wasn't over me. And Janet had said he wasn't ready to move on yet. But Vincent had never once brought it up to me. The only actual hint I'd ever had from him happened when we were kissing in his bathroom.

But while he had gotten lost in the kiss just as much as I had, it didn't mean he wanted to get back with me. He'd said so himself that his night with Victoria had been purely physical and he'd never had emotions tied up with her.

Who was to say that hadn't happened with us that night, too? The physical power that came from a man and a woman being in a small space could have been the real culprit there. Not feelings.

But then, Jaxon had said he'd heard Vincent crying when he'd gone to his room that night.

Ugh. I needed to stop trying to figure this out. I was just running around in circles in my mind.

"Did I say too much?" Ivy asked when I didn't say anything for a while.

I put the lid back on my lipstick. "No." I sighed. "You're fine. I'm just thinking."

Overthinking.

"And what are you thinking?"

"I don't know." I lifted a shoulder. "Just if it's even a good idea. I have no idea where Vincent stands on testing the waters with each other."

In fact, if anything, things had become more awkward between us since that night I'd stayed at his place—the drop-offs and pick-ups briefer than usual. Like he was avoiding me.

"Well, I don't want to rush you," she said. "It's definitely okay to take your time."

Especially since I wasn't trying to find a date to tomorrow's wedding anymore.

"Did you ever hear back from that Tyler guy?" she asked. "You haven't talked about him recently."

"No." My shoulders slumped. "I'm pretty sure he ghosted me."

Which was so weird. I'd thought we'd really connected that night. I would have talked to him for hours if he hadn't had to go to bed early.

"Maybe he's married and his wife found out," she said. "You did say he had his face hidden in all of his photos."

A sick feeling swirled in my stomach at the thought that he could have been slimy like that.

"Maybe that's it." I sighed, feeling even worse about my dating radar. "He did seem too good to be true."

Plus, what single guy went to bed at nine o'clock on a Saturday night? Sure, Vincent always went to bed early during football season, but that was because he needed the extra sleep to be at his peak performance on the field. Regular people didn't do that. Weekends were for staying up late.

"I kind of feel like I turned this conversation into a

big doom-and-gloom session," Ivy said. "Sorry about that."

I laughed. "It's okay. My love life is what it is."

"Well, I have a feeling things will turn up for you soon." She gave me a warm smile. "Now that you don't have the pressure of finding a date for Kira's wedding breathing down your neck, you can take time to figure out what you really want. I think the universe is just taking its time in putting the right person for you in your path."

"I hope so." I picked up my iPad to hold it closer to my face again.

"Hey, if it can happen for me," she said. "It can happen for anyone."

"It'd better." I glanced at the clock on the wall. I needed to hurry and put on my dress and heels if I was going to get to the chapel in Denver on time. "I should get going," I said. "Thanks for the chat."

"Make sure to let me know how things go," she said. "And remember, if the Dragon Ladies are rude to you when you see them, just remember you have a friend with a retired gossip blog that would be more than happy to revive it if you need me to exact some revenge."

"That's why we're friends." I laughed. "I'll talk to you later, Ivy."

"You'd better."

We waved goodbye to each other and ended the call.

And when I gave myself one last look in the mirror, inspecting my hair and makeup, I hoped this weekend would go well. Because seeing the Dragons' family without a date to use as armor was going to be interesting.

24

EMERSON

I ARRIVED at the church just as everyone was lining up to rehearse the ceremony.

"Sorry I'm late," I told Kira when I found her standing in the back of the line-up with her parents. "The roads were bad on I-70, so it took me longer than I expected to get here."

"That's okay." She smiled, looking stunning in her red pantsuit, her dark skin giving off the bride-to-be glow. "Vincent told us they were bad, so we figured that's what happened."

"Oh," I said, looking around for Vincent. But he was nowhere around.

Kira must have seen me looking for him because she pointed to the doors that led to the chapel and said, "He's already standing in the front with Derek."

"Of course." I nodded. I somehow forgot about that tradition for a minute.

"Anyway," she said. "You'll be walking down the aisle with Derek's high school buddy Landon." She looked around at the group of her and Derek's closest friends and family before pointing to a tall guy with auburn hair. "That's him," she said. "In the light blue button-up."

I looked at the guy she'd indicated whose back was to me, a little ball of nerves forming in my stomach at the prospect of walking down the aisle with a complete stranger. But I smiled the nerves away and said, "I guess I'll go introduce myself real quick."

Landon was even taller when I got up close—probably at least six-foot-three—which was always nice. It meant I would still be several inches shorter than him in my heels tomorrow. And from the set of his shoulders, I could tell that he was either an athlete or was just very good with his workout regimen.

He turned around when I approached, and I was met with a beautiful pair of dark brown eyes and a *very* nice-looking face.

Dang.

This Landon guy was hot.

"Are you Emerson?" he asked, seeming to take in my appearance as well.

"Yeah." I tucked some hair behind my ear, suddenly feeling shy for some reason. "That's me."

"I'm Landon." He held out his hand for me to shake. "Apparently, you're stuck with me for the next two days."

Stuck with him wasn't exactly a phrase I would have picked. And when I glanced at the other bridesmaids around us, I got the feeling several of them wouldn't mind trading places with me.

I turned away from the envious gazes and looked up at Landon. "Kira said you and Derek were friends in high school."

He nodded. "We go way back."

"Derek's from Utah, right?" I asked. "Do you still live there?"

"Yeah, I can't seem to leave." He shrugged a broad shoulder. "I teach Psychology at the University in our hometown."

A psychologist? "Does that mean you're going to psychoanalyze me?"

"No." He chuckled. "I'm off the clock, so you don't need to worry about that."

I wiped my forehead. "Well, that's good. Because I'm not sure I want to know what you would find."

I was about to ask him more when the wedding planner came through the chapel doors. She was a tall, spindly woman with red hair in a pixie cut. "It looks like everyone is here now," she said. "So how about we get this rehearsal started."

And with that, all the bridesmaids and groomsmen linked arms with their partner.

"Ready?" Landon held his arm out for me.

I slipped my arm in his and couldn't help but notice that his bicep was almost as big as Vincent's. I know I wasn't supposed to be comparing men to Vincent, but it was hard not to.

Either way, this psychology professor was definitely a nice distraction from the heavy conversation I'd had with Ivy earlier today. I wondered if he was single.

But just as I was trying to figure out a good way to ask him if he'd brought a date with him, the song "Marry Me" by Jason Derulo started playing through the speakers, indicating it was time for the wedding procession to start.

I tightened my grip on Landon's arm to keep myself upright, because the sound of the familiar music and the memories that instantly flooded my mind made my legs go weak under me.

"Are you okay?" Landon was looking at me with concern etched in his eyes.

My cheeks flushed with embarrassment, but I managed to stand up straight after a moment and said, "Yeah. I just lost my balance there for a sec."

"Okay."

I blinked a few times and stared ahead, attempting to steel the nerves swirling around inside me as Jason Derulo's rich voice sang the introduction with the piano accompaniment.

It had been a long while since I'd heard this song—but there had been a time when I'd listened to it several times a day, reliving the memory of the night Vincent had surprised me with something I'd never thought he'd do.

When we'd been married for a little over a year, this song was playing on the radio. It was several years old at the time already, but somehow, I hadn't heard it when it first came out. And I was instantly obsessed with it.

Jaxon was just a baby back then, so when I was stuck in the recliner nursing and rocking him for several hours a day, I ended up watching a lot of YouTube videos. And since I was the type of person who listened to their favorite song on repeat until I'd played it out, I had looked up the music video to this song, which had led me down the rabbit hole containing all sorts of videos where people had used this song.

I watched wedding proposals that had made me a little envious, since our engagement and wedding had been such a rushed thing. There were also videos that featured a compilation of some people's favorite couples from TV shows and all their romantic moments, the song playing in the background.

Then I stumbled upon a couple doing a ballroom-type dance to this song. And I was instantly captivated by it. I must have watched that dance on repeat for about an hour as Jaxon napped in my arms.

When Vincent got home from practice that day, I showed the video to him and told him we should take ballroom classes during the upcoming offseason so we could learn this dance.

He'd laughed and basically patted me on the head, telling me it was a cute idea, but he would never be caught dead taking ballroom classes.

So, with my bubble burst, I put the thought away and moved on to a new favorite song and other things—the thought of ballroom dancing with my husband getting shoved under the rug.

But then, on our anniversary weekend six months later, Vincent got my mom to watch Jaxon for the weekend and took me to a private dance studio where we had the very couple from the YouTube video teach us the choreography to their dance.

I'd thought he'd brushed me off, but apparently, he had been secretly practicing on his own in our home gym early in the morning when I was still sleeping, so he could eventually get to the point where he was confident enough to surprise me.

It was one of the best gifts anyone had ever given me, and it had showed me how much he truly loved me.

Because really, how many macho football players would learn a ballroom dance just to make their wife's silly dream come true?

Not many.

And even though we'd learned the choreography in the matter of a weekend, we'd danced in our kitchen to the song many nights over the next years.

I couldn't remember exactly when we'd stopped dancing together, but I was pretty sure it happened around the time we lost the baby and I'd sunk into a bad depression, throwing myself into my work and caring for Jaxon.

And then of course, we'd gotten divorced and hadn't danced since then.

But even though it had been a long time, the memories of what Vincent had done for me were as vivid in my mind as if they'd happened yesterday.

He really had loved me at one point. And I'd loved him back.

The wedding planner stepped up to me and Landon, breaking me out of the memory.

"When they reach the second-to-last pew," she said, gesturing to Kira's sister and Derek's brother who were walking down the aisle together in front of us. "It will be time for you to follow."

Right.

I blinked my eyes, trying to re-center myself back in

the present moment. It would be embarrassing if I messed up the whole wedding procession because I was too busy daydreaming about the highlights of my past.

When the couple in front of me were about ten feet away, the view ahead had cleared enough that I could see Derek and Vincent standing in the front of the chapel.

I sucked in a breath at the sight of Vincent. He was wearing a dark blue button-up shirt with the style of jeans that I'd always wanted him to wear on our date nights in the past because they looked so good on him.

And he'd gotten his hair cut since I'd last seen him.

Crap! He really wasn't supposed to look this good tonight. Not when I was trying to put off figuring out my feelings for him and just getting through the weekend.

But even though I'd been ogling Landon just a minute ago, he really had nothing on my ex. Because Vincent Lake had always been in a league all his own.

This was going to be awkward walking down the aisle to this song with him watching me.

"THANKS FOR BEING SUCH a great sport about all of this," Kira told me when we were done with the rehearsal portion of the night. "I know it wasn't your favorite idea to be in the wedding party with Vincent, but Derek and I really appreciate you being here with us."

I smiled at my friend. "It's no problem. I'm happy to be here."

Which was true.

Sure, my legs had wobbled all the way down the aisle as I tried not to look at Vincent—albeit unsuccessfully since I was stupid and wanted to see if he was watching me at all, or see if there was any sign that he was remembering us dancing to the song.

And though he hadn't been looking at me every time I glanced his way, he had looked my way enough for me to at least feel noticed.

When we were all standing in the front, while the pastor went over what Kira and Derek would need to do during the ceremony, I'd found myself watching him and remembering the day we'd vowed to love and cherish one another for the rest of our lives.

I'd only teared up a little at that part. And I didn't think he'd noticed.

He and Derek walked into the foyer of the church just a few feet away from Kira and me, and when they saw us, they walked over.

"How is my bride feeling?" Derek put his arm around Kira and kissed her on the forehead. "Getting cold feet yet?"

A wide grin stretched across Kira's cheeks. "My feet have never been more toasty."

"That's good." Derek squeezed her close again, and I couldn't help but smile at them. They were so in love. And it warmed my heart to see my friends so happy.

"You two are coming to the dinner at Rioja?" Derek asked, eyeing Vincent and then me.

"Of course," I said. "You know I love that place." Rioja had the best Mediterranean food in Denver, and I had been looking forward to eating their Petaluma chicken ever since Kira told me that was where the rehearsal dinner was going to be held.

"You'd better," Kira said. "You were the one who suggested it in the first place."

Derek turned to Vincent. "What about you?"

My gaze briefly drifted to Vincent, who stood with his fingers tucked in his pockets, as if he was uncomfortable with the dynamic of the four of us together like old times. But he said, "I'm coming. My mom and Arianna took Jaxon for the weekend so I can stay out late tonight."

"Great!" Derek smiled and took Kira's hand in his. "We'll see you guys over there, then."

When they were gone, I looked up at Vincent, feeling somewhat awkward being alone with him after the distance we'd had the past month.

"I guess I'd better head over there, too," I said, when nothing else came to mind.

But when our gazes met, there was an anxious look in his eyes that made me pause.

I furrowed my brow. "Is something wrong?"

"No." He shook his head and dug the toe of his shoe into the carpet. "I just—" He sighed—the way he always did when he was worried about telling me something. "I just wanted to let you know that I'm bringing a date to the wedding tomorrow."

My heart froze in my chest before plummeting to the earth, and it took a moment for it to remember I needed it to work in order to stay alive.

A date?

Vincent was bringing a date?

"I know the last time we spoke, I told you I hadn't started dating yet," he said the words quickly, his eyes wary. "So I figured I should let you know before tomorrow so it doesn't catch you off guard."

My mind was still trying to absorb the fact that he had a date.

Vincent was moving on?

Why did that make my chest hurt so much?

His expression became more worried the longer I took to respond, so I made myself say, "Th-thanks for the heads up," before he could wonder what was wrong with me.

Was this the part where I told him I was a loser and planning to come alone?

Man, for some reason I had expected him to not look for a date.

I wasn't ready for him to date yet.

He checked the time on his watch. "Anyway, we should probably get going before Derek and the other groomsmen eat all the food."

I nodded. "Yeah, his brothers looked pretty hungry."

But as I followed behind Vincent to the church's parking lot, the numbness washing over me told me I wasn't nearly as hungry as I'd been a few minutes ago.

25

EMERSON

"WHEN WE WERE at the church I had no idea you were Vincent Lake's ex," Landon whispered under his breath as we sat at the table in the private dining area at Rioja.

"Yeah, that's me," I said, scooting my chair closer to the table, still trying to regain my composure after learning Vincent was officially moving on.

For some reason it was hitting me harder than I thought it would. And with the conversation I'd had with Ivy still fresh on my mind—her pointing out to me that I was subconsciously comparing every guy I went out with Vincent—had me wondering in my head if I *was* still in love with him.

Because if I had really moved on, the thought of

seeing him with someone else tomorrow wouldn't have made me so sick to my stomach, would it?

Maybe I was just coming down with something.

"Is it weird being at events like this with him?" Landon asked, glancing at Vincent who was just taking his seat on the other side of the table. The tables were arranged in a long, banquet-style seating, so thankfully, he wasn't straight across from me but three chairs down instead.

"It's a little awkward," I said quietly, hoping Vincent couldn't hear. "But we have a kid together and see each other a couple times a week, so it's not too bad."

Though, seeing him chat with the various brides-maids when we'd walked in had definitely turned up the jealousy factor as I'd tried to figure out if one of them was his date for tomorrow.

Kira's college roommate was gorgeous and I knew she hung out with Derek and Kira here and there. Maybe they'd set them up.

But Kira would have warned me about something like that, wouldn't she?

"How old is your kid?" Landon asked, picking up his glass of water and taking a sip.

"He's four."

Landon smiled. "That's a fun age."

"Do you have kids?" I asked. I had noticed earlier

that he wasn't wearing a wedding band on his hand, but that didn't mean he couldn't have kids of his own.

"Not yet." He set his water back on the table. "But my brother has a couple of kids. I get to see them a lot."

"That's fun," I said. "Would you ever want kids of your own?"

"Sure." He shrugged. "I'd love to have one or two someday when I find the right girl." He shot me a smile.

It took me a moment to register it, but...was he flirting with me?

My cheeks warmed and I looked down briefly before swallowing and saying, "So I take it that you're single then."

"You would be correct." He nodded. "And what about you?"

"Same."

"Really?" He sat up a little straighter and furrowed his brow like he was actually surprised. "Are all the guys in Denver blind or something?"

My blush deepened.

Who knew talking to a near stranger could be so good for my bruised ego right now?

I picked up my glass, needing something to do with my hands. "I just haven't found the right guy yet, I guess."

"You never know." His brown-eyed gaze went from my eyes to my mouth, and then back to my eyes again before he leaned even closer and whispered, "Maybe you just did."

And when he winked at me, the warmth that had been on my cheeks throughout our conversation spread through my whole body.

Was he actually hinting that he might be interested in being that "right guy"? Because even though I barely knew anything about him, the thought that someone found me interesting in person after all my failed dates did good things for my soul.

He did say he only wanted one or two kids, right? That was better than Dave's basketball team.

So even though I knew the chances of anything actually going anywhere after this weekend, I decided to be flirtatious for a minute. I looked up through my eyelashes and said, "Maybe I just did."

And though I hadn't meant to, I found my gaze drifting toward Vincent to make sure he wasn't watching.

But he was looking straight at us. And from the dark look in his eyes, I imagined he may have been listening to every single word.

26

VINCENT

"WE'LL SEE YOU ALL TOMORROW," Derek said to the group of us still standing in the banquet room at Rioja after the dinner was over. "Thank you for spending the evening with us."

And with a wave from both him and Kira, they left hand in hand.

Most of the other people I knew from the wedding party had left, aside from Emerson who was still talking to the groomsman she'd been with all night. So instead of torturing myself by sticking around and watching Emerson flirt with another guy who even I had to admit was a good-looking guy, I followed after Derek and Kira and headed out to my truck.

I sat in my truck for a couple of minutes to check the

road conditions on my phone before I ventured onto I-70. The roads could get pretty dangerous when it was snowing, and I'd had a hard enough time getting to the church earlier. I didn't want to get stuck in a road closure.

CDOT's social media accounts said that the roads were clear, so I put my truck in gear to pull out of the parking lot. But just as I was about to back out of my spot, I noticed a figure in a familiar pink dress and white coat out of the corner of my eye.

I did a double take and realized it was Emerson, standing on the sidewalk and holding herself like she was shivering. I put my truck back into park.

When our eyes met, she walked to my door. I rolled down my window, confused.

"Hey," she said, tucking her hair behind her ear.

"Hey."

She pressed her lips together and glanced around quickly as if uncomfortable. Then she stepped even closer. "So, um, my car won't start. Do you think you could give me a jump?" She pointed to where her blue Mercedes was parked a few spaces away.

"Did you leave the lights on?" I asked, trying to figure out why it would be dead.

"I don't think so." She shrugged. "But maybe."

"Okay..." I said, looking around the cab of my truck, trying to remember where I'd put the jumper cables.

"Let me just pull over closer to your car and we can see about getting it started."

Relief showed in her face. "Thank you." She stepped back onto the sidewalk, and I pulled out of my spot and drove a few spaces down to where her car was parked.

I popped the hood of my truck, grabbed the jumper cables from the compartment under the passenger seat, then zipped up my coat. After pulling on my gloves, I climbed out of my truck into the cold night and walked over to where she stood in front of her car.

"I'm glad I caught you before you left," she said, her teeth chattering as she braced herself against the cold.

"I'm glad I decided to check CDOT first." I checked the front of her car. "If you'll pop your hood and give me your key, you can just sit in my truck while I see if we can get you started."

"Okay, thank you." She hurried to her driver's door, and a moment later, released the hood. I propped it up. After we switched key fobs and she went to sit in my warm truck, I hooked the cables to both of our batteries.

Then I indicated for her to start my truck. It started just fine, of course, and so I climbed into her car and pushed the button to start the engine.

Nothing happened.

I stepped on the brake again and pushed the ignition

button. But just like before, the engine didn't even make an attempt to turn over.

I frowned. Had I not connected the cables correctly?

I got out to make sure the cables had been attached properly. The black and red cable were indeed in the right spot, so I tried starting her car once more.

But it still didn't do anything.

Her car was only a couple of years old, so I doubted she needed the battery replaced already. Could it be her alternator?

I didn't know a lot about cars, but it seemed like this had happened to my mom's car before. Deciding I couldn't really do anything else with my limited skills, I climbed out of her car again and locked it up.

After removing the battery cables and shutting both our hoods, I went to the driver's side of my truck and opened the door.

"I think you might need a new alternator or something," I said, handing her back her key fob.

"Will I need to have it towed, then?" she asked.

"Probably." I nodded and gestured for her to scoot over to the passenger seat so I could climb in. "It'll be more expensive to call someone tonight, but I know a guy who would probably be able to help in the morning if you want me to give him a call."

"Oh." She blinked, seeming surprised. "You don't mind?"

"No." And to prove my point, I pulled out my phone. "I'll text him right now."

So I texted the guy who had fixed my truck the last time I'd had problems after practice. He responded immediately and said he'd have it towed to his shop and get to work on it first thing in the morning.

"There," I said, putting my phone in the back pocket of my jeans. "It's taken care of."

"Wow," she said, her tone surprised. "That was fast."

I shrugged. "Sometimes it helps to play for the Dragons."

"I guess so," she said, seeming relieved. "Is it okay if I get a ride home with you?"

"Of course," I said. "And I can just pick you up in the afternoon and drive you back here."

"But won't that be weird?" She gave me a wary look. "With your date and all? I don't exactly think she'd appreciate having your ex-wife along as a third wheel."

I smiled as I imagined what she was saying. That would definitely be weird. Especially since I'd been set up with Chelsea Stockton's sister and didn't really know anything about her personality.

So I said, "We don't need to worry about that. She lives in Denver so I can pick her up after we pick up your car."

"Okay, cool." She looked like she wanted to say

something more, but then seemed to rethink it and buckled her seatbelt instead.

After buckling my own seatbelt, I handed her the bag with the jumper cables. "Would you mind putting that in the compartment beneath you?"

"Sure." And when she took it from me, her fingers brushed against mine. Our eyes met briefly, and I wondered if she had felt the same spark of electricity that I had.

But she looked away the next moment and put the cables away.

I cleared my throat and pulled out of my parking spot to get on the road.

"So you and that Landon guy seemed to really hit it off," I said stupidly before realizing the last thing I wanted to talk about was her interactions with another man.

She looked at me with narrowed eyes, like she was surprised I was bringing it up. Then she said, "He's nice."

Nice.

What was that supposed to mean?

Was she into him?

Were they planning to hang out with each other at the wedding?

"He seemed pretty smitten with you," I offered, hoping she'd give me more insight into what she thought about him aside from him being nice. But when I glanced sideways to get a read on how she felt about my comment, her expression was just neutral.

After a short pause, she said, "I think he was just being nice."

"I doubt that."

She angled toward me. "You don't think a man and a woman can ever just talk without it having to mean anything?"

"When that woman is as beautiful as you, no."

I hadn't meant to say that either, but there it was, hanging in the air.

I grabbed the steering wheel tighter as I waited for her reaction. Hopefully, she wouldn't get after me for the compliment. I didn't want to mess up the good thing we had going so far this evening after all the uncomfortable interactions over the past month.

When she sat up straighter, a coy smile on her lips, I loosened my grip a little. "So, you think I look okay tonight?"

I would normally try to play down just how much I was still attracted to her, but there was just something about seeing her chatting with another man tonight that had me rethinking my whole strategy.

Since she seemed to be accepting compliments right now, I just went for it. "Yes, Emerson. You definitely look okay." And then because I was throwing all caution to the wind, I took my eyes off the road for a quick moment to take her in. "Better than okay."

"Better than okay?" She raised an eyebrow, and the smile on her lips told me she liked hearing that.

I nodded. "You know I think you're gorgeous. Even if we aren't married anymore, that's never going to change."

She gave me a soft, quiet look, where she seemed to study me. And I suddenly felt self-conscious under her scrutiny.

What did she think when she looked at me?

Did she still find me attractive?

Or had what I'd done to her ruined all my previous appeal?

I held my breath as I waited for her to say what she was thinking.

And after what seemed like a really long moment, she said, "You look really good too, Vincent."

My heart started beating again.

So at least I hadn't lost everything.

I rubbed my hand along my scruffy face that hadn't been shaved for a few days. "Even with this?"

"That's always been my favorite look on you," she said, her voice softer than it had been a moment ago.

Okay, now my heart was beating fast.

And when I glanced her way, I imagined I did see some attraction in her eyes in the moonlight.

Man, she was beautiful. Just looking at her made my insides constrict.

I cleared my throat. "I was kind of worried that after what happened at my house last month that you might think I looked like a big, scary Sasquatch today."

"No." She shook her head slowly. "I don't think you're scary at all. I was just caught off guard by everything."

I swallowed. "I'm sorry there was a reason for it to happen in the first place."

She nodded. "I know."

We were quiet for a while as we drove down the highway, passing snow-covered spruce trees. I thought about turning on the radio to give us something to listen to but decided not to. It was nice being able to sit comfortably in silence with someone else, lost in thought.

"Remember what we were talking about the last time we drove down this road together?" she asked, her voice somewhat melancholy.

Was she talking about when I'd said I hoped she'd be able to forgive me some day? Because I didn't want to bring that up if that wasn't it.

But I also didn't want her to think that I didn't remember our conversations. We'd obviously had some communication issues in the past and I didn't want her to think I hadn't been paying attention then.

I said, "Are you talking about when I said I hoped you'd be able to forgive me someday?"

She nodded, and when I glanced her direction, it looked like she was holding in some emotions. So I braced myself for whatever she was about to say.

She released a shaky breath, as if nervous, and then she looked at me again. "I think I realized today that I have forgiven you."

My heart froze and I blinked my eyes a few times, not sure I'd heard her right. And when I turned to her with my mouth open, I knew I must look shocked.

Because I was.

Of course, I'd always hoped that she'd be able to forgive me someday, but I never really dared to dream that she actually would.

It took a moment for me to speak, and when I did, my voice was thicker than usual. "You've forgiven me?"

She stared down at her hands in her lap and nodded. "No one is perfect. And I know you were under a lot of stress with your injury and I had become distant after we lost the baby."

"But that still doesn't excuse what I did."

She nodded again. "I know that. And of course I wish it never happened. But we all have things we wish we could take back. None of us are perfect. And..." She drifted off and lifted a shoulder, glancing over at me with an almost wistful look. "I can see that you've done everything you could to make up for it."

I'd certainly tried to. But it seemed like no amount of apologizing or groveling could ever be enough after what I'd done to her.

"You had a bad night," she continued. "Where you drank too much and were more susceptible to being influenced." She paused. "But no one is their biggest mistake."

Her eyes locked with mine, and I couldn't breathe as her words and their meaning washed over me.

No one is their biggest mistake.

She sighed. "You're a good man, Vincent. And you are such a good dad to Jaxon." She wiped at her eye, and her voice wobbled a little. "And I just think that it's time for me to allow myself to really heal. A big part of that is to stop looking at the past hurts for validation and focus more on what is happening now. Like right now, I'm sitting in this truck with one of the best men I know. You're not perfect. But neither am I. And I guess I just want to choose happiness now instead of pain."

I drew in a shaky breath as she spoke and I tried to keep myself together, my heart racing so fast and hard in my chest it was practically thrumming.

Don't cry. Don't cry. Don't cry.

I blew out a long breath and willed the tears pricking at the corners of my eyes to just stay inside. I didn't need to cry in front of Emerson right now. And I really needed to be able to see the road right now, too.

She must have noticed the huge wave of emotion I was trying to fight back, because she took off her seatbelt and scooted to the center of the bench seat. She buckled in next to me, and as I focused on the road, still trying to keep my emotions contained, I felt her stare on me.

Was she just waiting for me to cry?

But then, to my amazement, she leaned her head on my shoulder and slipped her arm through mine. "We're going to be okay," she whispered, gently kissing my shoulder.

And I couldn't keep the tears from falling as I felt the pieces of my heart that had been clawed apart because of my actions start to patch themselves back together.

27

EMERSON

"THANKS FOR THE RIDE," I said when Vincent pulled into my driveway.

I knew this was the part where I was supposed to unbuckle and walk inside the house, but I didn't want to move away from him.

I liked being next to him. He was warm and strong, and just being close to him had a calming effect on me.

And it felt like something really had shifted between us. We were both a little more *whole* at the end of our drive than we'd been at the beginning.

Was it so bad that I just wanted to live in this magic bubble for a little longer? Before we went to the wedding and I had to watch him and his date spend the day together?

Sure, I knew Landon would probably be happy to

keep me company tomorrow, and he'd even be a fun distraction. But somehow, that didn't make the prospect for tomorrow any better. We'd had fun talking tonight during dinner, but even though he was really cute and fun to talk to, he was missing the certain spark that I knew was possible with a guy.

A spark I knew was possible because I'd had it with Vincent.

"Want me to walk you to your door?" he asked, his voice low next to my ears.

I lifted my head off his shoulder for the first time since I'd put it there to look at him and said, "That would be nice."

So we climbed out of his truck and walked to the front door. But instead of typing in the passcode to unlock the door, I turned to face him.

He was so tall. Such a solid and comforting presence. There was some innate need that I had to feel protected and safe, and this hulk of a man had filled that need so perfectly.

I didn't want to say good night to him right now.

The other women in my divorced ladies Facebook group would probably tell me I was so stupid to want to spend time alone with my ex.

But I did.

I wanted to be alone with him.

I just wanted a night where we pretended things had never gone wrong and we were still together.

I didn't want to go inside and be by myself. I had spent half my nights alone over the past year and I didn't want to do it anymore.

So I looked up at his face on the dimly lit porch and asked, "Do you want to come in for a little while?" And then I held my breath as I watched the surprise register on his face.

I didn't know how I'd feel if he turned me down.

He bit his lip for a moment, as if trying to figure out what I meant with my invitation.

I said, "Just to hang out. You said your mom has Jaxon for the weekend, and I don't really feel like going to bed yet and would love some company." I shrugged. "Unless you already have plans for your night alone."

Like a late night with his date for tomorrow...

A sinking feeling came over me as I realized what he could have had planned.

But he ran his hand through his dark hair in the way that I'd always found so adorable and said, "Sure. I can hang out for a bit."

"Okay, cool." I sighed, relief instantly washing over me and leaving me feeling weak.

I typed in the passcode to my door and opened it. As I was flicking on the lights in the entryway, Vincent followed me in.

"Was that the same passcode we had when I lived here?" he asked.

I nodded as I kicked off my heels. "You were the one who installed it, so I never knew how to change it."

I guess I could have paid someone to help me or watched a YouTube video on how to do it, but I just hadn't really cared to. It wasn't like I needed to worry about him knowing the code to my house. He wasn't going to rob me or anything.

I opened the closet door to hang up my coat, but when I went to take it off, he was right there, helping me slip it off my shoulders.

"Thanks." I looked up at him through my lashes, feeling my cheeks heat up.

"No problem," he mumbled.

We hung up our coats, and as we walked down the hall toward the living room, I realized I hadn't really decided what we would be doing once we got there.

What did one do when they were hanging out with their ex?

A few options came to mind, but since I probably shouldn't be trying to kiss a guy who had a date with someone else the next day, I tried not to entertain that idea for very long.

There were lots of other things we could do. We'd always loved game nights in the past, or a movie would be nice. So I suggested one of those ideas.

He shrugged and said, "I was actually planning to watch that new murder movie that just came out when I got home tonight. Would you want to watch that?"

"Yes," I said enthusiastically. "I've been dying to see that one but never had anyone to go with when it was in the theater."

"I already have it on my VUDU account. I can just log in on your TV, if you want."

"That would be perfect." While he grabbed the remote from the drawer in the entertainment stand, I said, "I'm just going to hurry upstairs to change into something more comfortable real quick."

"Sure." He glanced over his shoulder then went back to logging into his account.

28

VINCENT

WHAT'S TAKING *her so long?* I wondered as I sat on the couch, waiting for Emerson to come back downstairs.

She'd gone up to change out of her dress at least ten minutes ago. Had she forgotten I was down here and decided to go to bed?

I was about to go upstairs to make sure she was okay when I heard a door open upstairs.

"Hey, Vincent," her voice called from the top of the stairs.

"Yeah?" I got to my feet and walked to the bottom of the staircase. And when I saw her at the top, she was still wearing the same tight-fitting pink dress from earlier. The one that had made it impossible not to stare at her when we were at the church earlier this evening.

Had I misheard her? Had she not really gone to her room to change?

But when our eyes met, she was ashen-faced.

"So, um..." She wrung her hands together. "I promise I'm not trying to seduce you or anything, but my zipper is stuck and I was wondering if you could help me out."

She wasn't trying to seduce me...

I gulped.

It was probably a good thing she prefaced her request with that because my insides instantly went jittery at the prospect of helping her.

Sure, I had helped her zip and unzip her dresses a thousand times when we'd been married, but for some reason, the thought of helping her with it today seemed so forbidden.

It took me a while to form a coherent sentence, but after what hopefully wasn't too obvious of a pause, I said, "S-sure. I can help."

And when I climbed the stairs I had to grip the handrail extra hard to keep my footing.

When I reached her, she led me into the bedroom we used to share. It had changed a lot since I'd last been in there. New teal curtains. New all-white bedding. New artwork on the walls. But it was still all very nice and clean like she'd always kept it, and it smelled faintly of her perfume.

"I think the fabric might be bunched around the zipper or something." She turned her back to me, sweeping her hair away from her neck so I could see the top of the zipper. "I tried to get it down, but it's such an awkward angle that I can't really get it on my own."

"Okay," I said, feeling even more jittery. "Let's see what I can do."

I moved close and tentatively took the zipper in my right hand. I tried tugging it down, just to see if it was simply the angle she'd been working with that was causing the issue. But like she had said, it didn't budge as if stuck on something.

So I stepped even closer, leaning my head down to get a better look. But then I caught a whiff of her shampoo. And she smelled amazing. Like happiness, and hope, and everything I wanted.

But because I needed to keep my head about me, I pushed away the feelings of attraction and focused on how the zipper was on the underside. It had caught on the woven pink fabric.

"You were right," I said, my voice froggy. "I just need to..." I trailed off as I pulled on the fabric and worked the zipper.

A few heartbeats later, it released.

"There," I said, pulling the zipper down until it rested at her lower waist, revealing a long triangle of skin on her back. "That should do the trick."

The sight of her skin with her lacy black bra underneath made my stomach muscles tighten and flip.

Daaaang. What was this girl doing to me?

Did she think I had superhuman restraint?

And before I could stop myself, I was trailing my fingers along that bare skin.

It was so soft. So smooth and warm.

And it made me want more.

"Emerson..." I whispered, stepping so my chest and torso pushed against her back as I spoke into her hair. But I didn't really know what I wanted to say, because I knew I shouldn't be asking what I wanted to ask.

She turned her face to the side so I could see her profile—she was peeking back at me from the corner of her eye. Like she was waiting for something. Waiting for me to decide what I was going to do next.

Was she feeling what I was feeling?

Was her whole body burning up with the same desire I had pulsing through my veins right now?

Her breathing did seem shallow. As if she was having just as hard a time as I was to keep her breathing steady.

I let my fingers slowly trace up her sides and then up and down her arms.

"I know you said you weren't trying to seduce me," I whispered into her soft hair. "But it's just..." I sighed, not knowing how to continue.

"I know," she whispered, her chest rising and falling. Then she turned to face me, her green eyes wide and hungry. "I wonder if this kind of thing ever goes away..."

She put her hands on my chest and let them slowly trail a path of fire along my torso, touching me in a way I hadn't been touched in so long.

"I don't think it does," I breathed. Because if anything, the pull I had for her was even stronger than it had been before.

I *wanted* her.

More than I wanted anything.

But I would let her decide what she wanted. I didn't have a lot of self-control where she was concerned, but I did know that if anything was ever going to happen between Emerson and me, it would be because she wanted it.

Her hands stopped at the top button of my shirt. I watched her, waiting—my heart in my throat.

She was just staring at my chest, like she was thinking hard about something.

Deciding where we would go next.

Then she patted my chest lightly and lifted her eyes to meet mine again. "I should probably finish changing into my pajamas so we can watch that movie."

"Okay." I nodded slowly, hoping my disappointment didn't show on my face. "I'll wait for you downstairs."

"I THOUGHT you might want to change into something more comfortable, too," Emerson's voice came from behind where I sat on her couch, waiting for her to come back downstairs.

It had taken a long time for my heart to get back to normal after our interaction in her room but putting some space between us had cleared my head enough to know that we had made the right choice.

Jumping back into bed right now would be a mistake.

I turned to watch her approach and saw she wore a white tank top—her black bra barely showing through the thin material—and a pair of black yoga pants.

It was like she was trying to test my self-control all night because she looked amazing.

But that wasn't the only thing I noticed. In her arms was my old football T-shirt from my time at the University of Alabama and my old gray sweats.

I furrowed my brow. "Where did those come from?"

"These were in the wash the day I packed everything of yours up." Her cheeks turned pink. She handed me the clothes and I lifted the shirt to inspect it.

"I thought these got lost in the move somehow." I looked at her. "What made you keep them?"

"I don't know." She sat on the arm of the couch next

to me and shrugged. "I planned to give them to you later, but as time went on I decided to keep them instead. I guess I wanted something to remember you by."

And I don't know what it was about her keeping something of mine that got to me, even when she'd been so mad at me, but I was momentarily speechless.

She hadn't wanted to totally erase me from her life after all.

"Anyway," she said. "Those are mine now. So while I'm fine letting you wear them while we watch the movie, you're going to have to give them back before you leave."

I couldn't help but smile. "For some reason I'm okay with that."

I wanted her to keep them.

But then I had another idea. "If you get to keep these, then I think it's only fair that I keep something of yours."

"You think so?" She smiled, her face open and unguarded. It was the kind of smile she used to give me when we were at our best. "And if you were to keep something, what would it be?"

I pursed my lips as I thought about it. Then I said, "If I could have anything of yours, I'd probably want a lock of your hair."

"My hair?" Her jaw dropped and she smacked my

arm. "Are you serious? Because that's almost as creepy as that porcelain doll was."

I laughed, loving teasing her. "Fine, so maybe I wouldn't really ask you to cut off your hair."

"Good. Because I would totally turn you down." She laughed. "Do you know how long it took me to get it this long?"

"No." I reached out and tentatively combed my fingers through her soft hair. "But it looks good."

It felt good, too. I'd always loved combing my fingers through her hair.

And when I saw goosebumps race across her skin with my touch, it told me she didn't mind me touching it right now, either.

This was progress.

She cleared her throat. "So, since we just nixed the whole lock-of-hair idea, what else would you keep?"

"I don't know." I thought about it, returning my hand to my lap. "I guess I'd probably want the quilt you used to bring to all the games before we got you the suite at the stadium." It was a green-and-white striped quilt that had always been easy to spot in the crowd among the black and gold Dragons' paraphernalia. Whenever I needed a boost during the game, I'd look for her in the crowd, see her smile and wave at me, and instantly feel better.

"Yeah?" she asked, seeming surprised by my choice.

"Yeah." I nodded.

And when she seemed to study me for a long moment, I couldn't help but wonder what she thought of my choice. Did she think it was odd that I still wanted something after everything that had happened?

"So what do you say?" I asked. "Think you can part with it?"

She pursed her pink lips then shrugged. "I'll have to think about it." She stood and turned on the lamp next to us. "Do you want any popcorn?"

"Sure," I said.

"Great. I'll pop some while you change."

29

EMERSON

"SO, I guess it's been a while since I wore this shirt." Vincent came out from the bathroom a minute later, wearing the clothes I'd given him.

The red T-shirt was a lot tighter on him than I remembered—leaving little to the imagination where his muscles were concerned.

Dang. He was ripped these days.

I let my gaze take in his physique. The fabric of the T-shirt was stretched tight across his sculpted biceps, his amazing pectoral muscles, and those broad shoulders of his.

Just looking at him right now seemed almost forbidden because of how it made me feel.

I gulped and turned back to the stove where I was popping popcorn.

Was I even strong enough to sit through a movie with him looking like that right next to me? I had a hard enough time not throwing myself in his arms when we were upstairs in my bedroom.

I drew in a deep breath, hoping it would help me remember my self-restraint. "Do you want the ranch popcorn seasoning on your popcorn?"

"Sure," he said, coming to stand beside me, leaning against the counter. "Want me to get a bowl?"

"Oh, yeah. That would be helpful," I said, not realizing until that moment that I had forgotten to grab one.

He went to the cupboard where we kept them and opened it. And when he reached up to grab the stainless steel bowl, the bottom of his shirt lifted just enough to show his toned torso.

I bit my lip as I watched him.

Was he trying to tempt me right now?

Because if so, it was totally working.

"Here you go," he said, coming back and setting the bowl on the counter beside me.

"Thanks," I said, stirring the handle of the stovetop popcorn popper.

"Want me to cue the movie to the beginning?" he asked.

"That would be great," I breathed, hoping he wouldn't notice how much his presence was affecting me.

Because the faster it was ready, the sooner I would be distracted by the movie instead of the hottie I was watching it with.

Yes, Vincent was a babe.

Stop thinking about it, Emerson.

The more I reminded myself of that fact, the harder it would be to not think of all the reasons why we should skip the movie and do something else.

Because doing something else would be a mistake.

Wouldn't it?

If only my hormones would just agree with my brain right now.

I finished with the popcorn and went back to the living room where Vincent was already sitting in one corner of the couch, the movie paused at the opening scene.

So I switched off the main lights, and since sharing a bowl of popcorn meant you had to sit by the other person, I took the couch cushion next to him.

"Ready?" he asked.

I nodded and handed him the popcorn bowl. "Ready."

He pressed the Play button, and within a few seconds, the movie started. As the screen panned over an old Victorian house where we saw a housekeeper setting up a dinner party, I told myself to relax. I'd watched hundreds of movies with Vincent before. This didn't need to be a big deal.

We were just two old friends hanging out on a Friday night. Nothing needed to happen.

I wouldn't even think about kissing him.

Nope, I definitely wouldn't think about kissing those beautiful, perfect lips of his that had a way of making me lose all track of time and space and reason.

And if he tried to kiss me—which he probably wouldn't since he had a date with another woman tomorrow—I would remind him of that fact.

Sure, our chemistry was off the charts and could apparently be ignited with the simplest of gestures, but that didn't mean we needed to act on it.

We were adults. We would act like it.

I peeked sideways at him, just to see if he seemed to be amped up about any of this like I was.

And when I did, he was looking at me, too.

I quickly turned back to the screen, which now had a woman in a 1920's flapper dress whispering something into the ear of a butler.

"You feel as awkward as I do?" he asked.

"Yes." I sighed, relieved that he had been the first to say it. But then I hurried to say, "Not that watching a movie with you is weird. Because it's not. It's good. And I'm glad we can do this. It's just..."

"It's just been a while."

I nodded. "Yeah."

"Well," he said with a sigh. "How about we don't think about how long it's been? Or any of the other things we might be worried about and just enjoy the movie?"

Other things we might be worried about?

Could he be thinking about the same things I was?

I pushed the thought away, because we were trying not to think about those things right now, and said, "Yes, let's do that."

With that seemingly settled, I allowed myself to nestle a little closer to his side and grabbed a handful of popcorn out of the bowl. I had waited months to watch this movie. I was determined to enjoy it.

And when the fancy guests on the screen started to arrive at the dinner party, Vincent lifted his arm and put it around my shoulders.

"Is this okay?" he whispered, the hesitant note in his voice totally melting my heart because it reminded me so much of the first time he'd done this very thing all those years ago.

"Yes, that's okay." I snuggled in closer, my heart beating faster.

How was it that so much could have happened between us and so much could have changed, yet he could still feel the same?

If Ivy hadn't said what she said earlier today, I probably would be questioning everything right now. Probably wouldn't have invited him inside in the first place.

But I was glad that I had. Because even if nothing ever happened between us after tonight, I was happy in this small moment in time. And being happy was something I hadn't truly felt for a very long time.

30

VINCENT

"EMERSON," I said, gently rubbing her back a few hours later. "We fell asleep."

But she didn't stir.

We had started watching a second movie after the first one ended, and apparently, we had both drifted off in the middle of it.

I was stretched across all three couch cushions on my side with a pillow tucked under my head, and she was nestled against me, her face curled into my chest. It was actually amazing she hadn't fallen off the couch from how little space there was for two people.

The TV logo bounced across the gray screen, telling me the movie must have ended a while ago. I looked at my watch. It was after two.

I really should get home.

So I rubbed my hand along her arm and tried to wake her again. "It's late. I should go."

But she just nestled even closer against me. And if my arm hadn't been falling asleep from the position I was in, I would probably just stay here forever.

"Emerson," I whispered against her ear.

"I'm too tired to move," she said drowsily.

"I'll carry you to your bed then," I said. "You'll sleep better there."

This definitely wouldn't be the first time I'd had to carry her to bed after a late night. Once Emerson hit a certain level of tiredness, it took a lot to get her to move.

After gathering some motivation of my own, I carefully maneuvered my way around her and off of the couch. Then squatting down low, I snuck my hands beneath her and lifted her into my arms.

She barely stirred as she cradled against me, and I was reminded of all the times I'd done this before. It's funny how you don't miss something until you're reminded of it again, but I suddenly missed being able to do things like this for her. Missed how she'd taken care of me, too.

I stepped around the popcorn bowl I'd placed on the floor earlier and carefully made my way up the stairs to her bedroom.

The door was partially open, so I pushed it with my foot and stepped into her moonlit room. It was surreal being here in the dark. Ghosts of days gone by almost lingering in the air.

I looked at the king-sized bed we used to share and tried to figure out where to put her.

Did she still sleep on the same side that she used to when we were married, like I still did?

Or had she taken advantage of having the space to herself and slept in the middle?

Deciding to just do what I used to do, I carried her to the left side. With a little effort I was able to pull the covers back. Then I gently lay her down on the bed, covering her with the fluffy white comforter.

She rolled to her side, facing out toward me.

So maybe she still slept where she always had?

I couldn't help but just watch her as she peacefully lay there. Her hair cascaded over her pillow, in soft curls. Her face was serene, the worries of her world wiped away as she dreamed.

She was beautiful. And I probably could have watched her all night. But I needed to go. So I bent close to her and gently pressed my lips against her forehead.

"Good night, Emerson," I whispered against her smooth, warm skin, catching the faint smell of her shampoo again. "Thank you for tonight."

When she didn't stir, I turned to leave. But before I could step away, her hand reached out and grabbed my pant leg.

I froze. Had she been awake?

"Stay," she whispered.

I frowned and looked back at her.

Had I heard her right? Or was my imagination just playing tricks on me?

When I didn't move, her eyes opened a little, her gaze lifting to meet mine. "It's late," she said, almost a soothing quality to her voice. "Just stay."

My stomach went to my throat and it took a moment for me to say, "Are you sure?"

She nodded her head drowsily. "I just want one night where I'm not alone."

My fingers tingled with those words because I too didn't want to be alone tonight. It was like living a dream that I never wanted to wake up from.

So once I managed to get my body to move, I went to the other side of the bed, pulled the covers back and climbed in. My body only released its pent-up tension when I rested my head on the pillow that had once been mine.

Emerson turned, so her body was facing me, but her eyes were still closed. "Good night, Vincent," she whispered, reaching out and putting her hand on my arm.

"Good night," I said, breathing through my nose so she wouldn't hear how hard of a time I was having breathing beside her.

She was quiet after that, and her hand slowly slipped off my arm, telling me that she was asleep again.

It took a while for my heartbeat to return to its regular speed as I watched Emerson's breathing deepen and become rhythmic. And as the minutes ticked by, I just studied the most beautiful woman I'd ever seen and thanked whatever forces were at work tonight for giving me a gift I didn't deserve. And even though it took a while longer, eventually my eyes grew heavy and I found sleep.

31

EMERSON

I WRINKLED my nose as sunlight woke me the next morning, and in the split second between being asleep and being awake, I realized I wasn't alone in my bed.

There was a heavy arm wrapped around my torso, and my back was enveloped by a warm and very familiar form.

I popped my eyes open as I realized what that meant.

Vincent had slept over.

In my bed.

I looked down at myself. I still wore the same tank and yoga pants I'd put on last night and I vaguely remembered him carrying me up the stairs.

And...

I pinched my eyes shut as I remembered asking him to stay with me.

I probably sounded like an idiot.

Well, at least I hadn't asked him for more than that.

But maybe he hadn't minded? Since *he* was the one currently spooning *me* in the middle of the bed.

Maybe it was possible he hadn't just done it because I sounded pathetically lonely.

He sighed deeply next to my ear and I knew he would be waking up soon. He always breathed like that just before he awoke, like he was just coming out of a deep sleep state or something.

Should I try to slip away before he realized we'd probably been cuddling most of the night? Because it had to be a subconscious thing, right? He wouldn't have just cuddled up to me like this if he was awake.

He drew in another long breath and his arm tightened around my torso as he pressed himself closer to my back. And I couldn't keep a smile from slipping onto my face, because it was just the same as waking up next to him had always been. We might have spent over a year apart, but the way we slept in the same bed hadn't changed.

I felt him move his face closer, like he was going to sniff my hair or kiss my neck, but then suddenly, his body went tense.

He just realized where he is and what he's doing.

An instant later, he let go of me, pushing himself away and rolling to the other side of the bed.

I chuckled and rolled around to face him. "Just in case you were hoping I was still asleep through all of that...I wasn't."

An embarrassed expression crossed his face for a second, but then his lips stretched into a wide smile. "Old habits die hard, I guess."

I nodded, my hair rubbing against my pillow. "It would seem so." Then I took in the T-shirt he was wearing. "Though it would seem not all things are the same. You did sleep with your shirt on. I don't know if I've ever seen that before."

He shrugged. "I figured it might be awkward if I slept in my usual sleepwear."

"I probably wouldn't have minded too much." I raised my eyebrows and bit my lip at the memory of how he used to sleep in his boxer briefs and nothing else.

And yeah, I had most definitely never complained about it.

His cheeks flushed and he covered his eyes with his arm and groaned. "You know it's dangerous for you to say things like that right now, don't you?"

"Why?" I asked, innocently.

He rolled over onto my side and gave me a good once-over. "Because it makes me want to pounce." And the fiery look in his eyes told me he wasn't exaggerating.

Daaaang.

Now it was my turn to blush—for my whole body to blush. I'd forgotten how much I'd missed this flirtatious side of him.

I said, "Good thing you have lots of self-control today, huh?"

He shook his head as if warning me not to tempt him. "I only have so much."

"But you're the star quarterback for the Denver Dragons. You don't get there without a strong will."

He raised a dark eyebrow, and I loved the way his brown eyes lit up before he said, "That's *very* different."

When his gaze went to my mouth for a split second, my stomach muscles tightened.

I really was pushing his buttons, wasn't I?

And I loved it.

But since I knew we probably shouldn't try doing what we were both very tempted to do, I shrugged and said, "Well, then. It's a good thing I have enough for the both of us."

"Whatever." He rolled his eyes and lay flat on his back. "I saw you checking me out."

I sat up and pushed the covers away, knowing if I didn't climb out of bed now I might be tempted to pounce on him myself.

"Well, since we both seem to be well aware of how attractive each of us is," I said as I slipped out of bed and onto the floor. "I'm going to go make some breakfast."

"That's probably a good idea." He nodded, his eyes raking me over as if to prove a point. "I'll be down in a minute."

MAKING breakfast with Vincent turned out to be really fun. He had changed back into the button-up shirt and jeans he'd worn to the rehearsal party last night—and though he still looked sexy in them, they helped me to be in a mind-frame that wasn't as distracted by his muscles as I'd been when he was wearing his old football shirt.

He made the bacon and eggs while I made the French toast and buttermilk syrup, and we only bumped up against each other a few times.

We had a good conversation as we ate, talking about what we had been up to lately. Me: working on a convenience store robbery case. Him: mainly just trying to keep up his training regimen with Cole and spending as much time with Jaxon as he could to make up for the busy football season.

He helped me clean up and even washed the pots and pans when we were done, and then he went back to his place to get ready for the wedding in a few hours.

All in all, it was a great Saturday morning. Very much like what we used to have before Jaxon was born, slow and easy and fun.

It almost made me excited about the prospect of going to Kira and Derek's wedding with him. Until I remembered he was only giving me a ride there because my car wasn't working. And, oh yeah, he still had a date.

Yeah, that was going to be fun to watch after the past fourteen hours of heaven.

At least the shop had called and said my car was already done and ready to be picked up. So I didn't have to worry about being that third wheel when Vincent went to pick up his date.

Who was she, anyway?

Was it someone he knew well?

Or just a casual date?

From the way he'd flirted with me all morning, it didn't seem like he was serious about anyone—at least I hoped he wouldn't flirt with me when he was dating someone else because that might make me rethink the whole forgiveness talk we'd had last night.

But whether I was ready to meet his date or not, I'd be running into her in a matter of hours.

"READY TO DO WHAT WE PRACTICED?" Landon asked a couple of hours later.

We were standing in the foyer of the church again, my arm linked through his as we waited for the wedding procession to start, much like we had done the night before. Only this time, he was all dressed up in a gray suit and navy-blue tie that matched the rest of the groomsmen standing around. And I wore the navy-blue bridesmaid's dress with a long, flowery skirt and low-waisted back that had been sitting in my closet for months. A pair of black strappy heels that hurt my feet but looked amazing completed my look.

"I guess so," I said, though I was a ball of nerves on the inside. I'd had such a good night and morning with Vincent, I didn't want to ruin it by seeing him with another woman.

I'd tried looking for him earlier, to see if he was standing somewhere talking to his date, but he'd apparently been with Derek since getting to the church.

I'd even tried poking my head through the back doors of the chapel to see if I could spot a woman sitting in the audience alone who might be his date, but at the same moment, Chelsea Stockton, the ringleader of the Dragon Ladies, had looked my way so I quickly stepped back.

Landon must have picked up on my anxiety with

those psychology skills of his because he narrowed his eyes and said, "Are you nervous?"

I sighed and met his dark brown eyes. "A little."

"Why?"

"Well..." I said, not sure if I should go into everything. I had seen him talking with a few other bridesmaids when I arrived, so I didn't think he'd really care if I told him I was worried about seeing my ex and his date. But it wasn't exactly nice to talk about feelings for another guy with one you'd kind of flirted with the night before.

"Does it have anything to do with your ex?" he asked, apparently reading my mind.

Maybe he wasn't just a psychologist but an actual mind-reader.

"Yeah." I pressed my lips together. "He brought a date with him, so this will be my first time seeing him with another woman."

I'd never actually *seen* him with Victoria, thankfully.

"Well, I'm pretty sure once his date sees you, she's going to feel just a *little* threatened."

I smiled. "You're too sweet, you know that?"

"I've been told that a time or two." He winked.

I bet he has. Just the sight of those cute dimples of his would have had me all over him.

You know, if I hadn't realized I still might be in love with my ex.

"If you'd like me to help you out in making him jealous," he said, a conspiratorial look in his eyes. "I don't really have anything better to do while we're here."

I raised an eyebrow. "I think those bridesmaids I saw flirting with you earlier might be a little disappointed if you did that."

"Maybe." He shrugged his broad shoulders. "But it's not every day you get to make the superstar, Vincent Lake, jealous of a college professor from Utah."

"Well..." I shook my head but couldn't keep a grin from stretching across my cheeks. "Let me first find out what his date looks like and maybe I'll take you up on your offer."

He patted my hand that was resting in the crook of his arm. "Just let me know."

The wedding planner appeared and looked over our group. "We'll be starting soon," she said. "Just remember what we went over last night, and I think we'll have a beautiful wedding today."

I turned back to look at Kira one more time before she became Mrs. Bailey. She looked beautiful in her white wedding gown with her arm slipped through her dad's. I caught her eye, and when she gave me an excitedly nervous smile, I gave her a thumbs-up and mouthed *good luck*.

She nodded and mouthed *thank you*. And in the

next moment, the song "Marry Me" started playing through the speakers.

Here we go.

I took a deep breath to steel my nerves as the wedding planner gestured to an usher to open the big doors ahead.

Everyone in the crowd turned to watch us.

Over the group of people on the groom's side of the room, I saw many old familiar faces that I hadn't seen in over a year—Vincent's teammates and their wives who had once been my tribe—albeit a tribe wherein I never felt like I ever completely belonged.

But when the few I'd been close to noticed me and waved or smiled, my heart burned in my chest as I realized that I really had missed them.

Landon bent his head down and whispered close to my ear, "It's our turn."

I lifted my chin, hoping it would help me feel confident what with all the eyes on me, and then we started our walk down the aisle.

I smiled at the crowd as I walked past them, but as the first chorus started to swell through the speakers, my gaze went to our destination at the front of the chapel and locked in on Vincent.

He wore the same suit and tie as all the other groomsmen, but somehow, the way the suit looked on him put all the other guys to shame. Even Landon, who appeared quite dapper today couldn't compare to him. It just suited him.

I expected Vincent to be watching the other bridesmaids and groomsmen who were nearing the front of the chapel, but even though I was several couples behind them, his eyes found mine.

"Looks like Vincent thinks you look as amazing in that dress as I thought," Landon spoke under his breath when Vincent continued to stare in our direction.

And the longer I looked at him, and the longer he stared back at me, I started to wonder if I might need my eyes checked or something because he really was just watching me the entire time.

I glanced around the room to see if I could spot who his date might be, because there was no way she was going to like seeing him watching me the way he did. But the only person in the crowd with a sour expression on her face was Chelsea Stockton. And since that seemed to be a permanent feature on her face whenever she was around me, I really didn't know what to think.

Maybe his date hadn't noticed?

Or maybe she didn't even know who I was, or anything about Vincent's past life?

I looked ahead again, and by this time, Landon and I had made it to the front of the chapel. I released my arm from his and we went our separate ways: Him to stand by Derek's brother, me to stand by a bridesmaid named Melissa.

The last of the bridesmaids and groomsmen made it to the front, followed by the flower girl and ring bearer.

"If you'll all stand for the bride," the pastor said to the crowd, gesturing upwards with her arms.

And in the next moment, Kira and her father appeared at the back of the church with huge smiles on their faces as the music changed to "Halo" by Beyoncé.

As they walked down the aisle, I watched Derek's reaction to seeing his bride. I'd always loved seeing the groom's reaction. And Derek didn't disappoint.

He had the biggest smile on his face, and maybe even a few tears in his eyes. But my favorite part was how obvious it was how much he loved her. It just emanated from all that he was.

Before I could look back to Kira and watch her walk toward the man of her dreams, my gaze slid over to Vincent. And my breath caught in my throat, my heart stuttering in my chest, because instead of watching Kira like I'd expected—like everyone else in the whole room was doing in that moment—Vincent was looking at me.

In the same way Derek was looking at Kira.

He was looking at me like he loved me.

32

EMERSON

THE WEDDING WAS BEAUTIFUL. Derek and Kira had written their own vows to read during the ceremony and by the time they were finished, there wasn't a dry eye in the room.

Once the ceremony was over and they were pronounced husband and wife, we all headed over to the Mile High Station for the dinner and reception.

When I walked into the big room filled with tables and a second-story balcony, many of the wedding guests were already seated at their assigned tables. But a group of Dragons players stood in a corner, chatting and patting each other on the back—like they were excited to see each other again after the past month of training on their own.

I was planning to just walk past them and make my

way to the front where a few of the other bridesmaids and groomsmen were already seated at the long tables, but then my eyes caught on Vincent standing in the crowd of football players.

I almost tripped on my dress, because I was surprised to see him with the guys instead of his date.

After the way he'd looked at me during the ceremony, I figured he'd at least try to cover for it and make his date feel less uncomfortable with the situation and stay by her side the rest of the evening.

But there wasn't a woman in the group.

Maybe she was in the bathroom?

Deciding I really shouldn't be that worried about it, I made my way around the outside edge of the room and headed toward the front.

I was almost there when Chelsea Stockton stepped in front of me. Her golden blonde hair was done in a tight updo. Her angular frame was looking more gaunt than usual in her black strapless dress. And her blue eyes still held the usual spite they always had when focused on me.

"Hey, Chelsea," I said, stumbling slightly with the surprise.

"Hey, Emerson," Chelsea said in her fake happy tone. "Long time no see."

"Yeah." I adjusted the strap on my dress. "It's been a while."

Why had she stopped me? What could she possibly have to say with that vindictive expression after a year of not seeing each other?

"It has been a while. I've been wondering what you've been up to." Her gaze dipped down, like she was checking out my hand for a second before looking back at my face. "I see you haven't gotten remarried yet."

"Um, nope," I said, wondering why she'd even be surprised about it. Did she know lots of women who jumped right into a new marriage after ending one?

"Are you here with anyone?" She glanced behind me, as if looking for someone. "You may not be married yet, but I bet you've at least been playing the field a little."

And here it was. She was trying to make me feel bad for being at the wedding alone.

Just like I had assumed she would when I'd gone on my hunt to find a date for tonight.

I swallowed. "I'm not dating anyone at the moment, so no, I didn't bring anyone with me."

"That's too bad." She pouted her lips and tutted. "It must be lonely in that big house of yours on the nights Vincent has Jaxon."

Yep, she was definitely trying to make me feel bad about my single status.

I was tempted to say I hadn't been too lonely last night with Vincent sleeping next to me, but then I thought better of it. I didn't need to stoop to Chelsea's level.

So I plastered as patient of a smile on my lips as I could and said, "As nice as it is to see you again, Chelsea, I'm going to go find my seat."

I was just stepping past her when she grabbed my arm. "Hold on."

I turned back to her, my eyebrows knitting together. "What?"

She sighed, and for a second, her overly confident demeanor faltered.

"I know you say you aren't dating anyone, but—" She leaned closer and whispered, "Are you the reason why Vincent called my sister this morning to cancel their date?"

My eyes widened and my mind raced for a moment as I took in what Chelsea had just said.

Chelsea's sister was the woman Vincent was supposed to be here with today?

And he'd cancelled?

"I don't know what you're talking about," I whispered back. "But if Vincent cancelled his date, it was because *he* didn't want to keep it."

"Whatever," Chelsea snapped, letting go of my arm like it had burned her. "You need to stop dragging him along. Just get over yourself and let the man move on."

I bristled and took a step back.

I hadn't been dragging him along.

Not purposely, anyway.

But instead of acknowledging any of that, I surprised myself by saying, "What if I don't want him to move on?"

She narrowed her icy blue eyes at me. Then, without a word, she huffed and walked away, back to the table where her minions, Sasha Perry and Kacie Roberts, were watching our interaction.

I just shook my head and frowned as she retreated.

"What was that about?" a deep voice said from beside me.

I turned to find Landon standing next to me with a glass of water in his hands, his gaze on me then to Chelsea.

I sighed and shrugged. "I really don't know."

He took a sip from his water then offered me his arm. "You can tell me about it at the table."

So I slipped my arm in his and let him lead me to the table at the front. But as we walked, the gravity of what Chelsea had been upset about hit me.

Vincent had cancelled his date after he'd left my house.

Was it too much to hope that it had something to do with the night and morning he'd spent with me?

"IS THIS SEAT TAKEN?" Vincent's voice sounded from behind me a few minutes later.

Derek and Kira had arrived after taking a few photos at the church, so the rest of the guests were just taking their seats. I'd noticed one of the bridesmaids Landon had been flirting with before the wedding eyeing him with a longing look in her eyes, so I'd let her take my seat next to him. And then I'd taken her seat—which was apparently right next to the one Vincent had been assigned to.

Gotta love it when things work out like that.

"I'm pretty sure that's your seat," I told him, my palms feeling slightly sweaty at the prospect of sitting next to him after what I'd just learned from Chelsea.

"Perfect." He pulled the chair out and then sat down. And when he scooted himself closer to the table, he was close enough that his leg rested against mine.

Well, if Chelsea hadn't wondered if something was going on between us earlier, she would definitely be wondering now.

"Is your date sitting by herself?" I asked, deciding to just find out from the get-go if what Chelsea had said was true.

He scrunched up his nose and guilt formed in his dark brown eyes. "She's actually not here."

"She's not?" I raised my eyebrows, hoping he'd continue.

He leaned closer, the smell of his delicious cologne wafting to my nose.

"I didn't think it would be fair for her to watch me stare at you all night," he whispered, giving me a meaningful look. "So when I drove home to get ready, I called her and cancelled."

He'd cancelled because of me.

I couldn't help but smile, my cheeks flushing.

He gave me a shy smile in return, like he was worried about my reaction to what he just admitted.

So I slipped my hand on his leg and gave it a gentle squeeze. "I'm glad you came alone."

He covered my hand with his warm, calloused one. "Me too." He leaned in closer and gently kissed me on the forehead, causing my heart to flutter before he said, "You looked beautiful walking down that aisle today."

I turned to him, feeling breathless with how tender and open he was being right now.

In front of all of his friends.

And I decided to be brave myself and said, "You looked really handsome, too."

He squeezed my hand, his brown eyes sparking with something. "Do you think you might be able to save me a dance tonight?"

I nodded slowly, feeling a smile stretching across my cheeks. "I think I can do that."

33

EMERSON

"CAN I walk you to your car?" Vincent asked after he'd helped me into my coat.

Derek and Kira had left in Derek's truck a few minutes before, and the wedding party was leaving after the fun night.

The evening had been magical. There really wasn't a better way to put it. Dinner was delicious, full of lots of flirtatious sideways glances, laughs, and a good amount of blushing from both of us. And after dinner, Vincent had taken me into his arms and we'd danced the night away.

It was amazing. If I had to name the top ten moments in my life, tonight would have made it on that list.

I really couldn't remember being this happy before.

It was like forgiving Vincent had given me the freedom I needed to open up myself again to what had been right for me all along.

I had been hurt and I was sure there would be more times in the future when I'd remember what he'd done and feel hurt all over again. But tonight I had chosen, once again, to let go of our past and just be with him— enjoy the feel of his strong arms around me as we'd danced. Savor the way his whispered comments in my ear sent chills racing across my skin. And revel at how the way he looked at me made my chest feel like it was bursting with sunshine.

I felt adored.

I felt cared for.

And even though he hadn't said it, I felt loved.

I'd pinched myself several times throughout the night, just to make sure I wasn't dreaming everything up, but so far, I hadn't woken up.

I never wanted to wake up from this. If it really was all just a dream, I wanted to live in this perfect dream land forever.

We had most definitely attracted several stares from the people who knew us and our story. Chelsea's eyes had practically bugged out of her skull when we'd walked past her hand in hand. Kira and Derek had glanced over at us with shock in their eyes when we'd joined them on the dance floor after their first dance.

And Cole had just stood at the edge of the crowd with his arms folded across his chest, wearing the smuggest and most pleased look I'd ever seen him wear.

And even though it was fun to shock our friends and the entire Dragons family, I really didn't care what they thought about what was going on between us. Because what they thought didn't matter. All that mattered was how Vincent and I felt about each other. Whatever we decided to do after tonight would only depend on us.

So as I buttoned up my coat, I looked up at Vincent and said, "Yes. I'd love for you to walk me to my car."

I'd also love for him to kiss me when he did it, but hopefully he could figure that out without me having to say so. Because after looking at his lips all night and feeling all the sparks igniting between us, I *needed* to kiss him. I needed him to kiss me so he would know that I wouldn't always react the way I had the last time. That it could have a happier ending tonight.

He finished buttoning his overcoat, took my hand in his big, strong one, and led me out into the beautiful February night. The sky was overcast with clouds, the night a bit warmer than the other nights we'd had recently.

"Tonight was really nice," I said as we strolled down the sidewalk together.

"It was nice," he said, shooting me a rueful kind of smile that made my insides jumble all together. He really did have a great smile. I'd missed seeing it over the past year.

"Are you picking up Jaxon from your mom's?" I asked, curious what the rest of his evening looked like.

"No." He shook his head. "She figured he'd be exhausted after all the fun she had planned for him today, so I'm going to pick him up in the morning."

"That's nice," I said.

"Yeah. They called earlier this afternoon and it sounded like they were having a great time together."

We walked quietly past a few cars and I tried to figure out what to say next. Would it be completely forward if I invited him to hang out again tonight?

We'd already spent more time together in the past twenty-four hours than we had in the last year, I didn't want him to feel like I was smothering him.

But when we made it to my car, I ended up not needing to figure out what to say because he sighed and said, "Thanks again for the great evening, but I should probably let you get home and rest."

Oh.

My heart sunk.

I managed to say, "Yeah, I guess it is getting late."

You know, if you considered nine o'clock late. It was the same time as when we'd left the restaurant last night. But I wouldn't bring it up.

If he wasn't interested in spending more time with

me, I wouldn't push it. I didn't want to have the sting of rejection be the last thing I felt with him tonight.

So I fished my key fob from the pocket of my coat and unlocked my car. "Thanks for walking me to my car."

He stepped closer, and my heart skipped a few beats when it looked like he might kiss me. But instead of a kiss, he put his hands on my arms and pulled me close before gently pressing his lips to my forehead.

My forehead...not my mouth.

I mean, it was sweet...but not exactly what I'd been hoping for after the fireworks I'd felt all night.

"I'll see you tomorrow when I bring Jaxon by," he said, rubbing his thumb across my chin.

"Okay." I nodded, fighting back the disappointment crashing over me. "I'll see you then."

He pulled me in for one more hug, so I let my body relax against him, breathing in his cologne and telling myself that even though it wasn't a kiss, it was still more than what we'd been doing two days ago.

Maybe he, like me, wasn't exactly sure where we were going to go after tonight, so he was playing it safe.

He pulled away from the hug. "Good night, Emerson."

"Good night, Vincent." Before I could let him see how disappointed I felt at the lackluster goodbye, I turned and climbed into my car.

As I drove home, I went over the evening through my mind.

I hadn't imagined all those sparks, had I?

He'd been smiling just as much as I had. And when I'd rested my head against his chest a few times as we'd danced, his heart had seemed to pick up at all the same times as mine had.

I was just coming to the Sutton Creek exit that would take me home when my phone started ringing through the car speakers. I glanced at the screen in the center of my dash and saw it was Vincent.

"Hello?" I said after pushing the answer button, wondering what he would be calling me about.

"Hi. Emerson?" He sounded out of breath for some reason.

"Yeah." I frowned. "Is something wrong?"

"No," he said. Then after a short pause, he said, "So, I feel like a huge idiot right now. I guess I'm still unsure about how to navigate this thing we have going on between us and I don't know...I'm second-guessing everything."

Hope bloomed in my chest as I waited for him to continue.

He was going to say more, right?

But when he was quiet for too long, I wondered if that was all he had called to say.

"What are you trying to say?" I asked when he remained quiet.

The exit sign came up, so I turned on the blinker to take the off ramp. I checked my rearview mirror and saw Vincent's dark gray truck right behind me. And his blinker was also on.

That was strange.

There were two exits in Sutton Creek and to get to his apartment, he should have taken the second one.

"I'm coming over," he said.

And then the song "Here I Am Again" from my favorite Korean Drama started playing through the car speakers again.

He'd hung up.

My heart raced as I drove the rest of the way to my house—anticipation throbbing in my veins as I wondered what he intended to do once he got there.

When I pulled into the garage, Vincent parked his truck right behind me on the driveway. By the time I had grabbed my coat from the passenger seat and climbed out of my car, he was already standing there next to me.

"What's going on?" I asked, my voice coming out higher pitched than normal when I noticed his disheveled look. He was still wearing his suit and over-coat, but his tie was gone—with the top button of his dress shirt undone. And his dark hair looked like he'd been running his fingers through it on the drive here.

But instead of explaining why he'd come over, he just grabbed my hand and pulled me toward the door that led into the house.

Once inside, he shut the door to the garage. But he didn't flick the lights on as expected. Instead, he just stood there in the darkness, his chest heaving, and said, "I know we already said good night, but I forgot to do something."

"You did?" I swallowed, the words sounding more like a gasp.

"I did."

I couldn't see a whole lot in the darkness, but I saw his head nod up and down.

He kissed the top of my head and his fingers slipped up my arm, along my shoulder, and behind my neck. With his lips hovering just over mine, he whispered, "I forgot to do this."

And then his soft lips gently pressed against mine. Once, then twice. Then again and again. He tasted like mint and happiness, and as he kissed me, shock waves went from my head and all the way down to my toes.

Finally.

I dropped the coat I'd all but forgotten I'd been holding and reached up to take his face in my hands. His jawline was freshly shaven, the skin so smooth and warm beneath my fingertips.

"I hope you don't mind me coming over," he said, his voice so low and raspy it made my insides melt.

"Definitely not," I mumbled back, my heart swelling in my chest over the fact that he too must have been thinking about kissing me earlier.

He'd probably just been hesitant after what happened the last time.

I let my hands travel down from Vincent's face to the lapel of his overcoat and pushed it down his shoulders, needing to feel more of him without the bulky fabric between us.

"Is that okay?" I asked.

"Yeah..." He sighed, sounding breathless. And I loved that I could still make him sound breathless after all this time.

I ran my hands under his jacket, along the thin fabric of his white button-up, feeling the solid contours of his chest and torso, loving how his body felt.

He responded by letting his fingers trace their way down my sides, rubbing his thumbs along my ribcage then squeezing my waist with his hands until they smoothed their way along my back and pulled my body closer to his. He was all lean muscle. And when he pressed me against the wall and flattened his body against mine, I could barely get myself to breathe.

Our bodies this close together felt incredible.

And I had missed this closeness so much.

I let my hands slide up his stomach and explore his torso. He was somehow stronger than he'd been a year ago, and I reveled in the feel of his muscles beneath my palms as his heart raced so fast it was probably keeping pace with mine.

His lips left my mouth to explore my throat, and my head fell back because his lips on my skin felt amazing. I let my hands explore the lines of his body, the tightly corded muscles just beneath the sleeves of his jacket.

"How is it possible I went so long without kissing you?" he asked, his voice husky and his breathing heavy like he'd just run a race.

"I was just wondering the same thing," I said as I pushed my fingers in his hair and tilted his head up to bring his mouth back to mine. He didn't hesitate to close the distance between our lips again, but this time, instead of a fast and hungry kiss, he slowed it down and deepened it.

My stomach muscles tightened, electricity shooting through my veins as his kisses took me back in time. But my feet were hurting after a night of dancing in heels, and I knew I wouldn't be able to stand in them much longer.

"I need to sit down." I gasped as I pulled away, my chest rising and falling with my labored breathing.

Vincent's eyes looked dazed for a moment before focusing again. He scanned the dark, moonlit room as if looking for a place for us to go. "You want to sit in there?" He nodded toward the living room.

"Yes," I said, and then he was pulling me behind him like he couldn't get to the couch fast enough. He sat down, and I was about to take the spot next to him when he tugged on my arm and pulled me sideways on his lap. And before I knew what was happening, he was reaching his hand behind my neck and we were kissing again.

This was crazy. We were acting like a couple of hormonal teenagers—acting like we had when we first started dating.

But when his arms encircled me, and his fingers grazed along the skin above the low backline of my dress, I didn't really care anymore because I didn't want this to stop. I wanted to kiss him all night if he'd let me.

His hands didn't remain at my back for long. They slowly slid up my sides and down again, ran along my stomach before finding their way to my back once more.

He sparked every molecule in my body to life as he kissed me over and over again. I dug my fingers into his scalp and he reacted by making a deep and masculine sound at the back of his throat, which made my fingers tremble at the thought that I could still make him moan.

He stared into my eyes for a moment, his pupils

blown wide as he looked me over, scanning over every inch of my face—and I couldn't help but feel so vulnerable. As if he could see all my flaws. But instead of turning away and telling me I didn't match up to what he wanted anymore, he murmured next to my lips, "You're so beautiful, Emerson." And then we were kissing again.

The intense, crackling heat continued to turn my brain into liquid as the kiss deepened, and all I could think of was that I wanted more of this. I needed to touch more of him. So I let my hands smooth their way along his shoulders and under his jacket. They traced their way down his chest, finding a path along the thin fabric of his shirt. They rubbed along his sides, but that still wasn't enough. I wanted to feel his skin.

My hands pushed their way across his back, untucking the bottom hem of his shirt so I could feel his hot skin on my fingertips.

"I see you're back to tempting me again like you were this morning," he mumbled against my mouth as I let my fingers travel from the back of his waist to the ribbed sides of his torso.

"I'm just refreshing my memory a little," I said, unable to keep a guilty smile from my lips.

"And how does the memory compare?" he asked.

"It's still a little fuzzy." I shrugged and looked down

at him coyly. "I think taking off your jacket might help though."

And when he tilted his head up like he was giving me permission to help him out of it, I didn't hesitate to push the jacket down his shoulders. Once he'd thrown the jacket to the floor, he said, "Now get back here," and we were lost in a kiss once more.

34

VINCENT

EMERSON TASTED EVEN BETTER than I remembered. And having her in my arms, her body pressed so close to mine, was the best I'd felt in a long time—even better than I'd felt when the Dragons made it to the playoffs.

And that dress she was wearing—

Well, let's just say I was having a very hard time not thinking of reasons to help her take it off.

And it was as if we were on the same wavelength, because just as I was thinking about that low backline and how easy it would be to slip the straps off her shoulders, her hands found their way to the collar of my dress shirt and she started unbuttoning it.

"What are you doing?" I asked, my brain barely coherent enough to form a sentence.

She'd already helped me take off my coat and suit coat. If she kept removing items of clothing, I wouldn't have much left soon.

While a huge part of me really wanted to end up in her bed again tonight, I knew we probably shouldn't. We needed to take things slowly.

One step at a time.

We hadn't even really talked about what any of this meant.

Sure, I knew how I felt about her. And I knew that if she were to tell me that she wanted to get together again, I'd do it in a heartbeat.

But that didn't mean it was the same for her. For all I knew, she had just gotten swept up in the romance of the weekend and might change her mind about kissing me tomorrow.

"I'm just unbuttoning the top few buttons," she said.

It was strange how that both relieved and disappointed me at the same time.

But even though she said she was just unbuttoning a few buttons, she ended up unbuttoning them all.

"We're just making out right now, right?" I asked, not sure in my foggy-minded state I was in the best place to interpret mixed signals.

"Sure," she said.

But her hands on my chest and arms and sides were telling me another story.

A story that every part of me—besides the tiny part of my brain that was still slightly coherent—wanted to help her tell.

She kicked off her heels and maneuvered herself so her knees were straddling my waist, the flowing skirt of her dress cascading over my lap.

This girl was going to be the death of me.

But I really couldn't think of a better way to die than tangled up with the woman I loved.

Yes, *loved.*

I had been smitten by this woman from the first time I saw her at one of Derek's parties, and I would be captivated with her until the day I died.

She was the spot of sunshine in the darkness, and I would always want to be with her.

I was just trying to decide whether I should tell her how I felt when my phone started ringing.

Emerson pulled her lips from mine and glanced at my jacket on the floor where my phone was.

"That's your mom's ringtone," she said, and I couldn't help but notice how swollen her lips were. "Do you think something's wrong with Jaxon?"

"Probably not," I said. My mom was a nurse, and if something was wrong with Jaxon, she'd know what to do better than I would.

He had probably gotten ahold of my mom's phone again and was just calling to say good night. He'd be okay if I missed his call one time.

But when I tried to pull Emerson's lips back to mine, she shook her head and climbed off of me. "You know I can't do anything else until I know he's okay."

Yes, I knew that well. Emerson's parenting instincts were always stronger than mine in times like this.

She fished my phone out of my jacket pocket and tossed it to me. I swiped to answer it before the call went to voicemail.

"Hello?" I said, hoping whoever was on the other line—Jaxon or my mom— wouldn't be able to tell that I was out of breath because I'd just been making out with my ex-wife.

"Hi, Dad," Jaxon said, his voice quiet like he was trying to be sneaky. He was probably hiding somewhere so my mom wouldn't know her grandson was a phone thief.

"What do you need, buddy?" I lifted my gaze to Emerson and saw her shoulders relax at the confirmation that it was our son instead of my mom.

Jaxon breathed heavily into the phone a few times, like he was trying to remember why he'd called. Then he said, "Oh, I just wanted to say good night."

"Good night, Jaxon. I love you."

"I love you too, Daddy."

A smile slipped onto my lips and I locked eyes with Emerson who mouthed, "He's okay?"

I nodded. That seemed to reassure her enough because she came right back to the couch and got back into the position she'd been in before.

"And Dad...?" Jaxon said.

"Yeah?" My voice came out higher than usual because just at that moment Emerson had decided to start kissing my neck.

"I want five cakes for my birthday."

This kid.

"You do?" I asked.

"Uh huh," he said excitedly. "I want a dinosaur cake, and a Big Hero 6 cake, and a..." he trailed off as if trying to remember the list he'd been compiling for the past few days.

Earlier this week he'd only wanted two cakes, now it was five.

"Those sound like great cakes," I said, hoping it would spur him to say goodbye so I could finish the call and get back to the woman currently driving me crazy with the kisses she was trailing from my neck to my collarbone.

"And a Batman cake," he said. "And Paw—"

"*Jaxon, did you steal my phone again?*" I heard what sounded like my mom's voice in the background.

A second later, Jaxon quickly said, "Bye, Dad," and then hung up.

When the line disconnected, I tossed my phone to

the side so I could show Emerson just what happened when she teased me like that.

35

VINCENT

"THIS IS A NICE SURPRISE," Emerson said when she walked into the kitchen the next morning. I had woken up before her and decided to make her favorite strawberry and Nutella crepes and green smoothie for breakfast

"I'm glad you like it." I glanced over my shoulder to take her in. She was wearing a silky pink button-up pajama top with matching pants, her hair falling out of the braid she'd put it in the night before.

And I couldn't help but think that she was beautiful like this.

I turned back to the crepe that was ready to flip, and she slipped her arms around my waist and kissed my back.

After flipping the crepe over, I closed my eyes and

just enjoyed the feel of her body pressed against my back, her head resting between my shoulder blades.

This was exactly how I wanted every morning to be from now on. It was perfect.

"Did you sleep well?" she mumbled.

I turned off the stove and scooped the crepe off the skillet and onto the top of the pile of crepes I had on the counter. "I did." Then I turned around to pull her in to my arms. "It was a good night."

She nestled against my chest, a slow smile slipping on her lips. "It *was* a good night."

After kissing on the couch for hours, we had stayed up talking and laughing, and yes, kissing even more until we could barely keep our eyes open. Then, when we realized we were human and really did need sleep to survive the next day, we had gone to her room and spent the night wrapped up in each other's arms.

It had been the perfect night.

This whole weekend had been amazing, actually.

And if it was up to me, I'd have it just go on forever.

We hadn't exactly talked about what was going on between us, or where we both saw us going from here. But if last night was any indication of what might come next, I had a lot of faith that when all was said and done, we'd be getting back together.

I didn't want to jinx it or anything, so I wasn't going to push the topic until it seemed like Emerson was ready to officially put a title on what we were. But for all intents and purposes, I was all in and excited about the direction we were headed.

"Should we eat?" Emerson asked after a minute.

I kissed the top of her head and breathed her in. "Sure."

So we each filled our plates and glasses and then took them to the table.

"This looks so good." Emerson picked up her knife and fork and started cutting in. "How did I get so lucky?"

I smiled, feeling my chest warm over how much she appreciated the small gesture. "I've been wondering the same thing all weekend."

And when our eyes met, she got a bashful look on her face, her cheeks tinged with pink.

She was adorable when she blushed.

"What time do you pick up Jaxon from your mom's today?"

"I was going to head over there around eleven. And then we were going to grab lunch and go to the Children's Museum for a few hours before I drop him off here."

"The Children's Museum?" Her eyebrow arched. "That sounds fun."

I nodded, inwardly debating whether to invite her to join us. I didn't want to scare her off by coming on too strongly, but I also didn't want her to think I didn't want her there with us if she was trying to drop hints.

So I cut into my crepe and said, "If you don't have any plans for today, we'd love to have you."

"Yeah?" she asked, putting a forkful of food in her mouth and chewing it thoughtfully. And I worried for a second that she was trying to think of a way to let me down nicely. But then she swallowed and said, "That sounds really nice, actually."

Relief filled me. "Awesome."

Her phone buzzed from where it sat on the table above her plate, her screen lighting up with a notification that said, "You have a new match."

When she looked at it to see what it said, she suddenly got a guilty expression on her face and flipped her phone over so it faced the tabletop.

"You don't want your ex-husband to see how popular you are with other men?" I asked in a playful tone.

"You saw that?" She sighed, looking flustered.

I nodded. "I can't really blame them, though. I'd swipe right on you, too." I winked so she knew it didn't bother me that she had guys interested in her.

She shook her head, her cheeks coloring. "So I guess you now know that I was so desperate to find a date for the wedding that I signed up for online dating."

"I actually found out about a month ago," I admitted, deciding it was time to come clean about something.

"You did?" She frowned, confused. "But I never said..."

I nodded. "You matched with Cole a while back."

Her jaw dropped. "What?" She shook her head. "There's no way. I would never match with Cole!"

"And yet you did." I chuckled, unable to keep a huge smile from my lips.

"I think I would remember swiping right on your best friend."

I lifted a shoulder. "You would...if you'd seen his face."

"What are you talking about?" Her eyebrows knitted together and I had a feeling she was catching on.

"Cole's middle name is Tyler..." I bit my lip and watched her face go through a range of emotions from confused to disbelief to shock.

"That was Cole?" she nearly shouted.

"The profile was his, at least."

"W-why did he swipe right on me?" She shook her head like she was realizing all sorts of things at once. "Why did he pretend to be a divorced guy? And why..." She narrowed her eyes. "Why did he ghost me? Was it some sort of twisted prank? Was he trying to get back at me for divorcing you?"

I shook my head quickly and took her hand in mine

before she could get too mad at my friend. Because if she was upset at him, she'd only end up being upset at me when I explained everything. And I really didn't want this to blow up in my face right now after having such a great weekend.

"It wasn't supposed to happen in the first place," I explained. "But Cole was showing me his profile and how the app worked, and when your face showed up on the screen, Jaxon got excited to see you and swiped right."

She seemed to take in everything I said and sat there for a moment processing it. "So he wasn't trying to date me?"

"No." I scooted my chair closer. Then before she could think it was because there was something wrong with her, I hurried and said, "Not because he doesn't think you're beautiful. Because he even admitted that any guy on that app would swipe right since you are gorgeous and your profile showed how fun and smart you are. But yeah, you're obviously just friends."

"Then why did he message me back? Why have that long conversation and ask if he could message me again?"

And here we were. To the part where she might get really mad at me and feel betrayed.

"It's kind of a long story..." I swallowed, trying to get up the nerve to explain what had happened that night.

"It is?"

"Yeah." I rubbed my neck, trying to figure out the best way to word everything. Then I said, "So, we were at the hotel the night before the playoff game when it happened. He had matched with you the night before, but we'd thought everything would be fine if he just didn't message you. But then you messaged him, so he came to my room to tell me about it and that he wanted to tell you it was him and the matching was all just an accident."

She nodded, not visibly upset yet as she listened.

"But then..." I ran a hand through my hair. "I saw it as a chance to finally have a real conversation with you and I couldn't pass up the opportunity."

"You wanted to talk to me?" she asked in a soft voice.

"Of course," I said, searching her green eyes. And when I saw what looked like hope in them, I dared to say, "I'd been trying to figure out all year how to get you to forgive me and give me another chance, so I took it."

She was quiet, taking it all in. Then she looked at me with confusion in her eyes. "Why did you ghost me after that? I messaged Tyler...you...a few times after that and got nothing."

I lifted my shoulders. "After that night at my apartment, I figured I was the last guy on earth you'd want to talk to, so I told Cole to delete the messages so you could move on and find a guy you could see a future with."

"I know I should probably be mad at you and Cole for doing that." Her eyes got a little teary, but she wiped at them and sighed. "But I guess I can't really blame you. And in a way, it's actually kind of sweet."

"So you're not mad?" I held my breath as I waited.

"No," she said. "I'm not mad." She squeezed my hand. "In fact, maybe I should give the app a five-star review."

I narrowed my eyes. "Why's that?"

She smiled. "Because in a roundabout way, it did help me find my perfect match."

My heart doubled over as I stared at her, trying to figure out if she was saying what I was hoping she was saying.

"You're not about to tell me there's another guy I need to be worried about, are you?" I asked.

"No," she said, giving me the most brilliant smile. "The guy I was talking about was you."

"I'LL JUST shower and change real quick," I said when Emerson and I got to my apartment a half hour later. "Then we can go."

"Sounds good," Emerson said, pulling out her phone

and sitting on the chair in my living room. "I'll just wait out here and catch up on some emails."

I rushed to my bedroom and took one of the fastest showers I'd ever taken. There were only so many hours in the day, and I wanted to make sure I spent as much time with Emerson today as I could.

Not a minute would be wasted.

I was just zipping up a clean pair of jeans when I heard my doorbell ring. Had my mom forgotten I was picking up Jaxon and had brought him back herself?

I did the button at the top of my pants and quickly pulled a shirt on over my wet hair. I was just opening my bedroom door when I heard Emerson talking to someone.

"Is this Vincent Lake's apartment?" a female voice I didn't recognize asked.

And when I walked around the corner and saw a woman with long dark hair talking to Emerson at the door, my heart stopped.

Victoria?

But when I got closer and had a better view, I saw it wasn't Victoria. Just someone who looked very much like her.

Who was this woman?

And what was she doing here?

When Emerson turned to me, her face was pale, like she'd just seen a ghost.

"This woman says she needs to speak to you." There was question and hurt in her eyes.

Did she think this was Victoria? Or did she think it was someone else I had been romantically involved with?

I swallowed, a sick feeling twisting in my gut.

"Hello?" I said, stepping beside Emerson in the entryway as I faced the woman with olive complected skin, high cheekbones, and blue eyes.

Could this be Victoria's sister? Because the resemblance was uncanny.

Like a ghost from my past showing up at the exact wrong moment.

The woman looked worried, as if she knew her reason for being here was going to cause a major disturbance to my life.

"Hi, Vincent." She eyed Emerson warily before meeting my gaze. "I'm sorry to show up like this, but..."

"Who are you?" I asked, unable to focus on what she had to say until I knew who she was.

"Oh sorry." She tucked some of her dark hair behind her ear, clearly flustered. "It's been a really long week."

I crossed my arms as I waited.

"I'm Amberley Barkume." She shook her head and closed her eyes for a second before looking up at me again. "My sister was Victoria Ruetzel."

"I can see the resemblance." My heart hammered in

my chest as I peeked at Emerson from the corner of my eye.

Please don't jump to conclusions. Please don't leave me.

I'd just gotten her back. If she thought for a minute that I still had something going on with Victoria, she'd never talk to me again.

But when I turned back to Amberley, I realized what she'd said. "Wait, did you say Victoria *was* your sister? Did something happen?"

Tears welled in the woman's eyes and she said, "She was in a skiing accident last weekend."

"Is she okay?"

I hadn't seen her for a year and four months, and all our interactions were tainted because of what they had turned into...but I was still a decent enough human that I didn't want her to be badly hurt.

"It's been a nightmare." Amberley shook her head, her lips trembling. "The funeral was yesterday and..." She looked at me then to Emerson, and then back at me. And a feeling of dread—the strength of which I hadn't felt since the night I came home and told Emerson that I'd slept with Victoria—flooded me.

"My husband and I have been trying to figure out what to do, but we already have three kids of our own and..." Amberley sighed and reached for something on the landing beside her that was hidden from my view.

And in a split second, my whole world dropped out from under me.

Because from behind the exterior wall of my apartment, Amberley had picked up a pink baby carrier. And inside that carrier, all cuddled up in a fuzzy pink elephant patterned blanket was a little baby girl who had to be less than a year old with dark hair and brown eyes.

The baby looked like me.

"I know my sister never told you about her because she thought Evelyn wasn't yours. She was in love with the guy she got back with after that night she had with you, and she was hoping the baby was his." Amberley had tears and sympathy in her eyes, like she knew just how her showing up today had the possibility to destroy everything I'd been working to rebuild with Emerson. "But I guess he had a paternity test done amid all the craziness of the past week, and that's when we realized Evelyn's biological father is actually you."

36

VINCENT

EMERSON EXCUSED herself from the room as soon as she realized what was going on, disappearing down the hall into Jaxon's bedroom. And though she hadn't said anything other than she was going to give Amberley and me some privacy to talk, the moment I looked into her eyes, I knew it was over.

Any reconciliation we might have going for us had gone down the drain as soon as the baby came into the picture.

She had forgiven me for cheating on her. She had forgiven me for betraying her and our marriage vows.

But she wouldn't be able to forgive this.

I had created a baby with another woman. I'd given another woman the one thing Emerson had craved the last few years—a baby girl. And if I knew her like I thought I did, there would not be a second olive branch extended to me from her.

The black fog that filled my body over the next hour as Amberley explained everything and introduced me to the baby—Evelyn—was like something I hadn't ever experienced before.

Fifteen seconds was all it could take to alter a person's life forever.

Fifteen seconds and life as I knew it was over.

I would get a paternity test, just to make sure that this woman I'd never met before was telling me the truth. But even with that in mind, I knew the moment I laid eyes on this little girl that she was mine.

Yes, she had Victoria's button nose and heart-shaped face. But her eyes were the same dark brown as Jaxon's and mine, and the way her dark hair was already showing a little curl was just how mine had been at that age.

"Anyway, I realize this was such a huge bomb to drop on you," Amberley said, setting Evelyn in my arms after telling me everything she knew about her and her routine. "And I wish Victoria would have been a little more responsible and figured out this whole paternity test long ago. But..." She sighed, her shoulders dropping as what looked like another wave of emotion swept over her. "I guess we always think we'll have more time than we really have."

I swallowed and nodded, the weight of this fifteen-pound infant feeling much heavier in my arms than it should have.

I have a daughter.

I kept saying the words in my mind over and over, but they still didn't seem real.

And I felt like such a horrible person, because when I'd found out Emerson and I had been expecting that baby we lost, I'd been overjoyed. I had been over the moon and anxious to welcome him or her into our family. But with this sweet, innocent baby who hadn't done a single thing wrong in the world, I just wanted to go back to this morning where I didn't know she even existed.

Amberley looked at her watch. "I have a plane to catch. But if you need anything, you can call me on the number I left in the diaper bag and I can do my best to help."

"Thanks," I said, feeling numb as I stood to walk her to my door.

Before leaving, she turned back to look at Evelyn in my arms once more. "Be a good baby for your dad, okay?"

Evelyn just smiled and continued to slobber all over her fist, happy to have the attention.

And then a moment later, Amberley left and I shut

the door to my apartment, wondering what the heck I was going to do with a baby.

Sure, I had been there when Jaxon was born, but I'd had Emerson to help me out then. And since she'd nursed him the full first year, I didn't even know how to make a bottle.

But I didn't have much time to think about how this baby was going to survive with such an inept and unprepared father because a minute later, Jaxon's bedroom door opened and Emerson's footsteps sounded in the hall.

I held my breath as I waited for her to turn the corner. When she came into view, her eyes were rimmed with red like she'd been crying.

My stomach rolled at the sight of her pain.

"Can we talk?" I asked, when she got closer.

But she just shook her head and wiped her mascara-streaked cheek with the back of her hand. "Not right now," she said, her voice wavering. "I'm going to go pick up Jaxon so your mom has time to run her errands before her shift at the hospital."

"Can we please just talk for a few minutes?" I grabbed her arm when she made a move to walk past me. "I'm going crazy here and just need to know what you're thinking right now."

When she looked up to meet my gaze, I saw the

same stoic look that I'd seen in them the night she had told me to get out of her house.

"I don't think you want to know what I'm thinking right now."

I let go of her arm and took a step back, feeling much like I did after a surprise tackle in a game. But I said, "You've reached your forgiveness threshold where I'm concerned then?"

"I don't know how I can come back from this, Vincent." And when she glanced down at the baby in my arms, the flash of pain in her eyes gutted me.

She looked back at me. "That should have been my baby," she whispered, her voice coming out sounding so tortured that it ripped me apart. And with those words, tears started streaming down her cheeks. "I should have been the only woman you had a child with."

"I'm *so* sorry, Emerson," I said, feeling like the worst human in the entire universe. "I'm so sorry that I did this to you."

"I know you are." She sniffled, her green eyes looking turquoise with all the tears she'd shed. "I'm sorry, too."

We just stood there, watching each other through our tears.

But apparently, she could only stand to look at me for so long because she stepped closer, kissed me on the cheek, and whispered, "Goodbye, Vincent."

Then without giving me a second glance, she walked out the door.

I hated how it didn't sound like she was saying goodbye for a couple of days, because it sounded like she was saying goodbye forever.

37

EMERSON

"DADDY NEEDS to give Baby Evelyn back," Jaxon said one Friday evening as we packed his overnight bag for him to go to Vincent's for the weekend. "She cries *forever.*"

It had been two weeks since Victoria's sister showed up with his baby.

Two weeks since all my hopes and dreams of resolving things with Vincent were crushed, and it felt like the world had split open on me again.

Two weeks where I had to tell myself daily that even though everything seemed to suck right now, it had to get better someday.

And two weeks where I'd stopped attempting to wear mascara all-together because it was pointless when I ended up crying it into a big mess on my face, anyway.

It was like I was back at square one again and trying to figure out a new direction for my life to go since the life with Vincent that I'd begun to piece together in my mind couldn't happen.

Not when he'd given someone else the baby that should have been mine.

So even though we'd exchanged Jaxon several times over the past two weeks, I'd managed to avoid seeing Vincent.

The betrayal was simply too raw right now. I just couldn't face him or his baby.

"I'm sorry she cries a lot. But she won't cry so much when she's older." I grabbed Jaxon's stuffed raccoon and dropped it in his backpack. "Did you know you used to cry all the time when you were little, too?"

"I did?" His brown eyes got all big and wide, like he couldn't imagine ever crying as much as his new baby sister.

I nodded. "But you grew out of it, so I'm sure Evelyn will, too."

I stumbled a little saying the baby's name, but hopefully Jaxon didn't notice that I too was having a difficult time accepting that she was a new, permanent part of his life.

Jaxon grabbed his baby blanket from his bed and handed it to me. "She makes Daddy too tired to play my game with me."

"She does?" I asked, feeling bad that he was feeling neglected with the new addition to his world.

He nodded and put his little hand on his hips and pouted. "She's ruining *everything*."

I sighed and pulled my little guy into my arms. Being the only child for almost five years had definitely not prepared him to share his dad's attention with someone else.

We were all having a rough time adjusting to this.

"I'm sorry." I ran my fingers through my son's blond hair and kissed his head. "I'm sure it'll get better soon. Sometimes you don't get to choose if you get a baby sister or not, and so you're just going to have to make the best of it."

He sighed and snuggled closer, wrapping his arms around me. "At least I still get my own room here. I's glad you didn't get a baby too."

And I knew it was just the innocent talk of a four-year-old but hearing those words about me never having a baby stabbed at my heart just a little harder today than they usually did.

I swallowed and fought back the tears threatening to spill out my eyes. "You won't have to worry about mommy ever having a baby."

Ever.

Jaxon pulled away from my arms and went to grab his stuffed cat to take with him, ready to move on to the next thing. But when he came back and looked at me, he said, "Why are you crying?"

I wiped at the tears that I apparently wasn't hiding very well and shook my head. "Mommy just gets sad about things sometimes."

He patted my arm with his little hand, "You're going to miss me tonight, aren't you?"

And I couldn't help but smile through my tears at just how small the world of a four-year-old was. "Yes, Jaxon. Of course, I'm going to miss you while you're at your dad's."

"HAVE A GOOD TIME WITH YOUR DAD," I told Jaxon when he climbed out of my car at Vincent's apartment. "I'll see you on Sunday night."

"Okay," he said, slipping his arms into the straps of his backpack. "I'll see you next time."

I smiled, loving the way he worded things. Four-year-olds were the cutest.

He shut the car door behind him, and then started walking up the sidewalk that led to Vincent's door.

I waited in my car, watching to make sure he made it in before I drove off. And when he disappeared inside, I pulled out of my parking spot and headed toward downtown to treat myself to a night on the town.

Sure, eating at a restaurant and clothes shopping by yourself weren't nearly as fun as they would be with a friend, but since everyone I knew was in a relationship these days, this was how I got to spend my Friday night.

After dinner at my favorite burger place and finding a few cute blouses and jeans on sale at Fiona's Boutique, I decided to head home to binge on the new K-Drama all the women in the K-Drama Addicts Facebook group had been talking about all week.

But when I opened the door of my car to put my shopping bags on the backseat, my eye caught on something black and white and furry.

Petrie.

I sighed.

Jaxon.

I really should know better by now than to let him carry that thing in his arms instead of putting it in his backpack with the rest of his overnight stuff.

I shut the car door and climbed into the driver's seat, wondering if he'd be okay without his stuffed cat for one night. But even as I debated in my mind over whether my four-year-old would miss it when he got tucked into his bed tonight, I knew what I needed to do.

So instead of heading toward the northeast end of town where I lived, I drove the opposite direction back to Vincent's apartment complex.

Maybe I'd get lucky and Jaxon would answer the door instead of Vincent.

After parking in one of the visitor's parking spots, I grabbed the scraggly black-and-white thing from the seat behind me and climbed out.

I heard a baby crying as soon as I stepped onto the short sidewalk that led up to Vincent's door.

Someone's not happy.

I knocked and the crying got louder before the door opened. And the man on the other side, with a little baby screaming in his big muscular arms, looked very different from the last time I'd seen him.

He didn't look like he'd shaved in weeks, his dark beard nice and full. His hair was going every which way, like he hadn't had a chance to run a comb through it since he woke up. And his signature white T-shirt that was usually bright white had several spit-up stains on the shoulder and chest.

Vincent was a wreck.

The dark circles under his eyes told me he hadn't had a goodnight's sleep in weeks.

"Hi," I said, feeling awkward for catching my ex at what looked like a really bad time. "Jaxon forgot this in my car earlier." I held up the toy and offered it to him.

He reached out to take it from me, but when he removed his arm from where it had rested under his baby's diapered bum, his arm came away with a creamy light green substance.

"Not again." He closed his eyes and let out a heavy sigh. Then he opened his eyes again and said, "Sorry. Looks like I need to give her another bath."

He trudged away from the door. And seeming to forget me, he disappeared down the hall where I guessed he planned to change and bathe his blowout baby.

Should I just set the toy inside the door and leave?

I stepped inside the apartment to survey the area and see what Jaxon might be up to, and what I saw inside was nothing like the last time I'd been here.

There were baby toys littered all over the living room rug. A baby swing sat in the middle of the floor between the living room and kitchen, a baby bouncer seat next to it. Pink and purple blankets and baby clothes were piled on one of the couch cushions, looking like they had been washed but had been waiting for who knows how long to be put away.

"Hi, Mommy," Jaxon said, bringing my attention to the kitchen counter where he was eating pizza and watching a cartoon on Vincent's iPad. "Do I get to come home now?"

"No." I shook my head and held up his toy. "I just came to drop off Petrie."

"Oh." He shook his head and gave a little laugh like he thought he was silly. "I forgot him."

"Yeah." I stepped closer and sat on the stool beside him, putting Petrie on the counter. "How are things going, anyway? Have you been having a good time with your dad and Evelyn?"

He just shrugged. "Daddy said I can watch movies all night."

I raised my eyebrows. "He did?" That did not sound like Vincent at all. Usually he was way more strict than me in how much screen time our son got.

But Jaxon just nodded, a gleeful look in his eyes. "Baby Evelyn's teeth are owie, so we get to watch movies all night to make her happy."

I imagined the movies were really to give Jaxon something to do while Vincent was dealing with a screaming infant, but I wouldn't correct him.

I looked around the room again and noticed several other things that were out of the ordinary from what I knew about how Vincent usually kept house. He had always been the type of person who washed his dishes or at least put them in the dishwasher as soon as he was done with his meal, but his kitchen sink was overflowing with dishes and bottles. The garbage was overflowing as well. And though it was the middle of March, the calendar on the wall was still on the month of February with Derek's wedding scribbled on the twenty-eighth.

Jaxon had always wanted to be held as a baby, especially the first nine months before he started crawling. Was it possible that Evelyn was even more needy?

But then again, having a baby suddenly appear in your life and having to take care of her on your own would definitely be overwhelming—especially if she was teething like Jaxon suggested.

I turned back to Jaxon. "Wanna help do something nice for your daddy?"

He narrowed his eyes, like he wasn't sure he wanted to agree to doing anything.

I said, "Your dad is giving Baby Evelyn a bath right now. I think it would be fun if we surprise him and clean up the toys before he gets back in here."

He looked at the toys on the floor. "But Baby Evelyn maked the mess."

"I know." I pushed pause on his show. "But I think it would be really nice for you to help out."

He sighed a long sigh, like it was a huge sacrifice for him to clean up a mess he didn't make. Then he said, "Fine."

So I helped him off the stool, and after he showed me the bins where the toys went, we started throwing the toys in them. By the time Vincent came back from cleaning up his daughter and changing her into a fresh diaper and footie pajamas, the living room floor was mostly clean.

The big man stopped when he saw what we'd done, and for a second it looked like he was fighting a wave of emotion as his jaw worked. "Thank you," he said, his voice deep and throaty.

I pushed my hands along the thighs of my jeans and stood, looking around at what we'd done, which honestly wasn't much in the grand scheme of things. "It was no problem."

But when I looked at Vincent again, it seemed like he was going to fall over from exhaustion. I was reminded of those early days with Jaxon and just how tired I had been all the time.

Sure, Vincent was used to pushing his body to the limits during football season, but this was an entirely different thing. He was raising a baby himself, whereas with me, I'd at least had someone to trade off with on the long nights and days. It was both physically and emotionally draining.

Not to mention the fact that I had also been avoiding him after getting both of our hopes up during the wedding weekend, so he was probably also dealing with some heartbreak like I was.

So I stepped toward him. "Let me take her for a little while," I said, holding out my arms. "I remember how hard it is to get showers in with a little one. I can give her a bottle or whatever she needs next while you take a few minutes to yourself."

He just stared at me, disbelief and surprise in his dark brown eyes. Like he couldn't believe I—the woman who had walked out on him and his baby two weeks ago —was actually offering to help him during his time of need.

I felt bad that I'd deserted him like that without even trying to talk about things. Yes, I felt vindicated in leaving him, but he'd been just as blindsided as I was.

"I'm really good with babies," I offered, reaching out for Evelyn again.

His eyes danced back and forth between mine, still unsure. But then his shoulders relaxed and he carefully handed me the dark, curly-haired baby in his arms.

And when I cradled her next to me, she was warm, smelled delicious, and was just the perfect amount of squishy.

For the longest time after the miscarriage and infertility diagnosis, I had refused to hold babies because I was bitter and didn't like being reminded of what I was missing out on. So I expected to be hit with even more of that bitterness when Vincent put Evelyn in my arms, especially since the circumstances of how she came to be were so triggering to me.

But strangely enough, I didn't feel any of that right then.

I maybe even liked how it felt to have a baby in my arms again.

"The formula is just over there." Vincent pointed to the kitchen island cluttered with dirty baby bottles, baby cereal boxes, and mail. "And there should be a clean bottle in the cupboard above the dishwasher." He ran a hand through his hair. "At least I think there was one left in there the last time I looked."

"Okay, I got it."

He looked back to me, both wariness and gratitude in his eyes. "Thank you, Emerson. I know helping me is probably the last thing you want to do right now."

I shook my head and gave him as confident a smile as I could muster. "It's no problem."

He hesitated for just a moment longer, as if he really was expecting me to throw Evelyn back into his arms and leave him high and dry, but then he slowly stepped back and went down the hall and into his bedroom.

So I turned my attention on the baby who was currently sucking on her fingers and drooling like there was no tomorrow, and said, "How about we get you that bottle."

38

EMERSON

JAXON and I played a round of Candy Land as I fed Evelyn her bottle at the kitchen island. I'd assumed she would be fussy since she'd been crying so hard when I first got there, but she'd been all smiles and just happy to fill her belly.

Which I guess I could understand. I was always more crabby when I was hungry, too.

I had just drawn the Plumpy card, sending me all the way back to the beginning of the game and Jaxon drew a double red to win, when Vincent came back into the room. He looked like a new man in a clean white V-neck shirt and black sweats, and he'd even trimmed his beard so it was down to the length of what I'd always called his sexy scruffy look.

"Feel better?" I asked, setting Evelyn's empty bottle on the counter.

"Much better." He nodded, running his fingers through his slightly damp hair. "Thank you again for letting me shower. I'm pretty sure that was the first one I've had since my mom was here on Monday night."

"Well, I'm glad you feel better," I said.

He glanced around awkwardly for a moment then said, "I guess I can take her so you can get back to your evening."

"Oh, yeah, sure." I stood from the stool and was about to put the baby in his arms when I noticed Jaxon's shoulders slump. He really had been missing out on his one-on-one time with his dad. And it wasn't like I really had anything to go home to. So I said, "Actually, I think Jaxon was really hoping you could read a story to him in his bed. If you don't mind doing that, I could rock Evelyn to sleep."

His eyes widened, probably surprised I was offering to help him even more. "Are you sure?"

"Yes," I said. "I think he'd love some time alone with his daddy."

Vincent nodded. "I have been a bit busy with the baby lately." Then he turned to Jaxon. "Would you like to sleep with me in my bed tonight, buddy?"

Jaxon's eyes lit up. "In your big bed?" And my heart

melted a little to see how excited he was to spend special time with his dad.

Vincent nodded and held out his hand for Jaxon to take. "It's been a long time since we had a guys' sleep-over. I think we should change that."

And that was all the encouragement Jaxon seemed to need to plop down off the bar stool, run to the book-shelf next to the couch to grab out a couple of board books, and then race down the hall to Vincent's room.

Vincent grabbed Jaxon's backpack that was on the floor by the fridge. He was about to disappear down the hall when he paused, as if he remembered something. He looked at me for a split second before his gaze slid to the little stuffed cat on the kitchen counter. "Can't forget this now, can we?" He held up Petrie.

I sighed, realizing I'd been holding my breath. "Definitely not."

A minute later it was just Evelyn and me left in the kitchen. I patted her back, trying to see if I could get out one more burp, and then grabbed what looked like a cozy blanket. We sat in the new rocking recliner Vincent had bought recently to see if I could get her to sleep.

As I rocked her and watched her big eyes drift shut, I waited to feel the resentment I'd had for this baby over the past two weeks since I found out she existed to resurface.

Because I should instinctively hate her, right?

This baby with dark brown hair was the product of one of the worst nights of my life.

Looking into her heart-shaped face, I could see a resemblance to both her mother and her father—two people who hadn't taken my feelings into account when they'd betrayed me.

But even as I waited to feel that hate and resentment flooding me, I just couldn't feel it anymore. Because this baby was amazingly sweet as I held her, completely innocent of her parents' mistakes.

And even though finding out she existed had rocked my world in a way, her life had been thrown into complete chaos.

She'd just lost her *mother*—the woman who had carried her for nine months, given birth to her, and then cared for her for the first eight months of her life. The person who had been her entire world until about three weeks ago had died.

And though this baby now had Vincent, and he was doing his best to take care of her, it wasn't the same as having a mother. Evelyn would never be able to get her mother back.

It wasn't like a divorce where if I really wanted to get my husband back I could still try. Death was permanent.

So despite all the anger I had felt over the past two

weeks, my heart went out to this little girl. And even though it was crazy and I couldn't understand how it was even possible, I couldn't help but feel little seeds of love growing for her, too.

She had the same eyes as her daddy. The same eyes he'd given to our son. And she was beautiful.

She had half of the DNA that my own little girl would have had.

So even though I didn't know what the future held for me and Vincent—or if there was even a chance for a future—I promised myself right then, with this sweet baby nuzzled against my chest, that I would at least try to be a positive influence in Evelyn's life. Because I would be tied to her in at least a small way since I was her brother's mother.

I'd make sure that even though Jaxon was having a hard time accepting his little sister and all the changes she brought with her right now, I would teach him to be a good big brother to her. Because that's what family did for each other.

So I just sat there, rocking back and forth for the next long while, soaking up all the sweetness of this beautiful baby in my arms. Then when my eyes started to feel heavy, I stood as slowly as I could so I wouldn't wake her and walked down to Jaxon's room that was now also her room.

A white crib was along the wall opposite of Jaxon's

full-size bed. I pulled out the blanket that was already in the crib, and then stood on my tiptoes so I could gently put Evelyn down into the crib without waking her.

This was always the trickiest part. But I must still have the muscle memory in place from all the times I'd had to put Jaxon in his crib because I managed to put her in there without startling her awake.

Go me!

After tiptoeing out of her room, I looked in on Vincent and Jaxon, wondering if Jaxon had roped his dad into reading each book five times since they'd been in there for so long. But when I peeked through the open door, I found two very tired boys, sleeping with a few books open on the bed between them—like Vincent had fallen asleep halfway through and Jaxon had decided he might as well just go to sleep, too.

I leaned against the doorframe and smiled. They were precious together. And Vincent was obviously exhausted because he never fell asleep sitting halfway up like that.

I walked into the room and lifted the covers over that big man, taking in the serene and unworried look on his face as he slept. I used to love watching him sleep back when we were married—he was always in the news and everyone in the world was always interested in what Vincent Lake was up to, but I loved that I was the only person who ever really got to see him like this.

I watched his chest rise and fall with his rhythmic breathing, and for the briefest moment, I had the urge to smooth my fingers along his cheek to see if his scruffy beard felt the same as I remembered.

But since I really didn't want to wake him or have him catch me having a sentimental moment, I turned my back to him to switch off the lamp on his nightstand. That was when I saw something that hadn't been there the last time I'd been in here, and my heart doubled over.

He had a photo of me from our trip to Mexico sitting on his nightstand—along with one of the little love notes I'd written him in a past life.

I put a hand to my chest, trying to cover the sudden surge of pain that surfaced.

He'd been holding onto things and memories from our marriage, just like I'd kept his clothes.

I didn't know if it was just because I was emotionally exhausted from everything or what, but the sight of this man's obvious enduring love for me despite all the obstacles in our path made fresh tears spring to my eyes.

Was it possible that our love story really wasn't over yet?

39

VINCENT

I WOKE THE NEXT MORNING, feeling more rested than I had in a long time. Feeling like a human instead of a zombie.

I sat up in bed and stretched, enjoying the bliss that comes from waking up naturally instead of being awoken by an alarm or a crying baby...

Wait.

I looked at the time on my watch.

It was seven twenty-three in the morning.

I had just slept for, like, nine hours straight.

Evelyn!

I jumped out of my bed and rushed down the hall to her and Jaxon's room. She always woke up at least once or twice during the night.

Had something happened to her?

Was she okay?

But when I walked into her room, my daughter wasn't the first human I saw. Instead, I found Emerson curled up under the covers on Jaxon's bed.

She'd stayed over?

A happy, squealing sound stole my attention next. And when I stepped up to the side of the crib, I found a very alert and very happy baby girl looking up at me with a smile. She kicked her legs when she saw me watching her and made gurgling sounds as if excited to see me.

I couldn't help but smile right back at her.

Being cute really was a survival skill for babies for all the trouble they sometimes caused.

Before she could make any more sounds that might wake Emerson, I picked Evelyn up and carried her out of the room, shutting the door behind me.

"Should we go change your diaper in the living room?" I asked Evelyn, holding her against my side as we walked down the hall.

She, of course, didn't answer since she couldn't talk, but I took her to the basket of diapers and wipes I kept in the living room to change her, anyway.

That was when I noticed something. My front living area that had been a complete wreck the night before was spotless. It even smelled fresh and clean.

I realized that not only had Emerson taken over the

night duty with Evelyn last night so I could get nine hours of uninterrupted sleep, but she had also washed the dishes, taken out the trash, and folded the pile of laundry I'd been meaning to get to for days.

Was she a superhero?

Because that woman put me to shame.

I was just feeding Evelyn her rice cereal in her high-chair when Jaxon came running down the hall.

"Good morning, buddy," I said, looking at him after Evelyn took a bite from her cereal.

"Hi, Dad." He ran over and gave me a hug. "I slept so good in your bed."

"That's good." I smiled, messing up his hair with my hand. "I slept good too."

He pulled away. Then he seemed to notice something was different about the living room and kitchen because he suddenly exclaimed, "It's beautiful in here!" There was a look of shock on his face.

"It is beautiful isn't it?" I chuckled. "I think your mommy did it for us."

His jaw dropped. "Mommy must be magical."

"I think she is," I said, feeling so undeserving of everything she had done for me in the past twelve hours. "Your mom is amazing."

EMERSON WOKE a little after nine and joined Jaxon, Evelyn, and me in the living room where Jaxon was showing the moves he'd learned in his karate class last week.

"Good morning, Mommy!" Jaxon said, running to her, mid hand-chop. "You sleeped here again?"

"I did." She gave him a sleepy-eyed smile. "I wanted to see how comfy your bed was."

Her gaze flickered to mine, reminding me of the other time she'd stayed here and how Jaxon had thought I'd been crying in his bed because it was more comfortable than mine.

Man, life could sure change a lot in a month and a half.

"Did you sleep good?" Jaxon asked.

She nodded, returning her attention back to him. "I slept all right. Baby Evelyn only woke me up once."

I cleared my throat. "Hey, thanks for taking care of her last night." I glanced around the room. "For taking care of pretty much everything, actually."

She sat on the arm of the couch. "It was no problem. I'm happy to help."

"Guess what, Mom?" Jaxon interrupted, not caring that his parents were already mid-conversation.

"What?" Emerson looked at him and smiled.

"Daddy says we get to go to the playground after

Evelyn's nap!" He said it with so much excitement you'd think I was taking him to Disneyland.

"He did?" Emerson asked, mirroring his enthusiasm.

He nodded. "Yeah."

"Well, that sounds like it'll be really fun."

"Super fun," he said. Then he raised his eyebrows like some sort of amazing idea had just occurred to him. "Can you come play with us, too? You can watch me go down the big, huge, slide."

"A big, huge slide?" She smiled, clearly loving how excited our son was.

He nodded. "I can do it all by *myself*!"

I didn't want to burst his bubble, but since I also didn't want Emerson to feel like we were trying to steal her whole weekend away from her, I said, "I'm sure your mom has lots of things to do today."

But Emerson surprised me by saying, "It actually sounds fun." She looked at me. "I just finished up a big case yesterday so my day is wide open, and if you don't mind, I'd be happy to join you guys at the playground."

"Really?"

She *wanted* to spend time with us?

With me?

Because while she had been super selfless and amazing to help me out last night, I figured the last thing she would want to do was spend time with me.

She nodded and said, "I actually went clothes shopping right before coming over here so I have some fresh clothes in my car. If Jaxon doesn't mind me using his bathroom, I could shower and get ready here, and then we could hang out."

I was momentarily speechless, trying to wrap my mind around what seemed like a one-eighty from two weeks ago when she'd basically said goodbye to giving me another chance.

Maybe she's just bored, I told myself so I wouldn't get my hopes up. *Maybe she just wants to hang out with Jaxon and it has nothing to do with me.*

But even as I tried to tell myself those things, the old familiar feeling of hope found its way into my heart.

40

EMERSON

"HAVE you figured out what you're going to do with Evelyn once the season starts up again?" I asked Vincent. We were sitting on a bench at the playground behind his apartment complex. Jaxon was having a blast running around on the grass with another boy his age and Vincent was feeding Evelyn peach yogurt melts as she sat in her stroller.

"I don't know." He sighed, setting a few more yogurt melts on the stroller tray. "But I should probably figure something out soon since training camp will be here before I know it."

"Yeah?" I asked.

He nodded. "I mean, my mom and Arianna have been helping me out here and there so I can still do a few workouts a week with Cole, but I know we can't keep it up in the long run. They both work full time and have their own lives to worry about."

"Have you considered getting a nanny?" I suggested, knowing a couple of the Dragons players had them.

"It's probably the best option I have," he said. "I've just been putting it off because I know once I start the interviewing process, the word will get out that I had a baby I didn't know about and the media will go nuts over that." He looked at me, a tired expression in his eyes. "I'm just not looking forward to all that. Dealing with everything on my own has already been hard enough, you know?"

I did know. I'd definitely wanted to live in my own little cocoon when all the crap hit the fan with us.

"I'm sure you'll figure something out," I said. And then before I could stop myself, I said, "And if worse comes to worst, I can always help out, too."

He pulled his head back, surprised. "You would watch Evelyn?"

"Sure." I shrugged. "I mean, she's not so bad when she's got a clean diaper and a full belly, right?"

"But I couldn't ask you to do that." He shook his head. "You shouldn't feel obligated to help me after everything."

"I know," I said, even though the me from two weeks and a year ago would have definitely agreed with him. "But I do like babies, and since I don't hate you or anything, I really wouldn't mind. It might even be fun to have a baby around."

He blinked his eyes and swallowed, like I'd surprised him again. Then he slowly said, "You don't hate me?" He gave me a guarded but hopeful look...like he had truly thought I could hate him.

"No." I met his wary gaze and gave him a cautious smile. "I don't hate you, Vincent."

"I honestly wouldn't blame you if you did." He held my gaze for the longest moment before swallowing and saying, "But thank you. I promise I'm going to do my best to deserve your forgiveness this time."

We watched Evelyn and Jaxon for a few minutes, each lost in our thoughts. And though a lot had happened between us, I couldn't help but feel like days such as today were exactly how I had always dreamed my weekends would be like from the time I was a little girl.

I liked the slow, lazy day. I enjoyed seeing Jaxon have such a great time in the seasonably warmer weather.

And yes, I even liked sharing the day with Vincent and Evelyn, too.

Having many more days like this would be one-hundred percent okay in my book.

"How was it holding Evelyn last night, anyway?" Vincent asked, breaking into my train of thought after

Jaxon ran past us again. "Was it hard after everything?" He raised his eyebrow, watching me.

I pulled the sleeves of my jacket over my hands and shrugged. "It actually wasn't as hard as I thought it would be."

"It wasn't?"

I rubbed my hand along my forearm. "No," I said. "I mean, I really wanted to hate her because of everything she reminded me of. But then I just couldn't." I sighed and met his brown-eyed gaze. "She's beautiful, Vincent."

He nodded slowly, looking down at his little girl who was now banging her hands on the stroller tray, wanting more of her snack. "She is." He smiled and poured a few more yogurt melts for her. Then he turned back to me. "Even more so when I've had a good night's sleep."

I smiled, putting my hand on his shoulder. "I know you're probably worried that you're screwing everything up, but you're doing a lot better than you think."

"I hope so. Because all I can think about is how good I am at messing everything up these days."

"I think we all have days like that," I said. "But the good news is that as long as we're still breathing, we get another chance."

He studied the ground, his jaw working for a moment. "Even when it's a third or fourth chance?"

"Yes, Vincent." I nodded. "Sometimes even then."

THE NEXT FEW weeks found me in a new normal—one that the longer it went on, the more attached to it I became.

Work was the same as usual, hard and monotonous sometimes, exhilarating on other times, but it was my evenings that had become my real joy—my evenings which I very rarely spent alone anymore since whenever I dropped off Jaxon at his dad's place, I usually ended up hanging out with them until bedtime.

And on the days I had Jaxon, we still ended up either going over to Vincent's place, bringing some takeout with us, or he and Evelyn would come hang out at our house and Vincent and I would cook together, trading off who held the baby if she was fussy.

It was like living my dream day every day.

And I never wanted it to end.

So when Vincent asked me if I wanted to go on a stroll with him one sunny spring evening when Arianna and Cole offered to watch Jaxon and Evelyn, I said yes.

When he tried to hold my hand as we walked down the sidewalk in the park, I let him. And that night, when he walked me to my door and gave me a tender kiss on the cheek, I went inside and relived the sweet moment over and over again, just bursting with pure joy because I was so happy.

So incredibly happy.

But even though I was so happy, I was also scared. Because it almost seemed too good to be true—that I could be on the cusp of everything I ever wanted: Having the man I had fallen in love with again love me back. Having the cutest son in the whole wide world call me Mom. Having the career and the home of my dreams.

And...if everything worked out in the way I was starting to dream it would...to have a daughter, too.

To be Evelyn's mom.

And so along with all the good things I had going in my life...I was so scared that it could all be taken away from me in a second. Because I had learned from past experiences that just when you thought everything was going your way, it usually meant the universe was getting ready to drop another bomb on you.

And I really, *really* didn't want anything to mess us up this time.

―――――

"THANKS FOR HAVING US OVER," Vincent said, standing from my couch one night after he and Evelyn had come over for dinner and a movie with Jaxon and me.

Jaxon had conked out on the loveseat a while ago with a blanket pulled over him. And I'd spent the movie nestled under Vincent's muscular arm as I cradled his sweet baby girl, just loving her warm and snuggly body against me as she slept.

"It was nice," I said, looking up at him. "I'm glad you two could come over."

"Me too." He grabbed Evelyn's car seat from the rug and set it on the couch next to me so I could slip her into it for her drive home.

And even though I wanted to hold her for a little longer, I slipped her out of her blanket and eased her from my arms and into her car seat.

As I strapped her in and covered her again with the purple blanket, I couldn't help but think it would be so much nicer to simply say goodnight instead of goodbye after nights like these.

To have them stay.

Once Evelyn was secured, Vincent took her car seat by the handle and I walked him to the front door.

And as we walked to the place where we'd be saying goodbye again for what was becoming more times than I wanted to count, a swelling filled my chest. A swelling that had been growing stronger and stronger as the weeks had gone by.

And I may not have consciously thought about it until this moment, but I knew what that feeling meant.

It meant that I loved him.

I loved Vincent.

He turned back to me before opening the door, and when our eyes locked, I wondered if he could see on my face all the emotions that revelation filled me with.

"Well, I better get going," he said as I was just trying to figure out how to tell him what I felt. "It's late."

And even though the words were just on the tip of my tongue, I instead said, "Yeah, it is late."

Come on, Emerson. Just spit out the words.

But when he stepped closer and kissed me on the forehead like he'd been doing a lot lately, I lost my nerve.

Admitting that I loved him after everything we'd been through was scary.

So instead of putting myself out there, I went with the safe option and avoided the scary conversation once again. "I'll see you soon."

He must not have picked up on the sudden turmoil swirling through me, because he simply gave me one more meaningful look—the kind of look that sent sparks through my whole body—and then opened the door to leave.

I leaned against the door frame and watched him walk to his truck in the driveway, and as he set Evelyn in the backseat, I knew that if I wanted to become a family again with that man I was so desperately in love with, I would be the one who'd need to make the grand gesture.

After all the times I'd rejected him this past year—all the times I'd told him that no amount of groveling would ever fix what he'd broken—I needed to let him know that his actions and constant steadiness had changed my mind when the initial words and pleading promises couldn't.

I wanted to show this man who was still punishing himself for the past that I didn't want to punish him anymore. That I wanted to put that dark period behind us and build a new life together.

Because he was the only person I wanted to be with. It had always been him for me and, as far as I was concerned, would only ever be him.

I just hoped Vincent was ready to take a leap with me.

41

VINCENT

EMERSON: **Jaxon and I thought it would be fun to have a picnic in the back yard on Saturday afternoon. Think you can come? I'd love to run some things by you.**

I looked at the text for about the hundredth time since Emerson had sent it to me on Monday. Even though I'd had all week to think about what she might want to run by me, I had no idea what it could be.

Okay, so that was a lie. I definitely had a few ideas of what it might be...I just didn't know if I should get too attached to any of them.

So on Saturday, after Evelyn woke up from her morning nap, I loaded her into the backseat of my truck and drove across town to the house I had been spending more and more time at recently.

I let out a long sigh as I drove. I hoped this picnic would go well.

She wouldn't have me come over just to call off whatever had been going on between us the past several weeks, would she?

I really hoped not.

My heart was in my throat as Evelyn and I waited for Emerson to answer her door. When she appeared in the entryway, wearing the same pink sundress she'd worn in the photo sitting on my nightstand with her hair cascading in curls around her face, she took my breath away.

"Hi," she said, looking up at me with those big green eyes of hers. "I'm glad you could make it."

"Thanks for inviting us over." I smiled nervously, still not sure what exactly to expect. "Sorry I didn't dress up more."

She took in my blue-and-green plaid button-up and jeans and smiled. "You look great." Then she turned to Evelyn who I had managed to dress in a pink-and-white striped dress with a bow on her head and said, "And you look adorable little Miss Evelyn."

She gave Evelyn's hand a gentle squeeze and my heart warmed with her greeting.

She really had accepted my daughter with so much more grace than I ever could have expected. It was amazing.

"Jaxon is already out back," she said. "So if you two want to follow me, we can start eating." She gestured for us to follow her, and as we did, I took her in.

She really was the most beautiful woman I had ever met. And if she hadn't avoided the conversation of what we were to each other every time I tried to bring it up, I would have been down on one knee again in a heartbeat.

Well, you know...if I wasn't scared to death that she'd reject me and crush all the hopes and dreams I'd been daring to dream these past few weeks.

We stepped onto the back porch. When Jaxon saw us, he came running toward me, giving me a hug around the legs. "Hi, Daddy!"

I smiled and patted him on the head. "Hey, bud. How are you?"

"I'm good." He gave me a big, toothy smile. "Mom made dinosaur sandwiches."

Before I could even respond, he grabbed my hand and started pulling me toward the grass where they had laid out the green-and-white quilt that, several weeks and a lifetime ago, I had told Emerson was the thing I'd keep to remember her by.

"You get to sit here." Jaxon pointed to one of the corners of the blanket. "Baby Evelyn goes here." He touched the back of the booster chair that had been his when he was a baby. "And Mommy sits here." He pointed to a spot next to where he'd told me to sit. And then he took a seat on the other side of the quilt.

As I put Evelyn into the booster seat and buckled her in, Emerson set a big picnic basket in the middle of the blanket.

I got myself to my spot and watched Emerson as she lowered herself to her knees. And I couldn't be sure, but as she started pulling out containers of food, it almost looked like she was nervous about something.

She was a fabulous cook and I'd always devoured everything she ever cooked, so she shouldn't be nervous about me not liking what she'd prepared. But what else was there to be nervous about?

Was it the thing she wanted to discuss with me?

She pulled out two plastic plates for the kids, and then two from the china set we'd received as a wedding gift.

"We really are being fancy today, aren't we?" I commented when she pulled out cloth napkins and champagne flutes as well.

Emerson's cheeks turned pink and Jaxon let out a loud giggle before covering his mouth, like he was just dying to say something.

I furrowed my brow and looked at Emerson and my son. "Is something going on that I don't know about?" Had I missed something? Jaxon had been talking a lot about what he wanted to do for his birthday party, but that still wasn't for a few weeks.

"I was waiting to do this next part after we'd filled our bellies." Emerson sighed and put her hands on her knees, sitting back on her feet. "But since Jaxon is just a *little* excited..." She turned and raised an eyebrow at Jaxon who was now bouncing up and down on his little bum. "Should we do it now?"

"Uh huh." He nodded enthusiastically.

"Okay," Emerson said. "You better get daddy's surprise then."

My surprise?

But before I could ask what kind of surprise they were talking about, Jaxon ran into the house and disappeared.

Emerson looked at me anxiously. "I promise we really did have this whole thing planned out and it was going to be really awesome, but—"

Jaxon burst through the back door again, this time hiding something behind his back.

I pressed my lips together and waited for him to approach, my chest tight with anticipation over what he would have there for me that required china and champagne.

He stepped onto the blanket again and knelt down next to Emerson so they were both facing me. And then,

Emerson knelt up again—this time though, putting one foot out so she was kneeling on one knee with the skirt of her dress falling around her.

Our gazes met, and when I saw moisture around the edges of her eyes, my heart swelled so big in my chest I thought it might burst.

Was she...?

I didn't dare think the words.

She licked her soft pink lips. "I know it's traditional for a man to be the one down on one knee," she said, her voice shaking slightly. "But I thought that since our love story has been a little unconventional, I might as well keep that going for us." She cleared her throat. "I know I've been all over the place this past year with where I wanted to go with you, but when I think about the future and what I want it to look like, you're in it. You, Jaxon, and Evelyn are all there."

"I know neither of us is perfect," she continued. "And we will always have our ups and downs as we go through life. But there isn't anyone else in the entire world that I want to do this thing called life with. So..." She turned to Jaxon and held her hand out for whatever was behind his back.

He looked at her hand for a moment, but instead of handing his mom the present, his eyes got real big, his chest puffed out, and he blurted, "Will you marry us!?"

Yep, my four-year-old son completely stole Emerson's thunder.

This kid of ours was kind of amazing sometimes.

Emerson shook her head and smiled, eternally patient with our cute kid. "What Jaxon means is..." She looked at me again, her eyes shimmering in the afternoon sunlight. "Will you marry *me* again, Vincent?" She reached behind Jaxon since he still wasn't handing over what she wanted. And a moment later, she was holding a familiar-looking ring box and gazing at me with so much hope and love in her eyes I felt lightheaded. "Will you be a family with us again? You and Evelyn and Jaxon and me?"

And when she opened the box, it revealed the wedding band she'd given me all those years before. The ring that, I guess until very recently, had been in the top drawer of my nightstand at my apartment.

I looked at Emerson again, knowing full well I had tears in my eyes. And it took me a moment to find my words, because I had suddenly gotten all choked up.

But I managed to say, "Yes," my voice coming out all gravelly. "Yes, I would love to marry you again." I got to my own knees and held my arms out for Emerson and Jaxon. "I want nothing more than to be a family with you again."

When they both found their way into my arms, I hugged them close and held them tight. And I couldn't keep the tears I'd been holding back for the past minute from falling as I realized this was the first time in over a year we had had a family hug like this, with the three of us together.

It was the perfect moment.

Jaxon pulled away first and Emerson kissed me on the cheek. Then she said, "Thanks for saying yes," before resting her head against my shoulder.

I sighed and wrapped my arms around her in an embrace.

"I love you," I whispered and kissed her on the forehead. "I love you so much, Emerson."

"I love you too." She slipped her arms around my torso and gave me a squeeze.

And we just stayed there on the blanket for a moment, as the feeling of peace and hope and happiness fell over us.

But of course, since four-year-olds are not the most patient beings, Jaxon looked at us and said, "Isn't you going to put on your ring, Dad?"

I chuckled. "I guess I'd better," I said, dropping my arms from his mother.

Emerson took the white gold wedding band out of the box and held it up. "How about we see if this thing still fits?"

So I gave her my left hand. And when she pushed it onto my ring finger, it slipped on with ease. Like it was always meant to be there.

I pulled Emerson to my side again and studied my left hand for a moment.

"How did you two get this, anyway?" I asked, loving the way it felt to have it on my finger again.

She shrugged, her expression sneaky as she looked at Jaxon. "Do you want to tell Daddy how we got it?"

A huge grin stretched across Jaxon's cheeks. "I sneaked in your room and stole it for Mom."

"That's right." Emerson nodded. "I asked him if he knew if Daddy still had his wedding ring, and he knew just where to find it."

I guess that shouldn't surprise me too much. He did love sneaking through my things when I wasn't watching closely.

Evelyn, who had been sitting so happily through the past few minutes decided that now was the time to let us know that her needs needed to be met and started banging her hands on the tray in front of her.

"Think we should start this picnic now?" Emerson raised an eyebrow.

"I guess so," I mumbled. "But not until I get a kiss."

And when I pulled her into my arms for a quick kiss, I couldn't help but feel like everything was finally right in my world. I also realized that even though I would never willingly choose to relive the past year and a half, going through the turmoil made this life-changing moment even sweeter.

Just like the hardest games in football made for the sweetest victories, this victory of winning Emerson back into my life for good was more than I ever could have asked for.

EPILOGUE

EMERSON

FOUR YEARS LATER

"DOES Vincent really not have any idea?" Arianna asked me. We were waiting in the team box at the Mercedes-Benz Stadium in New Orleans after one of the biggest games of my husband's career.

I shook my head, unable to resist smiling at the secret I'd been keeping for the past few weeks.

"I don't think he has a clue."

But why would he? Neither of us had *ever* expected for this to happen. In fact, I probably never would have even known until my pants started getting tighter if it wasn't for the morning sickness.

"He's gonna freak." Arianna laughed. "I mean,

when you, Jaxon, and Evelyn showed up with those matching Dragons jerseys, I thought they were cute. But..." She looked at the back of Evelyn's jersey again where she sat on the floor in front of us, coloring in her coloring book. "This is so amazing."

I smiled, looking at the words "big sister" on the back of my sweet daughter's black and gold jersey. Tears crinkled at the corners of my eyes as I thought about how amazing it really was.

I wasn't supposed to be able to get pregnant. It just wasn't in the cards for me. And yet, by some kind of miraculous force, it had happened.

And now Vincent just needed to finish those interviews on the field so he could find out that not only had he just won the Super Bowl, but he was going to have a big surprise coming this summer that would keep him much busier than he ever expected to be during retirement.

Yes, the best quarterback in the league who had won Player of the Year three years in a row was ending his football career on a high note at age thirty-five and retiring so he could spend more time with his family.

Because family was more important than anything to that wonderful man.

"Oh! Look! They're coming," one of the other teammate's wives said, getting to her feet.

And a moment later, the guys, who I'm sure were both exhausted and exhilarated after the hard-won game, came trickling inside the family room with huge smiles on their faces.

Cole came in and his gaze immediately found Arianna who had jumped up the moment he came through the door and ran to give him a big hug.

Yeah, Cole wasn't only scoring in the end zone, he'd finally gotten out of the friend zone, too.

A few other guys came in and were immediately greeted by their loved ones.

I stood and blew out a breath as I tried to see over the heads of the big, tall guys coming through the doors.

He had to be coming here with them, right?

He wouldn't make me wait even longer, would he?

But I didn't have to wait much longer because a big ball of nerves filled my stomach when I saw the top of Vincent's head appear in the doorway.

"Daddy!" Evelyn squealed when she saw him glance around the room. And he must have heard her over the crowd because a second later, his gaze zeroed in on us.

He pushed his way through the crowd of families and football players, the smile on his face growing wider and wider the closer he got to us.

"You did it!" Evelyn said, throwing her arms around

his neck as he swooped our four-year-old up into his arms.

"We did." He kissed her on the cheek.

Jaxon went up to his dad's side next and gave him the loving yet slightly awkward hug of an eight-year-old boy. "Good job, Dad," he said. "That was a cool game."

Vincent mussed Jaxon's blond hair with his hand. "Thanks, buddy."

He put Evelyn back on the floor and turned to me with open arms. "And now for the woman I've been dying to see all day."

I smiled and went into his embrace, hugging him tight. "That was an amazing game," I said, kissing his cheek before resting my head against his chest. "What a way to end your career."

He squeezed me. "What a great way to start the next chapter of my life."

"Speaking of next chapters..." I said, taking the perfect segue that he'd given me. "Can you kids come here and show your dad your new jerseys?"

Vincent pursed his lips together as our kids stood side by side facing him.

"Those are some nice jerseys," he said. But from the dip of his dark eyebrows and the confused look on his face, I could tell he was wondering what was so special about them that required attention.

So I said to the kids, "Okay, now how about you show him the back."

The kids both turned around so their backs were to their dad. And above the number seventeen, where the last name Lake would typically be, were the words "big brother" on Jaxon's jersey and the words "big sister" on Evelyn's.

I watched Vincent for his reaction and knew the moment he realized what we were trying to tell him because he immediately started blinking back tears and the biggest look of shock came on his face.

"You're pregnant?" He stared at me, his voice quiet with awe. "We—" He gave his head a shake and sighed. "We're going to have a baby?"

"We are." I smiled and nodded, tears finding their way back into my own eyes. "I'm twelve weeks along. I'm due the middle of August."

"August?" He blinked his eyes again, like he still couldn't believe it.

"Yes, August," I said, my insides practically bursting over the secret I'd been keeping from everyone. "But the doctor says we should plan on having the babies in July."

He went still, his whole body frozen. Then he blinked his eyes a few times and said, "Wait? Did you just say *babies*? As in, not just one but multiple?"

"We're having twins."

And I vaguely noticed that we had an audience—the kids and several other Dragons' family members watching us with shocked expressions as they overheard what we were talking about—but I just focused on Vincent and hoped he wasn't about to go into cardiac arrest with this last bit of news.

Because his eyes were as big as saucers and it looked like he was about to fall over.

"T-twins?" he asked. "As in, two babies?"

I smiled and couldn't help but laugh. "Yes, honey. Twins typically means two babies."

And that was when that big man of mine sat down on the chair next to him and pushed his hands through his dark hair.

"I can't believe this." He reached for my hand to pull me onto his lap.

"I couldn't either when I found out." I sat down, slipping my arms behind his neck. "But it's good news, right?"

"Of course," he said, his voice reassuring as he rubbed my back with his hands. "It's the best news." Then he said, "How on earth did you keep this a secret from me for so long?"

"It was so hard," I said. "But I thought it might be nice to make sure you at least have something to celebrate today in case the game didn't go like we'd hoped."

"Well, it's probably a good thing you did because I'm sure I would've had a hard time concentrating if you had told me earlier." He shook his head. "Twins? Really?"

I rubbed a hand along my tummy, which was barely showing any signs that there were two babies in there. "Your retirement just got a lot more exciting."

He pulled me closer and pressed a kiss to my temple. "And here I thought I was just going to let you be my sugar momma while I hung out at home playing video games all day."

I laughed, knowing that even without two babies in his future, this man would never be able to just sit around the house for long. I was pretty sure coaching Jaxon's football and basketball teams and being Evelyn's dance dad was more likely on the horizon than anything else.

But I said, "You'll just have to play the video games during naptime."

He chuckled. "Since I'm sure two babies will be perfectly well behaved enough to always sleep at the same time."

I lifted a shoulder. "You never know. They are yours, and so of course with your DNA, they can't help but be amazing at everything."

He kissed my hair. "Pretty sure that when they do

turn out to be amazing, all the credit should go to their mother."

Read Arianna and Cole's Story Next

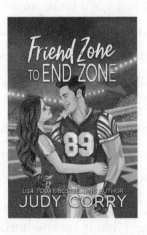

Dating Coach Rule #1: Don't fall for your client, especially if he's your best friend.

Grab your copy here!

NOTE FROM THE AUTHOR:

Why hello, lovely reader!

If you're reading this, it means you made it to the end! And it also means that you are one of my favorite people. ;)

Thank you so much for taking a chance on Her Football Star Ex! I've written several books now, and while all of them are pieces of my heart put in print, Emerson and Vincent's story was definitely one of my babies. I've had their story in my head for several years, so finally having it in book form is amazing, and sharing it with you wonderful readers is even better.

If you enjoyed reading this book and have the time, I'd love to hear your thoughts in a brief, honest review.

Always grateful,

Judy Corry

WANT A FREE BOOK? SIGN UP!

I hope you enjoyed HER FOOTBALL STAR EX! If you haven't already, please sign up for my newsletter so you can stay up to date on my latest book news. Plus, you'll get two FREE books by me, just for signing up! https://subscribepage.com/judycorry

Join the Corry Crew on Facebook: https://www.facebook.com/groups/judycorrycrew/

Follow me on Instagram: @judycorry
Follow me on TikTok: @judycorry

Also By Judy Corry

Rich and Famous Series:

Assisting My Brother's Best Friend (Kate and Drew)

Hollywood and Ivy (Ivy and Justin)

Her Football Star Ex (Emerson and Vincent)

Friend Zone to End Zone (Arianna and Cole)

Stolen Kisses from a Rock Star (Maya and Landon)

Eden Falls Academy Series:

The Charade (Ava and Carter)

The Facade (Cambrielle and Mack)

The Ruse (Elyse and Asher)

The Confidant (Scarlett and Hunter)

The Confession (Nash and Kiara)

Ridgewater High Series:

When We Began (Cassie and Liam)

Meet Me There (Ashlyn and Luke)

Don't Forget Me (Eliana and Jess)

It Was Always You (Lexi and Noah)

My Second Chance (Juliette and Easton)

My Mistletoe Mix-Up (Raven and Logan)

Forever Yours (Alyssa and Jace)

Standalones:

Protect My Heart (Emma and Arie)

Kissing The Boy Next Door (Lauren and Wes)

<u>Coming Soon:</u>

Hideaway With You (Addie and Evan)

EXCERPT FROM FRIEND ZONE TO END ZONE

"You know this whole thing is happening today because of me, right?" I said to my best friend, Arianna, who was sitting next to me at her brother's wedding reception.

"Emerson and Vincent got re-married all because of you?" She arched a dark eyebrow, looking away from the happy couple as they glided on the dance floor that had been set up in the middle of their backyard. "And how do you figure that?"

I shrugged. "I accidentally matched with Emerson on that dating app you said I should sign up for, and voila! They're married."

Sure, their four-year-old son was the one who had accidentally swiped right on his mom's photo when I came across her profile on Meet Your Match one day. So technically, he should get some credit for getting his

parents back together again. But I'd created the somewhat anonymous profile that she'd liked enough to
swipe right on, so I was basically an accidental
matchmaker.

"And how many piña coladas have you had
tonight?" Arianna asked. "Because I'm *pretty* sure
Vincent and Emerson are the ones who deserve most of
the credit for reclaiming their happily-ever-after."

"Whatever. It was totally all me."

She shook her head and laughed, her long, dark
brown curls bouncing around her face with the movement. "For all your bragging about being a matchmaker,
you seemed to have forgotten to actually use that app for
yourself."

And here we were again. Back to her teasing me
about being one of the only single guys on the Denver
Dragons NFL team.

But sadly, this time around I couldn't claim the
excuse of being too busy to date, since it was the off-
season and the only thing I had going on were my
morning workouts with her brother: the quarterback to
my wide-receiver and good friend, Vincent Lake. So I
picked up my drink, swirled it around a bit before
raising my eyebrow and saying, "I just haven't matched
with anyone interesting enough to tempt me."

Arianna's jaw dropped immediately, and I had to
work to keep a grin from my face because I knew exactly

what she was going to say to my arrogant-sounding statement.

"Excuse me?" she said, the shock in her voice every bit as obvious as I expected. "Did you seriously just say that?"

"Say what?" I gave her my most innocent expression, feigning ignorance.

She just stared at me with her big brown eyes. "I never thought I'd see the day when you got too big for your britches, Cole Kekoa."

"Too big for my britches?" I looked down at my navy-blue dress pants. "Have my butt-sculpting exercises been working then?"

"Seriously?" She smacked my arm. "I was talking about the whole *no one is handsome enough to tempt me* line you just said." Arianna shook her head. "You sound just like Mr. Darcy at the ball in *Pride and Prejudice.*"

Yeah...I knew I did.

Normally, a professional football-playing, deep-sea fishing, ax-throwing, manly man like myself would pretend not to know who this Mr. Darcy character was that Arianna was referencing. But since I was best friends with a woman who was obsessed with romance movies—and I frequently let her talk me into watching them with her since her jerk boyfriend couldn't be bothered enough to meet her halfway on their movie nights—

I had seen pretty much every film adaption of Jane Austen's famous book.

And yes, I also knew the quote she was referencing by heart because my brain couldn't help but remember stupid information like that.

So instead of denying the fact that I knew exactly what she was talking about, I said, "I think the exact quote is, 'She is tolerable; but not handsome enough to tempt me; I am in no humor at present to give consequence to young ladies who are slighted by other men.'"

Arianna put a hand on her hip. "So you won't meet any of those girls you're matching with because they're single and have a reason to be on the dating app in the first place?"

"I only said that because I knew it would rile you up." I gave her a mischievous grin before taking another sip of my drink. "I wasn't actually making a dig at the girls on the website. I'm sure there are a lot of great women on there."

"And yet you signed up for the dating app like four months ago and still haven't even met one girl for coffee."

I shrugged, the sleeves of my suit coat tightening with the movement. "Coffee is gross."

"Fine. Then tea, or one of those Dole whips you love so much." She let out an exasperated sigh. "I'm sure there are girls out there obsessed with pineapple just as much as you are."

Arianna and her brother always made fun of my obsession with pineapple-flavored anything but having been born in Hawaii and growing up with my Hawaiian dad, I couldn't help love the fruit. It must have been in my half-Polynesian blood or something.

And since I really was a walking billboard for all things pineapple, I took another sip from my piña colada and said, "But don't you understand that me not having a girlfriend is actually only a good thing for you?"

She crossed her arms and pressed her glossy pink lips together before saying, "And how do you figure that?"

"Well, if I had a girlfriend, I wouldn't be hanging out at this table with you right now. And you would be sitting all alone. So really, me being lazy only benefits you."

I had expected her to laugh, or at least smile since we'd been joking around all night, but when her expression turned serious instead, I realized I'd hit a nerve.

She folded the teal paper napkin in front of her on the table and said, "Well, if Chad hadn't *forgotten* about my brother's wedding and agreed to go to Tallahassee for work instead of being my plus-one, I wouldn't need you to entertain me."

"Sorry," I mumbled. "Bad reasoning on my part."

"It's okay." She set her elbows on the table and rested her delicate chin in her hands, the position and the way her silver bridesmaid dress fell over her slender shoulders making her look even more petite than usual. "Obviously, I'm still a bit mad at Chad for not being here."

She and Chad had been dating for three years, and while I really wanted to point out that even after all this time, Chad still only thought about Chad, I didn't. Me pointing out the many flaws I saw in the guy always put Arianna on the defensive, and I really didn't feel like letting her boyfriend ruin what had so far been a pretty fun night.

"Anyway," she said, sitting up taller. "We were talking about your love-life problems and not mine. Let me look at this app of yours and see if I can help you out."

And since I just wanted to make Arianna happy and keep her mind off Chad, I unlocked my phone, opened it up to the dating app I'd only signed up for because of her, and handed it to her.

She looked at the screen for a minute, tapping it a few times. Then with her dark eyebrows knitted together, she turned to me and said, "You've been matching with tons of women but not messaging them. Why?"

"What?" I asked. "I'm supposed to actually message the girls?"

"Duh." She sighed and shoved my arm. "How can you of all people be doing this wrong? I know you got like a 3.8 GPA in college and you haven't had a single concussion since then."

"Well," I said, taking my phone back from her and slipping it into the pocket of my suit coat. "If someone would take time out of her busy schedule to be my dating coach like she promised, maybe I'd be doing better at this."

"You don't need me to help you get a girl," she said. "I mean, if you simply uploaded a photo that actually showed your face instead of your back, or not hide your face behind a huge fish, you'd have every single woman from Denver to Vail swiping right."

"Are you saying you think I'm hot?" I raised an eyebrow and shot her a flirtatious look.

She shoved my arm again. "Maybe if you would let me cut your hair, I'd say that."

"Ouch." I pretended to be hurt.

But in reality, I knew she only said that because she was a beautician and had been begging me to let her cut my long, curly black hair ever since we became friends three years ago.

It was just something, like my lack of having a love life, that I had claimed not to have time for.

I mean, once you started cutting it short you had to maintain it, and who had time to get haircuts once a month when you were busy playing football?

Okay, so maybe I was just a little lazy...

"You don't even know what I look like with short hair," I said. "What if I actually look worse?"

"Impossible," she said. Then she held up a finger to quiet me, as if she knew I was totally about to twist her words into making it seem like she'd just said it was impossible for me to look worse than I already did. "With your bone structure, big brown eyes, and jawline, showing more of your face would not be a bad thing. In fact, I think you just keep the hair to spite me."

"Not to spite you exactly..." I said.

She sighed.

"How about this," I said. "You agree to give me those special dating lessons like you promised and I will let you cut my hair."

"Really?" Her deep brown eyes lit up.

And even though I was probably going to regret letting her do it, I nodded. "I'm sure it will take a lot of work to turn me into Prince Charming, so I guess allowing you to cut my hair is probably a fair payment for your professional services."

"Oh, you're going to pay me for the haircut, too."

I laughed. "Okay, fine."

She took a sip of her champagne then scooted her

chair away from the table. "And since I'm going to be the best dating coach you've ever seen, we're going to start with dancing lessons right now."

I groaned. Because even though I didn't really suck at dating—I simply sucked at *trying* to date for reasons I couldn't tell her—I really did need a lot of help on the dance floor.

But when she grabbed my hand and started pulling me toward the wedding guests who were currently slow dancing to Vincent and Emerson's song, "Return to Love" by Andrea Boccelli, I let her—it was probably my one chance to dance with my gorgeous best friend without her boyfriend glaring at me from across the room.

Read more from Friend Zone to End Zone here.

ABOUT THE AUTHOR

Judy Corry is the USA Today Bestselling Author of Contemporary and YA Romance. She writes romance because she can't get enough of the feeling of falling in love. She's known for writing heart-pounding kisses, endearing characters, and hard-won happily ever afters.

She lives in Southern Utah with the boy who took her to Prom, their four awesome kids, and two dogs. She's addicted to love stories, dark chocolate and chai lattes.

Made in the USA
Monee, IL
27 July 2024